THE

BRITISH ESSAYISTS:

WITH

PREFACES

BIOGRAPHICAL, HISTORICAL,

AND CRITICAL,

BY THE

REV. LIONEL THOMAS BERGUER,

LATE OF ST. MARY HALL, OXON; FELLOW (EXTRAORDINARY) OF THE
ROYAL MEDICAL SOCIETY OF EDINBURGH.

IN FORTY-FIVE VOLUMES.

VOL. XXII.

LONDON:

PRINTED FOR J. AND A. ARCH, CORNHILL; PRINCES STREET;
BALDWIN AND CO.

W. Baynes and Son, Paternoster-Row; A. K. Newman and Co. Ogle, Square;
McMillan, New Bond Street; E. Lumley; Ridgway; J. Bohte, Strand;
J. H. Bohn, Old Bond-street; Baldwin and Cradock, Strand; W. Wright,
Fleet-street; T. Bumpus, Strand; H. Sharpe; T. Boys; W. Grapel, and
Robinson and Ranse, Liverpool; Hall and Blackburn, T. Robertson, &c. and
H. S. Baynes and Co., Edinburgh; R. M. Tims, and J. Cumming, Dublin.

1823.

THE

BRITISH ESSAYISTS;

WITH

PREFACES

2356

BIOGRAPHICAL, HISTORICAL,

AND CRITICAL,

BY THE

REV. LIONEL THOMAS BERGUER,

LATE OF ST. MARY HALL, OXON: FELLOW EXTRAORDINARY OF THE
ROYAL MEDICAL SOCIETY OF EDINBURGH.

IN FORTY-FIVE VOLUMES.
VOL. XXII.

LONDON:

PRINTED FOR T. AND J. ALLMAN, PRINCES STREET,

HANOVER SQUARE:

W. Baynes and Son, Paternoster Row; A. B. Dulau and Co. Soho Square;
W. Clarke, New Bond Street; R. Jennings, Poultry; J. Hearne, Strand;
R. Triphook, Old Bond Street; Westley and Parrish, Strand; W. Wright,
Fleet Street; C. Smith, Strand: H. Mozley, Derby: W. Grapel, and
Robinson and Sons, Liverpool: Bell and Bradfute, J. Anderson, jun. and
H. S. Baynes and Co. Edinburgh: M. Keene, and J. Cumming, Dublin.

1823.

BRITISH ESSAYISTS.

CONTENTS TO VOL. XXII.

RAMBLER.

No. 160—208.

Nullius addictus jurare in verba magistri,
Quo me cunque rapit tempestas, deferor hospes.—Hor.

Printed by J. B. Dove, S. John's Square

THE

RAMBLER.

No. 166. SATURDAY, SEPTEMBER ...

RAMBLER.

—— Inter se convenit ursis.

Beasts of each kind their fellows spare,
Nor lives in amity with bear.

No. 160—208

"THE world," says Locke, "has people of all
sorts." As in the general hurry produced by the
superfluities of some, and necessities of others, no
man needs to stand still for want of employment, so
in the innumerable gradations of ability, and the
less varieties of study and inclination, no employment can be vacant for want of a man qualified to
discharge it.

Such is probably the natural state of the universe,
but it is so much deformed by interest and passion,
that the benefit of this adaptation of men to things
is not always perceived. The folly or the penury of
those who set their services to sale, inclines them to
invest of qualifications which they do not possess...

THE

RAMBLER.

N° 160. SATURDAY, SEPTEMBER 28, 1751.

———— Inter se convenit ursis.—Juv.

Beasts of each kind their fellows spare ;
Bear lives in amity with bear.

'THE world,' says Locke, ' has people of all sorts.' As in the general hurry produced by the superfluities of some, and necessities of others, no man needs to stand still for want of employment; so in the innumerable gradations of ability, and endless varieties of study and inclination, no employment can be vacant for want of a man qualified to discharge it.

Such is probably the natural state of the universe, but it is so much deformed by interest and passion, that the benefit of this adaptation of men to things is not always perceived. The folly or indigence of those who set their services to sale, inclines them to boast of qualifications which they do not possess, and attempt business which they do not understand ; and they who have the power of assigning to others the task of life, are seldom honest or seldom happy in their nominations. Patrons are corrupted by avarice, cheated by credulity, or overpowered by resistless solicitation. They are sometimes too strongly influenced by honest prejudices of friendship, or the prevalence of virtuous compassion. For, whatever cool reason may direct, it is not easy for a man of tender and scrupulous goodness to overlook the immediate effect of his own actions, by turning his eyes upon remoter consequences, and to do that which must give present pain, for the sake of obviating evil yet unfelt, or securing advantage in time to come. What is distant is in itself obscure, and, when we have no wish to see it, easily escapes our notice, or takes such a form as desire or imagination bestows upon it.

Every man might, for the same reason, in the multitudes that swarm about him, find some kindred mind with which he could unite in confidence and friendship; yet we see many straggling single about the world, unhappy for want of an associate, and pining with the necessity of confining their sentiments to their own bosoms.

This inconvenience arises in like manner from struggles of the will against the understanding. It is not often difficult to find a suitable companion, if every man would be content with such as he is qualified to please. But if vanity tempts him to forsake his rank, and post himself among those with whom no common interest or mutual pleasure can ever unite him, he must always live in a state of unsocial separation, without tenderness and without trust.

There are many natures which can never approach within a certain distance, and which, when any irregular motive impels them towards contact, seem to start back from each other by some invincible repulsion. There are others which immediately cohere whenever they come into the reach of mutual attraction, and with very little formality of preparation, mingle intimately as soon as they meet. Every man, whom either business or curiosity has thrown at large into the world, will recollect many instances of fondness and dislike, which have forced themselves upon him without the intervention of his judgment; of dispositions to court some and avoid others, when he could assign no reason for the preference, or none adequate to the violence of his passions; of influence that acted instantaneously upon his mind; and which no arguments or persuasions could ever overcome.

Among those with whom time and intercourse have made us familiar, we feel our affections divided in different proportions without much regard to moral or intellectual merit. Every man knows some whom he cannot induce himself to trust, though he has no reason to suspect that they would betray him; those to whom he cannot complain, though he never observed them to want compassions; those in whose presence he never can be gay, though excited by invitations to mirth and freedom; and those from whom he cannot be content to receive instruction, though they never insulted his ignorance by contempt or ostentation.

That much regard is to be had to those instincts of kindness and dislike, or that reason should blindly follow them, I am far from intending to inculcate: It is very certain that by indulgence we may give them strength which they have not from nature, and almost every example of ingratitude and treachery proves, that by obeying them we may commit our happiness to those who are very unworthy of so great a trust. But it may deserve to be remarked, that since few contend much with their inclinations, it is generally vain to solicit the good-will of those whom we perceive thus involuntarily alienated from us; neither knowledge nor virtue will reconcile antipathy; and though officiousness may for a time be admitted, and diligence applauded, they will at last be dismissed with coldness or discouraged by neglect.

Some have indeed an occult power of stealing upon the affections, of exciting universal benevolence, and disposing every heart to fondness and friendship. But this is a felicity granted only to the favourites of nature. The greater part of mankind find a different reception from different dispositions; they sometimes obtain unexpected caresses from those whom they never flattered with uncommon regard, and sometimes exhaust all their arts of pleasing without effect. To these it is necessary to look round, and attempt every breast in which they find virtue sufficient for the foundation of friendship; to enter into the crowd, and try whom chance will offer to their notice, till they fix on some temper congenial to their own, as the magnet rolled in the dust collects the fragments of its kindred metal from a thousand particles of other substances.

Every man must have remarked the facility with which the kindness of others is sometimes gained by those to whom he never could have imparted his own. We are by our occupations, education, and habits of life, divided almost into different species, which regard one another for the most part with scorn and malignity. Each of these classes of the human race has desires, fears, and conversation, vexations and merriment, peculiar to itself; cares which another cannot feel; pleasures which he cannot partake; and modes of expressing every sensation, which he cannot understand. That frolic which shakes one man with laughter will convulse another with indignation: the strain of jocularity which in one place obtains treats and patronage, would in another be heard with indifference, and in a third with abhorrence.

To raise esteem we must benefit others, to pro-

cure love we must please them. Aristotle observes
that old men do not readily form friendships, because
they are not easily susceptible of pleasure. He
that can contribute to the hilarity of the vacant hour,
or partake with equal gust the favourite amusement,
he whose mind is employed on the same objects,
and who therefore never harasses the understanding
with unaccustomed ideas, will be welcomed with
ardour, and left with regret, unless he destroys
those recommendations by faults with which peace
and security cannot consist.

It were happy if, in forming friendships, virtue
could concur with pleasure; but the greatest part of
human gratifications approach so nearly to vice, that
few who make the delight of others their rule of
conduct, can avoid disingenuous compliances; yet
certainly he that suffers himself to be driven or allured from virtue, mistakes his own interest, since
he gains succour by means, for which his friend, if
ever he becomes wise, must scorn him, and for which
at last he must scorn himself.

Nº 161. TUESDAY, OCTOBER 1, 1751.

Οἵη γὰρ φύλλων γενεὴ, τοιήδε καὶ Ἀνδρῶν.—Hom.

Frail as the leaves that quiver on the sprays,
Like them man flourishes, like them decays.

'TO THE RAMBLER.

'SIR,

' You have formerly observed that curiosity often
terminates in barren knowledge, and that the mind
is prompted to study and inquiry rather by the un-

easiness of ignorance, than the hope of profit. Nothing can be of less importance to any present interest than the fortune of those who have been long lost in the grave, and from whom nothing now can be hoped or feared. Yet to rouse the zeal of a true antiquary, little more is necessary than to mention a name which mankind have conspired to forget: he will make his way to remote scenes of action through obscurity and contradiction, as Tully sought amidst bushes and brambles the tomb of Archimedes.

'It is not easy to discover how it concerns him that gathers the produce, or receives the rent of an estate, to know through what families the land has passed, who is registered in the Conqueror's survey as its possessor, how often it has been forfeited by treason, or how often sold by prodigality. The power or wealth of the present inhabitants of a country cannot be much increased by an inquiry after the names of those barbarians, who destroyed one another twenty centuries ago, in contests for the shelter of woods or convenience of pasturage. Yet we see that no man can be at rest in the enjoyment of a new purchase till he has learned the history of his grounds from the ancient inhabitants of the parish, and that no nation omits to record the actions of their ancestors, however bloody, savage, and rapacious.

'The same disposition, as different opportunities call it forth, discovers itself in great or little things. I have always thought it unworthy of a wise man to slumber in total inactivity, only because he happens to have no employment equal to his ambition or genius ; it is therefore my custom to apply my attention to the objects before me, and as I cannot think any place wholly unworthy of notice that affords a habitation to a man of letters, I have collected the history and antiquities of the several garrets in which I have resided.

Quantulacunque estis, vos ego magna voco.

How small to others, but how great to me!

'Many of these narratives my industry has been able to extend to a considerable length; but the woman with whom I now lodge has lived only eighteen months in the house, and can give no account of its ancient revolutions; the plasterer having, at her entrance, obliterated, by his white-wash, all the smoky memorials which former tenants had left upon the ceiling, and perhaps drawn the veil of oblivion over politicians, philosophers, and poets.

'When I first cheapened my lodgings, the landlady told me, that she hoped I was not an author, for the lodgers on the first floor had stipulated that the upper rooms should not be occupied by a noisy trade. I very readily promised to give no disturbance to her family, and soon dispatched a bargain on the usual terms.

'I had not slept many nights in my new apartment before I began to inquire after my predecessors, and found my landlady, whose imagination is filled chiefly with her own affairs, very ready to give me information.

'Curiosity, like all other desires, produces pain as well as pleasure. Before she began her narrative, I had heated my head with expectations of adventures and discoveries, of elegance in disguise, and learning in distress; and was somewhat mortified when I heard that the first tenant was a tailor, of whom nothing was remembered but that he complained of his room for want of light; and, after having lodged in it a month, and paid only a week's rent, pawned a piece of cloth which he was trusted to cut out, and was forced to make a precipitate retreat from this quarter of the town.

'The next was a young woman newly arrived

from the country, who lived for five weeks with great regularity, and became, by frequent treats, very much the favourite of the family, but at last received visits so frequently from a cousin in Cheapside, that she brought the reputation of the house into danger, and was therefore dismissed with good advice.

' The room then stood empty for a fortnight; my landlady began to think that she had judged hardly, and often wished for such another lodger. At last an elderly man of grave aspect read the bill, and bargained for the room at the very first price that was asked. He lived in close retirement, seldom went out till evening, and then returned early, sometimes cheerful, and at other times dejected. It was remarkable, that whatever he purchased, he never had small money in his pocket, and though cool and temperate on other occasions, was always vehement and stormy till he received his change. He paid his rent with great exactness, and seldom failed once a week to requite my landlady's civility with a supper. At last, such is the fate of human felicity, the house was alarmed at midnight by the constable, who demanded to search the garrets. My landlady assuring him that he had mistaken the door, conducted him up stairs, where he found the tools of a coiner; but the tenant had crawled along the roof to an empty house, and escaped; much to the joy of my landlady, who declares him a very honest man, and wonders why any body should be hanged for making money when such numbers are in want of it. She however confesses that she shall for the future always question the character of those who take her garret without beating down the price.

' The bill was then placed again in the window, and the poor woman was teased for seven weeks by innumerable passengers, who obliged her to climb with them every hour up five stories, and then disliked the prospect, hated the noise of a public street, thought the stairs narrow, objected to a low ceiling, required the walls to be hung with fresher paper, asked questions about the neighbourhood, could not think of living so far from their acquaintance, wished the windows had looked to the south rather than the west, told how the door and chimney might have been better disposed, bid her half the price that she asked, or promised to give her earnest the next day, and came no more.

'At last, a short meagre man, in a tarnished waistcoat, desired to see the garret, and when he had stipulated for two long shelves, and a larger table, hired it at a low rate. When the affair was completed, he looked round him with great satisfaction, and repeated some words which the woman did not understand. In two days he brought a great box of books, took possession of his room, and lived very inoffensively, except that he frequently disturbed the inhabitants of the next floor by unseasonable noises. He was generally in bed at noon, but, from evening to midnight, he sometimes talked aloud with great vehemence, sometimes stamped as in a rage, sometimes threw down his poker, then clattered his chairs, then sat down in deep thought, and again burst out into loud vociferations ; sometimes he would sigh as oppressed with misery, and sometimes shake with convulsive laughter. When he encountered any of the family he gave way or bowed, but rarely spoke, except that as he went up stairs he often repeated,

$$\text{—}\text{Ὃς ὑπέρτατα δώματα ναίει,}$$
This habitant th' aerial regions boast ;

hard words, to which his neighbours listened so often, that they learned them without understanding them. What was his employment she did not venture to ask him, but at last heard a printer's boy inquire for the author.

' My landlady was very often advised to beware of this strange man, who, though he was quiet for the present, might perhaps become outrageous in the hot months; but as she was punctually paid, she could not find any sufficient reason for dismissing him, till one night he convinced her, by setting fire to his curtains, that it was not safe to have an author for her inmate.

' She had then, for six weeks, a succession of tenants, who left her house on Saturday, and, instead of paying their rent, stormed at their landlady. At last she took in two sisters, one of whom had spent her little fortune in procuring remedies for a lingering disease, and was now supported and attended by the other: she climbed with difficulty to the apartment, where she languished eight weeks without impatience or lamentation, except for the expense and fatigue which her sister suffered, and then calmly and contentedly expired. The sister followed her to the grave, paid the few debts which they had contracted, wiped away the tears of useless sorrow, and, returning to the business of common life, resigned to me the vacant habitation.

' Such, Mr. Rambler, are the changes which have happened in the narrow space where my present fortune has fixed my residence. So true it is that amusement and instruction are always at hand for those who have skill and willingness to find them; and so just is the observation of Juvenal, that a single house will shew whatever is done or suffered in the world.

                                        I am, Sir, &c.'

N° 162. SATURDAY, OCTOBER 5, 1751.

Orbus es, et locuples, et Bruto consule natus ;
 Esse tibi veras credis amicitias?
Sunt veræ ; sed quas Juvenis, quas pauper habebas :
 Qui novus est, mortem diligit ille tuam.—Mart.

What old, and rich, and childless too,
 And yet believe your friends are true ?
Truth might perhaps to those belong,
 To those who lov'd you poor and young ;
But, trust me, for the new you have,
 They'll love you dearly—in your grave.—F. Lewis.

One of the complaints uttered by Milton's Samson,
in the anguish of blindness, is, that he shall pass
his life under the direction of others ; that he cannot
regulate his conduct by his own knowledge, but
must lie at the mercy of those who undertake to
guide him.

There is no state more contrary to the dignity of
wisdom than perpetual and unlimited dependance,
in which the understanding lies useless, and every
motion is received from external impulse. Reason
is the great distinction of human nature, the faculty
by which we approach to some degree of association
with celestial intelligences ; but as the excellence of
every power appears only in its operations, not to
have reason, and to have it useless and unemployed,
is nearly the same.

Such is the weakness of man, that the essence of
things is seldom so much regarded as external and
accidental appendages. A small variation of trifling
circumstances, a slight change of form by an artificial dress, or a casual difference of appearance, by
a new light and situation, will conciliate affection
or excite abhorrence, and determine us to pursue or

to avoid. Every man considers a necessity of compliance with any will but his own, as the lowest state of ignominy and meanness; few are so far lost in cowardice or negligence, as not to rouse at the first insult of tyranny, and exert all their force against him who usurps their property, or invades any privilege of speech or action. Yet we see often those who never wanted spirit to repel encroachment or oppose violence, at last, by a gradual relaxation of vigilance, delivering up, without capitulation, the fortress which they defended against assault, and laying down unbidden the weapons which they grasped the harder for every attempt to wrest them from their hands. Men eminent for spirit and wisdom often resign themselves to voluntary pupillage, and suffer their lives to be modelled by officious ignorance, and their choice to be regulated by presumptuous stupidity.

This unresisting acquiescence in the determination of others, may be the consequence of application to some study remote from the beaten track of life; some employment which does not allow leisure for sufficient inspection of those petty affairs, by which nature has decreed a great part of our duration to be filled. To a mind thus withdrawn from common objects, it is more eligible to repose on the prudence of another, than to be exposed every moment to slight interruptions. The submission which such confidence requires, is paid without pain, because it implies no confession of inferiority. The business from which we withdraw our cognizance, is not above our abilities, but below our notice. We please our pride with the effects of our influence thus weakly exerted, and fancy ourselves placed in a higher orb, from which we regulate subordinate agents by a slight and distant superintendence. But whatever vanity or abstraction may suggest, no man can safely do that by others which might be done by himself; he that indulges negligence will quickly become ignorant of his own affairs; and he that trusts without reserve will at last be deceived.

It is however impossible but that, as the attention tends strongly towards one thing, it must retire from another; and he that omits the care of domestic business, because he is engrossed by inquiries of more importance to mankind, has at least the merit of suffering in a good cause. But, there are many who can plead no such extenuation of their folly; who shake off the burden of their station, not that they may soar with less encumbrance to the heights of knowledge or virtue, but that they may loiter at ease and sleep in quiet; and who select for friendship and confidence not the faithful and the virtuous, but the soft, the civil, and compliant.

This openness to flattery is the common disgrace of declining life. When men feel weakness increasing on them, they naturally desire to rest from the struggles of contradiction, the fatigue of reasoning, the anxiety of circumspection; when they are hourly tormented with pains and diseases, they are unable to bear any new disturbance, and consider all opposition as an addition to misery, of which they feel already more than they can patiently endure. Thus desirous of peace, and thus fearful of pain, the old man seldom inquires after any other qualities in those whom he caresses, than quickness in conjecturing his desires, activity in supplying his wants, dexterity in intercepting complaints before they approach near enough to disturb him, flexibility to his present humour, submission to hasty petulance, and attention to wearisome narrations. By these arts alone many have been able to defeat the claims of kindred and of merit, and to enrich themselves with presents and legacies.

Thrasybulus inherited a large fortune, and augmented it by the revenues of several lucrative employments, which he discharged with honour and dexterity. He was at last wise enough to consider, that life should not be devoted wholly to accumulation, and therefore retiring to his estate, applied himself to the education of his children, and the cultivation of domestic happiness.

He passed several years in this pleasing amusement, and saw his care amply recompensed; his daughters were celebrated for modesty and elegance, and his sons for learning, prudence, and spirit. In time the eagerness with which the neighbouring gentlemen courted his alliance, obliged him to resign his daughters to other families; the vivacity and curiosity of his sons hurried them out of rural privacy into the open world, from whence they had not soon an inclination to return. This however he had always hoped; he pleased himself with the success of his schemes, and felt no inconvenience from solitude till an apoplexy deprived him of his wife.

Thrasybulus had now no companion; and the maladies of increasing years having taken from him much of the power of procuring amusement for himself, he thought it necessary to procure some inferior friend who might ease him of his economical solicitudes, and divert him by cheerful conversation. All these qualities he soon recollected in Vafer, a clerk in one of the offices over which he had formerly presided. Vafer was invited to visit his old patron, and being by his station acquainted with the present modes of life, and by constant practice dexterous in business, entertained him with so many novelties, and so readily disentangled his affairs, that he was desired to resign his clerkship, and accept a liberal salary in the house of Thrasybulus.

Vafer, having always lived in a state of dependance, was well versed in the arts by which favour is obtained, and could without repugnance or hesitation accommodate himself to every caprice, and echo every opinion. He never doubted but to be convinced, nor attempted opposition but to flatter Thrasybulus with the pleasure of a victory. By this practice he found his way into his patron's heart, and having first made himself agreeable, soon became important. His insidious diligence, by which the laziness of age was gratified, engrossed the management of affairs; and his petty offices of civility, and occasional intercessions, persuaded the tenants to consider him as their friend and benefactor, and to entreat his enforcement of their representations of hard years, and his countenance to petitions for abatement of rent.

Thrasybulus had now banqueted on flattery, till he could no longer bear the harshness of remonstrance, or the insipidity of truth. All contrariety to his own opinion shocked him like a violation of some natural right, and all recommendation of his affairs to his own inspection was dreaded by him as a summons to torture. His children were alarmed by the sudden riches of Vafer, but their complaints were heard by their father with impatience, as the result of a conspiracy against his quiet, and a design to condemn him, for their own advantage, to groan out his last hours in perplexity and drudgery. The daughters retired with tears in their eyes, but the son continued his importunities till he found his inheritance hazarded by his obstinacy. Vafer triumphed over all their efforts, and continuing to confirm himself in authority, at the death of his master, purchased an estate, and bade defiance to inquiry and justice.

Nº 163. TUESDAY, OCTOBER 8, 1751.

Mitte superba pati fastidia, spemque caducam
Despice ; vive tibi, nam moriere tibi.—SENECA.

Bow to no patron's insolence ; rely
On no frail hopes ; in freedom live and die.—F. LEWIS.

NONE of the cruelties exercised by wealth and power upon indigence and dependance is more mischievous in its consequences, or more frequently practised with wanton negligence, than the encouragement of expectations which are never to be gratified, and the elation and depression of the heart by needless vicissitudes of hope and disappointment.

Every man is rich or poor, according to the proportion between his desires and enjoyments ; any enlargement of wishes is therefore equally destructive to happiness with the diminution of possession, and he that teaches another to long for what he never shall obtain, is no less an enemy to his quiet, than if he had robbed him of part of his patrimony.

But representations thus refined exhibit no adequate idea of the guilt of pretended friendship ; of artifices by which followers are attracted only to decorate the retinue of pomp, and swell the shout of popularity, and to be dismissed with contempt and ignominy, when their leader has succeeded or miscarried, when he is sick of show, and weary of noise. While a man, infatuated with the promises of greatness, wastes his hours and days in attendance and solicitation, the honest opportunities of improving his condition pass by without his notice ; he neglects to cultivate his own barren soil, because he expects every moment to be placed in regions of spontaneous fertility, and is seldom roused from his delusion, but by the gripe of distress which he cannot resist, and the sense of evils which cannot be remedied.

The punishment of Tantalus in the infernal regions affords a just image of hungry servility, flattered with the approach of advantage, doomed to lose it before it comes into his reach, always within a few days of felicity, and always sinking back to his former wants.

Καὶ μὴν Τάνταλον εἰσεῖδον χαλέπ᾽ ἄλγε᾽ ἔχοντα,
Ἑσταότ᾽ ἐν λίμνη, ἡ δὲ προσέπλαζε γενείω·
Στεῦτο δὲ διψάων πιέειν δ᾽ οὐκ εἶχεν ἑλέσθαι.
Ὁσσάκι γὰρ κύψει᾽ ὁ γέρων, πιέειν μενεαίνων,
Τοσσαχ᾽ ὕδωρ ἀπολέσκετ᾽ ἀναβροχὲν ἀμφὶ δὲ ποσσὶ
Γαῖα μέλαινα φάνεσκε· καταζήνασκε δὲ δαίμων.
Δένδρεα δ᾽ ὑψιπέτηλα κατακρήθεν χέε καρπὸν,
Ὄγχναι καὶ ῥοιαί, καὶ μηλέαι ἀγλαόκαρποι,
Συκαῖ τε γλυκεραὶ, καὶ ἐλαῖαι τηλεθόωσαι.
Τῶν ὁπότ᾽ ἰθύσει᾽ ὁ γέρων ἐπὶ χερσὶ μάσασθαι,
Τάσδ᾽ ἄνεμος ῥίπτασκε ποτὶ νέφεα σκιόεντα.

'I saw,' says Homer's Ulysses, 'the severe punishment of Tantalus. In a lake whose waters approached to his lips, he stood burning with thirst, without the power to drink. Whenever he inclined his head to the stream, some deity commanded it to be dry, and the dark earth appeared at his feet. Around him lofty trees spread their fruits to view; the pear, the pomegranate, and the apple, the green olive, and the luscious fig, quivered before him, which, whenever he extended his hands to seize them were snatched by the winds into clouds and obscurity.'

This image of misery was perhaps originally suggested to some poet by the conduct of his patron, by the daily contemplation of splendour which he never must partake, by fruitless attempts to catch at interdicted happiness, and by the sudden evanescence of his reward, when he thought his labours almost at an end. To groan with poverty, when all about

him was opulence, riot, and superfluity, and to find
the favours which he had long been encouraged to
hope, and had long endeavoured to deserve, squan-
dered at last on nameless ignorance, was to thirst
with water flowing before him, and to see the fruits
to which his hunger was hastening, scattered by
the wind. Nor can my correspondent, whatever he
may have suffered, express with more justness or
force the vexations of dependance.

' To the Rambler.

'Sir,

'I am one of those mortals who have been courted
and envied as the favourites of the great. Having
often gained the prize of composition at the university, I began to hope that I should obtain the same
distinction in every other place, and determined to
forsake the profession to which I was destined by
my parents, and in which the interest of my family
would have procured me a very advantageous settlement. The pride of wit fluttered in my heart, and
when I prepared to leave the college, nothing entered my imagination but honours, caresses, and
rewards, riches without labour, and luxury without
expense.

'I however delayed my departure for a time, to
finish the performance by which I was to draw the
first notice of mankind upon me. When it was completed I hurried to London, and considered every
moment that passed before its publication, as lost in
a kind of neutral existence, and cut off from the
golden hours of happiness and fame. The piece
was at last printed, and disseminated by a rapid sale;
I wandered from one place of concourse to another,
feasted from morning to night on the repetition of
my own praises, and enjoyed the various conjectures
of critics, the mistaken candour of my friends, and

the impotent malice of my enemies. Some had read the manuscript, and rectified its inaccuracies; others had seen it in a state so imperfect, that they could not forbear to wonder at its present excellence; some had conversed with the author at the coffee-house; and others gave hints that they had lent him money.

'I knew that no performance is so favourably read as that of a writer who suppresses his name, and therefore resolved to remain concealed, till those by whom literary reputation is established had given their suffrages too publicly to retract them. At length my bookseller informed me that Aurantius, the standing patron of merit, had sent inquiries after me, and invited me to his acquaintance.

'The time which I had long expected was now arrived. I went to Aurantius with a beating heart, for I looked upon our interview as the critical moment of my destiny. I was received with civilities, which my academic rudeness made me unable to repay; but when I had recovered from my confusion, I prosecuted the conversation with such liveliness and propriety, that I confirmed my new friend in his esteem of my abilities, and was dismissed with the utmost ardour of profession and raptures of fondness.

'I was soon summoned to dine with Aurantius, who had assembled the most judicious of his friends to partake of the entertainment. Again I exerted my powers of sentiment and expression, and again found every eye sparkling with delight, and every tongue silent with attention. I now became familiar at the table of Aurantius, but could never, in his most private or jocund hours, obtain more from him than general declarations of esteem, or endearments of tenderness, which included no particular promise, and therefore conferred no claim. This frigid reserve somewhat disgusted me, and when he complained of three days' absence, I took care to inform him with how much importunity of kindness I had been detained by his rival Pollio.

'Aurantius now considered his honour as endangered by the desertion of a wit, and lest I should have an inclination to wander, told me that I could never find a friend more constant or zealous than himself; that indeed he had made no promises, because he hoped to surprise me with advancement, but had been silently promoting my interest, and should continue his good offices, unless he found the kindness of others more desired.

'If you, Mr. Rambler, have ever ventured your philosophy within the attraction of greatness, you know the force of such language introduced with a smile of gracious tenderness, and impressed at the conclusion with an air of solemn sincerity. From that instant I gave myself up wholly to Aurantius, and as he immediately resumed his former gaiety, expected every moment a summons to some employment of dignity and profit. One month succeeded another, and in defiance of appearances I still fancied myself nearer to my wishes, and continued to dream of success, and wake to disappointment. At last the failure of my little fortune compelled me to abate the finery which I hitherto thought necessary to the company with whom I associated, and the rank to which I should be raised. Aurantius, from the moment in which he discovered my poverty, considered me as fully in his power, and afterward rather permitted my attendance than invited it; thought himself at liberty to refuse my visits, whenever he had other amusements within reach; and often suffered me to wait, without pretending any necessary business. When I was admitted to his table, if any man of rank equal to his own was present, he took occasion to mention my writings, and commend my ingenuity, by which he intended to apologize for the confusion of distinctions, and the improper assortment of his company; and often called upon me to entertain his friends with my productions, as a sportsman delights the squires of his neighbourhood with the curvets of his horse, or the obedience of his spaniels.

'To complete my mortification, it was his practice to impose tasks upon me, by requiring me to write upon such subjects as he thought susceptible of ornament and illustration. With these extorted performances he was little satisfied, because he rarely found in them the ideas which his own imagination suggested, and which he therefore thought more natural than mine.

'When the pale of ceremony is broken, rudeness and insult soon enter the breach. He now found that he might safely harass me with vexation; that he had fixed the shackles of patronage upon me, and that I could neither resist him nor escape. At last, in the eighth year of my servitude, when the clamour of creditors was vehement, and my necessity known to be extreme, he offered me a small office, but hinted his expectation that I should marry a young woman with whom he had been acquainted.

'I was not so far depressed by my calamities as to comply with this proposal; but knowing that complaints and expostulations would but gratify his insolence, I turned away with that contempt with which I shall never want spirit to treat the wretch who can outgo the guilt of a robber without the temptation of his profit, and who lures the credulous and thoughtless to maintain the show of his levee,

and the mirth of his table, at the expense of honour,
happiness, and life.   I am, Sir, &c.

LIBEERALIS.'

N° 164.   SATURDAY, OCTOBER 12, 1751.

——Vitium, Gaure, Catonis habes.—MART.

Gaurus pretends to Cato's fame;
And proves——by Cato's vice, his claim.

DISTINCTION is so pleasing to the pride of man,
that a great part of the pain and pleasure of life
arises from the gratification or disappointment of an
incessant wish for superiority, from the success or
miscarriage of secret competitions, from victories
and defeats, of which, though they appear to us of
great importance, in reality none are conscious except ourselves.

Proportionate to the prevalence of this love of
praise is the variety of means by which its attainment is attempted. Every man, however hopeless
his pretensions may appear to all but himself, has
some project by which he hopes to rise to reputation; some art by which he imagines that the notice
of the world will be attracted; some quality, good
or bad, which discriminates him from the common
herd of mortals, and by which others may be persuaded to love, or compelled to fear him. The as-
cents of honour, however steep, never appear inaccessible; he that despairs to scale the precipices, by
which learning and valour have conducted their favourites, discovers some by-path, or easier acclivity,
which, though it cannot bring him to the summit,
will yet enable him to overlook those with whom he

is now contending for eminence; and we seldom require more to the happiness of the present hour, than to surpass him that stands next before us.

As the greater part of human kind speak and act wholly by imitation, most of those who aspire to honour and applause propose to themselves some example which serves as the model of their conduct and the limit of their hopes. Almost every man, if closely examined, will be found to have enlisted himself under some leader whom he expects to conduct him to renown; to have some hero or other, living or dead, in his view, whose character he endeavours to assume, and whose performances he labours to equal.

When the original is well chosen and judiciously copied, the imitator often arrives at excellence which he could never have attained without direction; for few are formed with abilities to discover new possibilities of excellence, and distinguish themselves by means never tried before.

But folly and idleness often contrive to gratify pride at a cheaper rate: not the qualities which are most illustrious, but those which are of easiest attainment, are selected for imitation; and the honours and rewards which public gratitude has paid to the benefactors of mankind, are expected by wretches who can only imitate them in their vices and defects, or adopt some petty singularities, of which those from whom they are borrowed, were secretly ashamed.

No man rises to such a height as to become conspicuous, but he is on one side censured by undiscerning malice, which reproaches him for his best actions, and slanders his apparent and incontestable excellences; and idolized on the other by ignorant admiration, which exalts his faults and follies into virtues. It may be observed, that he by whose intimacy his acquaintances imagine themselves digni-

fied, generally diffuses among them his mien and his
habits; and indeed without more vigilance than is
generally applied to the regulation of the minuter
parts of behaviour, it is not easy, when we converse
much with one whose general character excites our
veneration, to escape all contagion of his peculiarities, even when we do not deliberately think them
worthy of our notice, and when they would have excited laughter or disgust had they not been protected
by their alliance to nobler qualities, and accidentally
consorted with knowledge or with virtue.

The faults of a man loved or honoured, sometimes steal secretly and imperceptibly upon the wise
and virtuous, but by injudicious fondness or thoughtless vanity are adopted with design. There is scarce
any failing of mind or body, any error of opinion or
depravity of practice, which, instead of producing
shame and discontent, its natural effects, has not at
one time or other gladdened vanity with the hopes of
praise, and been displayed with ostentatious industry
by those who sought kindred minds among the wits
or heroes, and could prove their relation only by si-
militude of deformity.

In consequence of this perverse ambition, every
habit which reason condemns may be indulged and
avowed. When a man is upbraided with his faults,
he may indeed be pardoned if he endeavours to run
for shelter to some celebrated name; but it is not to
be suffered that, from the retreats to which he fled
from infamy, he should issue again with the confidence of conquests, and call upon mankind for
praise. Yet we see men that waste their patrimony
in luxury, destroy their health with debauchery, and
enervate their minds with idleness, because there have
been some whom luxury never could sink into contempt, nor idleness hinder from the praise of genius.

This general inclination of mankind to copy characters in the gross, and the force which the recommendation of illustrious examples adds to the allurements of vice, ought to be considered by all whose character excludes them from the shades of secrecy, as incitements to scrupulous caution and universal purity of manners. No man, however enslaved to his appetites, or hurried by his passions, can, while he preserves his intellects unimpaired, please himself with promoting the corruption of others. He whose merit has enlarged his influence, would surely wish to exert it for the benefit of mankind. Yet such will be the effect of his reputation, while he suffers himself to indulge in any favourite fault, that they who have no hope to reach his excellence will catch at his failings, and his virtues will be cited to justify the copiers of his vices.

It is particularly the duty of those who consign illustrious names to posterity, to take care lest their readers be misled by ambiguous examples. That writer may be justly condemned as an enemy to goodness, who suffers fondness or interest to confound right with wrong, or to shelter the faults which even the wisest and the best have committed from that ignominy which guilt ought always to suffer, and with which it should be more deeply stigmatized when dignified by its neighbourhood to uncommon worth, since we shall be in danger of beholding it without abhorrence, unless its turpitude be laid open, and the eye secured from the deception of surrounding splendour.

N° 165. TUESDAY, OCTOBER 15, 1751.

ʼΗν νέος, ἀλλὰ πένης ; νῦν γηρῶν, πλούσιος εἰμί.

ʼΩ μόνος ἐκ πάντων οἰκτρὸς ἐν ἀμφοτεροῖς·

Ος τότε μὲν χρῆσθαι δυνάμην, ὁπότ᾽ οὐδὲ ἓν εἴχον·

Νῦν δ᾽ ὁπότε χρῆσθαι μὴ δύναμαι, τότ᾽ ἔχω.—ANTIPHILUS.

Young was I once and poor, now rich and old;
A harder case than mine was never told;
Blest with the pow'r to use them—I had none;
Loaded with riches now, the pow'r is gone.—F. LEWIS.

'TO THE RAMBLER.

'SIR,

' THE writers who have undertaken the unpromising task of moderating desire, exert all the power of their eloquence, to shew that happiness is not the lot of man, and have by many arguments and examples proved the instability of every condition by which envy or ambition are excited. They have set before our eyes all the calamities to which we are exposed from the frailty of nature, the influence of accident, or the stratagems of malice; they have terrified greatness with conspiracies, and riches with anxieties, wit with criticism, and beauty with disease.

' All the force of reason, and all the charms of language, are indeed necessary to support positions which every man hears with a wish to confute them. Truth finds an easy entrance into the mind when she is introduced by desire, and attended by pleasure; but when she intrudes uncalled, and brings only fear and sorrow in her train, the passes of the intellect are barred against her by prejudice and passion; if she sometimes forces her way by the batteries of argument, she seldom long keeps possession of her conquests, but is ejected by some favoured enemy, or at best obtains only a nominal sovereignty, without influence and without authority.

'That life is short we are all convinced, and yet suffer not that conviction to repress our projects or limit our expectations; that life is miserable we all feel, and yet we believe that the time is near when we shall feel it no longer. But to hope happiness and immortality is equally vain. Our state may indeed be more or less imbittered, as our duration may be more or less contracted; yet the utmost felicity which we can ever attain will be little better than alleviation of misery, and we shall always feel more pain from our wants than pleasure from our enjoyments. The incident which I am going to relate will shew, that to destroy the effect of all our success, it is not necessary that any signal calamity should fall upon us, that we should be harassed by implacable persecution, or excruciated by irremediable pains; the brightest hours of prosperity have their clouds, and the stream of life, if it is not ruffled by obstructions, will grow putrid by stagnation.

'My father resolving not to imitate the folly of his ancestors, who had hitherto left the younger sons encumbrances on the eldest, destined me to a lucrative profession; and I being careful to lose no opportunity of improvement, was at the usual time in which young men enter the world, well qualified for the exercise of the business which I had chosen.

'My eagerness to distinguish myself in public, and my impatience of the narrow scheme of life to which my indigence confined me, did not suffer me to continue long in the town where I was born; I went away as from a place of confinement, with a resolution to return no more, till I should be able to dazzle with my splendour those who now looked upon me with contempt, or reward those who had paid honours to my dawning merit, and to shew all who had suffered me to glide by them unknown and neglected, how much they mistook their interest in omitting to propitiate a genius like mine.

'Such were my intentions when I sallied forth into the unknown world, in quest of riches and honours, which I expected to procure in a very short time; for what could withhold them from industry and knowledge? He that indulges hope will always be disappointed. Reputation I very soon obtained; but as merit is much more cheaply acknowledged than rewarded, I did not find myself yet enriched in proportion to my celebrity.

'I had however in time surmounted the obstacles by which envy and competition obstruct the first attempts of a new claimant, and saw my opponents and censurers tacitly confessing their despair of success, by courting my friendship and yielding to my influence. They who once pursued me, were now satisfied to escape from me; and they who had before thought me presumptuous in hoping to overtake them, had now their utmost wish, if they were permitted at no great distance quietly to follow me.

'My wants were not madly multiplied as my acquisitions increased, and the time came at length, when I thought myself enabled to gratify all reasonable desires, and when, therefore, I resolved to enjoy that plenty and serenity which I had been hitherto labouring to procure, to enjoy them while I was yet neither crushed by age into infirmity, nor so habituated to a particular manner of life as to be unqualified for new studies or entertainments.

'I now quitted my profession, and to set myself at once free from all importunities to resume it, changed my residence, and devoted the remaining part of my time to quiet and amusement. Amidst innumerable projects of pleasure which restless idleness incited me to form, and of which most, when they came to the moment of execution, were rejected for others of no longer continuance, some accident revived in my imagination the pleasing ideas of my native place. It was now in my power to visit those from whom I had been so long absent, in such a manner as was consistent with my former resolution, and I wondered how it could happen that I had so long delayed my own happiness.

'Full of the admiration which I should excite, and the homage which I should receive, I dressed my servants in a more ostentatious livery, purchased a magnificent chariot, and resolved to dazzle the inhabitants of the little town with an unexpected blaze of greatness.

'While the preparations that vanity required were made for my departure, which, as workmen will not easily be hurried beyond their ordinary rate, I thought very tedious, I solaced my impatience with imagining the various censures that my appearance would produce, the hopes which some would feel from my bounty, the terror which my power would strike on others; the awkward respect with which I should be accosted by timorous officiousness; and the distant reverence with which others, less familiar to splendour and dignity, would be contented to gaze upon me. I deliberated a long time, whether I should immediately descend to a level with my former acquaintances, or make my condescension more grateful by a gentle transition from haughtiness and reserve. At length I determined to forget some of my companions, till they discovered themselves by some indubitable token, and to receive the congratulations of others upon my good fortune with indifference, to shew that I always expected what I had now obtained. The acclamations of the populace I purposed to reward with six hogsheads of ale, and a roasted ox, and then recommended to them to return to their work.

' At last all the trappings of grandeur were fitted, and I began the journey of triumph, which I could have wished to have ended in the same moment, but my horses felt none of their master's ardour, and I was shaken four days upon rugged roads. I then entered the town, and having graciously let fall the glasses, that my person might be seen, passed slowly through the street. The noise of the wheels brought the inhabitants to their doors, but I could not perceive that I was known by them. At last I alighted, and my name, I suppose, was told by my servants, for the barber stept from the opposite house, and seized me by the hand with honest joy in his countenance, which, according to the rule that I had prescribed to myself, I repressed with a frigid graciousness. The fellow, instead of sinking into dejection, turned away with contempt, and left me to consider how the second salutation should be received. The next friend was better treated, for I soon found that I must purchase by civility that regard which I expected to enforce by insolence.

' There was yet no smoke of bonfires, no harmony of bells, no shout of crowds, nor riot of joy; the business of the day went forward as before; and after having ordered a splendid supper, which no man came to partake, and which my chagrin hindered me from tasting, I went to bed, where the vexation of disappointment overpowered the fatigue of my journey, and kept me from sleep.

' I rose so much humbled by these mortifications, as to inquire after the present state of the town, and found that I had been absent too long to obtain the triumph which had flattered my expectation. Of the friends whose compliments I expected, some had long ago moved to distant provinces, some had lost, in the maladies of age, all sense of another's prosperity, and some had forgotten our former intimacy amidst care and distresses. Of three whom I had resolved to punish for their former offences by a longer continuance of neglect, one was, by his own industry, raised above my scorn, and two were sheltered from it in the grave. All those whom I loved, feared, or hated, all whose envy or whose kindness I had hopes of contemplating with pleasure, were swept away, and their place was filled by a new generation with other views and other competitions; and among many proofs of the impotence of wealth, I found that it conferred upon me very few distinctions in my native place.   I am, Sir, &c.

SEROTINUS.'

N° 166. SATURDAY, OCTOBER 19, 1751.

Semper eris pauper, si pauper es, Æmiliane :
Dantur opes nulli nunc, nisi divitibus.—-Mart.

Once poor, my friend, still poor you must remain ;
The rich alone have all the means of gain.—Edw. Cave.

No complaint has been more frequently repeated in all ages than that of the neglect of merit associated with poverty, and the difficulty with which valuable or pleasing qualities force themselves into view, when they are obscured by indigence. It has been long observed, that native beauty has little power to charm without the ornaments which fortune bestows, and that to want the favour of others is often sufficient to hinder us from obtaining it.

Every day discovers that mankind are not yet convinced of their error, or that their conviction is without power to influence their conduct; for poverty still continues to produce contempt, and still obstructs the claims of kindred and of virtue. The eye of wealth is elevated towards higher stations, and seldom descends to examine the actions of those who are placed below the level of its notice, and who in distant regions and lower situations are struggling with distress, or toiling for bread. Among the multitudes overwhelmed with insuperable calamity, it is common to find those whom a very little assistance would enable to support themselves with decency, and who yet cannot obtain from near relations what they see hourly lavished in ostentation, luxury, or frolic.

There are natural reasons why poverty does not easily conciliate affection. He that has been confined from his infancy to the conversation of the lowest classes of mankind, must necessarily want those accomplishments which are the usual means of attracting favour; and though truth, fortitude, and probity, give an indisputable right to reverence and kindness, they will not be distinguished by common eyes, unless they are brightened by elegance of manners, but are cast aside like unpolished gems, of which none but the artist knows the intrinsic value, till their asperities are smoothed and their incrustations rubbed away.

The grossness of vulgar habits obstructs the efficacy of virtue, as impurity and harshness of style impair the force of reason, and rugged numbers turn off the mind from artifice of disposition and fertility of invention. Few have strength of reason to over-rule the perceptions of sense; and yet fewer have curiosity or benevolence to struggle long against the first impression: he therefore who fails to please in his salutation and address, is at once rejected, and never obtains an opportunity of shewing his latent excellences or essential qualities.

It is indeed not easy to prescribe a successful manner of approach to the distressed or necessitous, whose condition subjects every kind of behaviour equally to miscarriage. He whose confidence of merit incites him to meet without any apparent sense of inferiority the eyes of those who flattered themselves with their own dignity, is considered as an insolent leveller, impatient of the just prerogatives of rank and wealth, eager to usurp the station to which he has no right, and to confound the subordinations of society; and who would contribute to the exaltation of that spirit which even want and calamity are not able to restrain from rudeness and rebellion.

But no better success will commonly be found to attend servility and dejection, which often give pride the confidence to treat them with contempt. A request made with diffidence and timidity is easily denied, because the petitioner himself seems to doubt its fitness.

Kindness is generally reciprocal; we are desirous of pleasing others, because we receive pleasure from them; but by what means can the man please, whose attention is engrossed by his distresses, and who has no leisure to be officious; whose will is restrained by his necessities, and who has no power to confer benefits; whose temper is perhaps vitiated by misery, and whose understanding is impeded by ignorance?

It is yet a more offensive discouragement, that the same actions performed by different hands produce different effects, and instead of rating the man by his performances, we rate too frequently the performance by the man. It sometimes happens in the combinations of life, that important services are performed by inferiors; but though their zeal and activity may be paid by pecuniary rewards, they seldom excite that flow of gratitude, or obtain that accumulation of recompense, with which all think it their duty to acknowledge the favour of those who descend to their assistance from a higher elevation. To be obliged is to be in some respect inferior to another; and few willingly indulge the memory of an action which raises one whom they have always been accustomed to think below them, but satisfy themselves with faint praise and penurious payment, and then drive it from their own minds, and endeavour to conceal it from the knowledge of others.

It may be always objected to the services of those who can be supposed to want a reward, that they were produced not by kindness but interest; they are therefore, when they are no longer wanted, easily disregarded as arts of insinuation, or stratagems of selfishness. Benefits which are received as gifts from wealth, are exacted as debts from indigence; and he that in a high station is celebrated for superfluous goodness, would in a meaner condition have barely been confessed to have done his duty.

It is scarcely possible for the utmost benevolence to oblige, when exerted under the disadvantages of great inferiority; for by the habitual arrogance of wealth, such expectations are commonly formed as no zeal or industry can satisfy; and what regard can he hope, who has done less than was demanded from him?

There are indeed kindnesses conferred which were never purchased by precedent favours; and there is an affection not arising from gratitude or gross interest, by which similar natures are attracted to each other, without prospect of any other advantage than the pleasure of exchanging sentiments, and the hope of confirming their esteem of themselves by the approbation of each other. But this spontaneous fondness seldom rises at the sight of poverty which every one regards with habitual contempt, and of which the applause is no more courted by vanity, than the countenance is solicited by ambition. The most generous and disinterested friendship must be resolved at last into the love of ourselves; he therefore whose reputation or dignity inclines us to consider his esteem as the testimonial of desert, will always find our hearts open to his endearments. We every day see men of eminence followed with all the obsequiousness of dependance, and courted with all the blandishments of flattery, by those who want nothing from them but professions of regard, and who think themselves liberally rewarded by a bow, a smile, or an embrace.

But those prejudices which every mind feels more or less in favour of riches, ought, like other opinions which only custom and example have impressed upon us, to be in time subjected to reason. We must learn how to separate the real character from extraneous adhesions and casual circumstances, to consider closely him whom we are about to adopt or to reject; to regard his inclinations as well as his actions; to trace out those virtues which lie torpid in the heart for want of opportunity, and those vices that lurk unseen by the absence of temptation; that when we find worth faintly shooting in the shades of obscurity, we may let in light and sunshine upon it and ripen barren volition into efficacy and power.

Nº 167.   TUESDAY, OCTOBER 22, 1751.

Candida perpetuo reside, Concordia lecto,
    Tamque pari semper sit Venus æqua jugo.
Diligat ipsa senem quondam, sed et ipsa marito
    Tunc quoque cùm fuerit, non videatur anus.—MART.

Their nuptial bed may smiling concord dress,
And Venus still the happy union bless!
Wrinkled with age, may mutual love and truth
To their dim eyes recall the bloom of youth.—F. LEWIS.

'TO THE RAMBLER.

'SIR,

'IT is not common to envy those with whom we cannot easily be placed in comparison. Every man sees without malevolence the progress of another in the tracks of life, which he has himself no desire to tread, and hears, without inclination to cavils or contradiction, the renown of those whose distance will not suffer them to draw the attention of mankind from his own merit. The sailor never thinks it necessary to contest the lawyer's abilities; nor would the Rambler, however jealous of his reputation, be much disturbed by the success of rival wits at Agra or Ispahan.

'We do not therefore ascribe to you any superlative degree of virtue, when we believe that we may inform you of our change of condition without danger of malignant fascination; and that when you read of the marriage of your correspondents Hymenæus and Tranquilla, you will join your wishes to those of their other friends for the happy event of a union in which caprice and selfishness had so little part.

'There is at least this reason why we should be

less deceived in our connubial hopes than many who enter into the same state, that we have allowed our minds to form no unreasonable expectations, nor vitiated our fancies, in the soft hours of courtship, with visions of felicity which human power cannot bestow, or of perfection which human virtue cannot attain. That impartiality with which we endeavoured to inspect the manners of all whom we have known was never so much overpowered by our passion, but that we discovered some faults and weaknesses in each other; and joined our hands in conviction, that as there are advantages to be enjoyed in marriage, there are inconveniences likewise to be endured; and that, together with confederate intellects and auxiliary virtues, we must find different opinions and opposite inclinations.

'We however flatter ourselves, for who is not flattered by himself as well as by others on the day of marriage, that we are eminently qualified to give mutual pleasure. Our birth is without any such remarkable disparity as can give either an opportunity of insulting the other with pompous names and splendid alliances, or of calling in upon any domestic controversy the overbearing assistance of powerful relations. Our fortune was equally suitable, so that we meet without any of those obligations which always produce reproach or suspicion of reproach, which, though they may be forgotten in the gaieties of the first month, no delicacy will always suppress, or of which the suppression must be considered as a new favour, to be repaid by tameness and submission, till gratitude takes the place of love, and the desire of pleasing degenerates by degrees into the fear of offending.

'The settlements caused no delay; for we did not trust our affairs to the negotiation of wretches who would have paid their court by multiplying stipula-

tions. Tranquilla scorned to detain any part of her
fortune from him into whose hands she delivered up
her person; and Hymenæus thought no act of baseness more criminal than his who enslaves his wife
by her own generosity, who by marrying without a
jointure condemns her to all the dangers of accident
and caprice, and at last boasts his liberality, by
granting what only the indiscretion of her kindness
enabled him to withhold. He therefore received on
the common terms the portion which any other woman might have brought him, and reserved all the
exuberance of acknowledgment for those excellences which he has yet been able to discover only in
Tranquilla.

'We did not pass the weeks of courtship like those
who consider themselves as taking the last draught
of pleasure, and resolve not to quit the bowl without
a surfeit, or who know themselves about to set happiness to hazard, and endeavour to lose their sense
of danger in the ebriety of perpetual amusement,
and whirl round the gulf before they sink. Hymenæus often repeated a medical axiom, that *the suc-
cours of sickness ought not to be wasted in health.* We
know that however our eyes may yet sparkle, and our
hearts bound at the presence of each other, the time
of listlessness and satiety, of peevishness and discontent, must come at last, in which we shall be driven
for relief to shows and recreations; that the uniformity of life must be sometimes diversified, and
the vacuities of conversation sometimes supplied.
We rejoice in the reflection that we have stores of
novelty yet unexhausted, which may be opened when
repletion shall call for change, and gratifications yet
untasted, by which life, when it shall become vapid
or bitter, may be restored to its former sweetness and
sprightliness, and again irritate the appetite, and
again sparkle in the cup.

' Our time will probably be less tasteless than that of those whom the authority and avarice of parents unite almost without their consent in their early years, before they have accumulated any fund of reflection, or collected materials for mutual entertainment. Such we have often seen rising in the morning to cards, and retiring in the afternoon to doze, whose happiness was celebrated by their neighbours, because they happened to grow rich by parsimony, and to be kept quiet by insensibility, and agreed to eat and to sleep together.

' We have both mingled with the world, and are therefore no strangers to the faults and virtues, the designs and competitions, the hopes and fears of our contemporaries. We have both amused our leisure with books, and can therefore recount the events of former times, or cite the dictates of ancient wisdom. Every occurrence furnishes us with some hint which one or the other can improve, and if it should happen that memory or imagination fail us, we can retire to no idle or unimproving solitude.

' Though our characters, beheld at a distance, exhibit this general resemblance, yet a nearer inspection discovers such a dissimilitude of our habitudes and sentiments, as leaves each some peculiar advantages, and affords that *concordia discors*, that suitable disagreement which is always necessary to intellectual harmony. There may be a total diversity of ideas which admits no participation of the same delight, and there may likewise be such a conformity of notions, as leaves neither any thing to add to the decisions of the other. With such contrariety there can be no peace, with such similarity there can be no pleasure. Our reasonings, though often formed upon different views, terminate generally in the same conclusion. Our thoughts, like rivulets issuing from distant springs, are each impregnated in its course with various mixtures, and tinged by infusions unknown to the other, yet at last easily unite into one stream, and purify themselves by the gentle effervescence of contrary qualities.

'These benefits we receive in a greater degree, as we converse without reserve, because we have nothing to conceal. We have no debts to be paid by imperceptible deductions from avowed expenses, no habits to be indulged by the private subserviency of a favoured servant, no private interviews with needy relations, no intelligence with spies placed upon each other. We considered marriage as the most solemn league of perpetual friendship, a state from which artifice and concealment are to be banished for ever, and in which every act of dissimulation is a breach of faith.

'The impetuous vivacity of youth, and that ardour of desire, which the first sight of pleasure naturally produces, have long ceased to hurry us into irregularity and vehemence; and experience has shewn us that few gratifications are too valuable to be sacrificed to complaisance. We have thought it convenient to rest from the fatigue of pleasure, and now only continue that course of life into which we had before entered, confirmed in our choice by mutual approbation, supported in our resolution by mutual encouragement, and assisted in our efforts by mutual exhortation.

'Such, Mr. Rambler, is our prospect of life, a prospect which, as it is beheld with more attention, seems to open more extensive happiness, and spreads by degrees into the boundless regions of eternity. But if all our prudence has been vain, and we are doomed to give one instance more of the uncertainty of human discernment, we shall comfort ourselves amidst our disappointments, that we were not betrayed but by such delusions as caution could not

escape, since we sought happiness only in the arms
of virtue.

We are, Sir, your humble servants,

HYMENÆUS,

TRANQUILLA.'

Nº 168. SATURDAY, OCTOBER 26, 1751.

————————Decipit
Frons prima multos, rara mens intelligit
Quod interiore condidit cura angulo.—PHÆDRUS.

The tinsel glitter, and the specious mien,
Delude the most; few pry behind the scene.

IT has been observed by Boileau, that 'a mean or
common thought expressed in pompous diction, generally pleases more than a new or noble sentiment
delivered in low and vulgar language; because the
number is greater of those whom custom has enabled
to judge of words, than whom study has qualified to
examine things.'

This solution might satisfy, if such only were offended with meanness of expression as are unable
to distinguish propriety of thought, and to separate
propositions or images from the vehicles by which
they are conveyed to the understanding. But this
kind of disgust is by no means confined to the ignorant or superficial; it operates uniformly and universally upon readers of all classes: every man,
however profound or abstracted, perceives himself
irresistibly alienated by low terms; they who profess the most zealous adherence to truth are forced
to admit that she owes part of her charms to her ornaments; and loses much of her power over the soul,

E 3

when she appears disgraced by a dress uncouth or ill-adjusted.

We are all offended by low terms, but are not disgusted alike by the same compositions, because we do not all agree to censure the same terms as low. No word is naturally or intrinsically meaner than another; our opinion therefore of words, as of other things arbitrarily and capriciously established, depends wholly upon accident and custom. The cottager thinks those apartments splendid and spacious, which an inhabitant of palaces will despise for their inelegance; and to him who has passed most of his hours with the delicate and polite, many expressions will seem sordid, which another, equally acute, may hear without offence; but a mean term never fails to displease him to whom it appears mean, as poverty is certainly and invariably despised, though he who is poor in the eyes of some, may by others be envied for his wealth.

Words become low by the occasions to which they are applied, or the general character of them who use them; and the disgust which they produce arises from the revival of those images with which they are commonly united. Thus if, in the most solemn discourse, a phrase happens to occur which has been successfully employed in some ludicrous narrative, the gravest auditor finds it difficult to refrain from laughter, when they who are not prepossessed by the same accidental association, are utterly unable to guess the reason of his merriment. Words which convey ideas of dignity in one age, are banished from elegant writing or conversation in another, because they are in time debased by vulgar mouths, and can be no longer heard without the involuntary recollection of unpleasing images.

When Macbeth is confirming himself in the horrid

purpose of stabbing his king, he breaks out amidst
his emotions into a wish natural to a murderer:

> ————Come, thick night!
> And pall thee in the dunnest smoke of hell,
> That my keen knife see not the wound it makes;
> Nor heav'n peep through the blanket of the dark,
> To cry, Hold, hold!

In this passage is exerted all the force of poetry, that
force which calls new powers into being, which em-
bodies sentiment, and animates matter; yet perhaps
scarce any man now peruses it without some disturbance of his attention from the counteraction of the
words to the ideas. What can be more dreadful
than to implore the presence of night, invested not
in common obscurity, but in the smoke of hell?
Yet the efficacy of this invocation is destroyed by
the insertion of an epithet now seldom heard but in
the stable, and *dun* night may come or go without
any other notice than contempt.

If we start into raptures when some hero of the
Iliad tells us that δορυ μαινεται, his lance rages with
eagerness to destroy; if we are alarmed at the terror
of the soldiers commanded by Cæsar to hew down
the sacred grove, who dreaded, says Lucan, lest the
axe aimed at the oak should fly back upon the
striker,

> ————Si robora sacra ferirent,
> In sua credebant redituras membra secures.

> None dares with impious steel the grove to rend,
> Lest on himself the destin'd stroke descend;

we cannot surely but sympathize with the horrors of
a wretch about to murder his master, his friend, his
benefactor, who suspects that the weapon will refuse
its office, and start back from the breast which he is
preparing to violate. Yet this sentiment is weak-
ened by the name of an instrument used by butchers

and cooks in the meanest employments; we do not
immediately conceive that any crime of importance
is to be committed with a *knife;* or who does not, at
last, from the long habit of connecting a knife with
sordid offices, feel aversion rather than terror?

Macbeth proceeds to wish, in the madness of guilt,
that the inspection of heaven may be intercepted,
and that he may, in the involutions of infernal darkness, escape the eye of Providence. This is the utmost extravagance of determined wickedness; yet
this is so debased by two unfortunate words, that
while I endeavour to impress on my reader the energy
of the sentiment, I can scarce check my risibility,
when the expression forces itself upon my mind; for
who, without some relaxation of his gravity, can hear
of the avengers of guilt *peeping through a blanket?*

These imperfections of diction are less obvious to
the reader, as he is less acquainted with common
usages; they are therefore wholly imperceptible to a
foreigner, who learns our language from books, and
will strike a solitary academic less forcibly than a
modish lady.

Among the numerous requisites that must concur
to complete an author, few are of more importance
than an early entrance into the living world. The
seeds of knowledge may be planted in solitude, but
must be cultivated in public. Argumentation may
be taught in colleges, and theories formed in retirement; but the artifice of embellishment, and the
powers of attraction, can be gained only by a general converse.

An acquaintance with prevailing customs and fashionable elegance is necessary likewise for other purposes. The injury that grand imagery suffers from
unsuitable language, personal merit may fear from
rudeness and indelicacy. When the success of Æneas
depended on the favour of the queen upon whose

coasts he was driven, his celestial protectress thought him not sufficiently secured against rejection by his piety or bravery, but decorated him for the interview with preternatural beauty. Whoever desires for his writings or himself, what none can reasonably contemn, the favour of mankind, must add grace to strength, and make his thoughts agreeable as well as useful. Many complain of neglect who never tried to attract regard. It cannot be expected that the patrons of science or virtue should be solicitous to discover excellences, which they who possess them shade and disguise. Few have abilities so much needed by the rest of the world as to be caressed on their own terms; and he that will not condescend to recommend himself by external embellishments, must submit to the fate of just sentiment meanly expressed, and be ridiculed and forgotten before he is understood.

Nº 169.　TUESDAY, OCTOBER 29, 1751.

Nec pluteum cædit, nec demorsos sapit ungues.—PERSIUS.

No blood from bitten nails those poems drew;
But churn'd, like spittle, from the lips they flew.—DRYDEN.

NATURAL historians assert, that whatever is formed for long duration arrives slowly to its maturity. Thus the firmest timber is of tardy growth, and animals generally exceed each other in longevity, in proportion to the time between their conception and their birth.

The same observation may be extended to the offspring of the mind. Hasty compositions, however they please at first by flowery luxuriance, and spread in the sunshine of temporary favour, can seldom endure the change of seasons, but perish at the first blast of criticism, or frost of neglect. When Apelles was reproached with the paucity of his productions, and the incessant attention with which he retouched his pieces, he condescended to make no other answer, than that *he painted for perpetuity*.

No vanity can more justly incur contempt and indignation than that which boasts of negligence and hurry. For who can bear with patience the writer who claims such superiority to the rest of his species, as to imagine that mankind are at leisure for attention to his extemporary sallies, and that posterity will reposite his casual effusions among the treasures of ancient wisdom?

Men have sometimes appeared of such transcendent abilities, that their slightest and most cursory performances excel all that labour and study can enable meaner intellects to compose; as there are regions of which the spontaneous products cannot be equalled in other soils by care and culture. But it is no less dangerous for any man to place himself in this rank of understanding, and fancy that he is born to be illustrious without labour, than to omit the cares of husbandry, and expect from his ground the blossoms of Arabia.

The greatest part of those who congratulate themselves upon their intellectual dignity, and usurp the privileges of genius, are men whom only themselves would ever have marked out as enriched by uncommon liberalities of nature, or entitled to veneration and immortality on easy terms. This ardour of confidence is usually found among those who, having not enlarged their notions by books or conversation, are persuaded, by the partiality which we all feel in our own favour, that they have reached the summit of excellence, because they discovered none higher than themselves, and who acquiesce in the first

thoughts that occur, because their scantiness of
knowledge allows them little choice, and the narrowness of their views affords them no glimpse of perfection, of that sublime idea which human industry
has from the first ages been vainly toiling to approach.   They see a little, and believe that there is
nothing beyond their sphere of vision, as the Patue-
cos of Spain, who inhabited a small valley, conceived
the surrounding mountains to be the boundaries of
the world.   In proportion as perfection is more dis-
tinctly conceived, the pleasure of contemplating our
own performances will be lessened; it may therefore
be observed, that they who most deserve praise are
often afraid to decide in favour of their own performances; they know how much is still wanting to
their completion, and wait with anxiety and terror
the determination of the public.   ' I please every
one else,' says Tully, ' but never satisfy myself.'

It has often been inquired, why, notwithstanding
the advances of latter ages in science, and the assistance which the infusion of so many new ideas
has given us, we still fall below the ancients in the
art of composition.   Some part of their superiority
may be justly ascribed to the graces of their language, from which the most polished of the present
European tongues are nothing more than barbarous
degenerations.   Some advantage they might gain
merely by priority, which put them in possession of
the most natural sentiments, and left us nothing but
servile repetition or forced conceits.   But the greater
part of their praise seems to have been the just reward of modesty and labour.   Their sense of human
weakness confined them commonly to one study,
which their knowledge of the extent of every science engaged them to prosecute with indefatigable
diligence.

Among the writers of antiquity I remember none

except Statius who ventures to mention the speedy production of his writings, either as an extenuation of his faults, or a proof of his facility. Nor did Statius, when he considered himself as a candidate for lasting reputation, think a closer attention unnecessary, but amidst all his pride and indigence, the two great hasteners of modern poems, employed twelve years upon the Thebaid, and thinks his claim to renown proportionate to his labour.

> Thebais, multâ cruciata limâ,
> Tentat, audaci fide, Mantuanæ
>   Gaudia famæ.
>
> Polish'd with endless toil, my lays
> At length aspire to Mantuan praise.

Ovid indeed apologises in his banishment for the imperfection of his letters, but mentions his want of leisure to polish them as an addition to his calamities; and was so far from imagining revisals and corrections unnecessary, that at his departure from Rome, he threw his Metamorphoses into the fire, lest he should be disgraced by a book which he could not hope to finish.

It seems not often to have happened that the same writer aspired to reputation in verse and prose; and of those few that attempted such diversity of excellence, I know not that even one succeeded. Contrary characters they never imagined a single mind able to support, and therefore no man is recorded to have undertaken more than one kind of dramatic poetry.

What they had written they did not venture in their first fondness to thrust into the world, but considering the impropriety of sending forth inconsiderately that which cannot be recalled, deferred the publication, if not nine years, according to the direction of Horace, yet till their fancy was cooled after the raptures of invention, and the glare of novelty had ceased to dazzle the judgment.

There were in those days no weekly or diurnal writers; *multa dies, et multa litura,* much time, and many rasures, were considered as indispensable requisites; and that no other method of attaining lasting praise has been yet discovered, may be conjectured from the blotted manuscripts of Milton now remaining, and from the tardy emission of Pope's compositions, delayed more than once till the incidents to which they alluded were forgotten, till his enemies were secure from his satire, and what to an honest mind must be more painful, his friends were deaf to his encomiums.

To him, whose eagerness of praise hurries his productions soon into the light, many imperfections are unavoidable, even where the mind furnishes the materials as well as regulates their dispositions, and nothing depends upon search or information. Delay opens new veins of thought, the subject dismissed for a time appears with a new train of dependant images, the accidents of reading or conversation supply new ornaments or allusions, or mere intermission of the fatigue of thinking enables the mind to collect new force and make new excursions. But all those benefits come too late for him, who, when he was weary with labour, snatched at the recompense, and gave his work to his friends and his enemies, as soon as impatience and pride persuaded him to conclude it.

One of the most pernicious effects of haste, is obscurity. He that teems with a quick succession of ideas, and perceives how one sentiment produces another, easily believes that he can clearly express what he so strongly comprehends; he seldom suspects his thoughts of embarrassment, while he preserves in his own memory the series of connexion,

F

or his diction of ambiguity, while only one sense is present to his mind. Yet if he has been employed on an abstruse or complicated argument, he will find, when he has a while withdrawn his mind, and returns as a new reader to his work, that he has only a conjectural glimpse of his own meaning, and that to explain it to those whom he desires to instruct, he must open his sentiments, disentangle his method, and alter his arrangement.

Authors and lovers always suffer some infatuation, from which only absence can set them free; and every man ought to restore himself to the full exercise of his judgment, before he does that which he cannot do improperly, without injuring his honour and his quiet.

N° 170. SATURDAY, NOVEMBER 2, 1751.

Confiteor; si quid prodest delicta fateri.—Ovid.

I grant the charge; forgive the fault confess'd.

'To the Rambler.

'Sir,

'I am one of those beings, from whom many, that melt at the sight of all other misery, think it meritorious to withhold relief; one whom the rigour of virtuous indignation dooms to suffer without complaint, and perish without regard; and whom I myself have formerly insulted in the pride of reputation and security of innocence.

'I am of a good family, but my father was burdened with more children than he could decently support. A wealthy relation, as he travelled from

London to his country-seat, condescending to make him a visit, was touched with compassion of his narrow fortune, and resolved to ease him of part of his charge, by taking the care of a child upon himself. Distress on one side, and ambition on the other, were too powerful for parental fondness, and the little family passed in review before him, that he might make his choice. I was then ten years old, and without knowing for what purpose I was called to my great cousin, endeavoured to recommend myself by my best courtesy, sung him my prettiest song, told the last story I had read, and so much endeared myself by my innocence, that he declared his resolution to adopt me, and to educate me with his own daughters.

‘ My parents felt the common struggles at the thought of parting, and *some natural tears they dropp'd, but wip'd them soon.* They considered, not without that false estimation of the value of wealth which poverty long continued always produces, that I was raised to higher rank than they could give me, and to hopes of more ample fortune than they could bequeath. My mother sold some of her ornaments to dress me in such a manner as might secure me from contempt at my first arrival; and when she dismissed me, pressed me to her bosom with an embrace that I still feel, gave me some precepts of piety, which, however neglected, I have not forgotten, and uttered prayers for my final happiness, of which I have not yet ceased to hope that they will at last be granted.

‘ My sisters envied my new finery, and seemed not much to regret our separation; my father conducted me to the stage-coach with a kind of cheerful tenderness; and in a very short time, I was transported to splendid apartments and a luxurious table, and grew familiar to show, noise, and gaiety.

‘ In three years my mother died, having implored

a blessing on her family with her last breath. I
had little opportunity to indulge a sorrow which
there was none to partake with me, and therefore
soon ceased to reflect much upon my loss. My
father turned all his care upon his other children,
whom some fortunate adventures and unexpected
legacies enabled him, when he died four years after
my mother, to leave in a condition above their expectations.

‘ I should have shared the increase of his fortune,
and had once a portion assigned me in his will; but
my cousin assuring him that all care for me was
needless, since he had resolved to place me happily
in the world, directed him to divide my part amongst
my sisters.

‘ Thus I was thrown upon dependance without
resource. Being now at an age in which young
women are initiated into company, I was no longer
to be supported in my former character, but at considerable expense; so that partly lest I should waste
money, and partly lest my appearance might draw too
many compliments and assiduities, I was insensibly
degraded from my equality, and enjoyed few privileges above the head servant, but that of receiving
no wages.

‘ I felt every indignity, but knew that resentment
would precipitate my fall. I therefore endeavoured
to continue my importance by little services and
active officiousness, and for a time preserved myself
from neglect, by withdrawing all pretences to competition, and studying to please rather than to shine.
But my interest, notwithstanding this expedient,
hourly declined, and my cousin's favourite maid began to exchange repartees with me, and consult me
about the alterations of a cast gown.

‘ I was now completely depressed; and though I
had seen mankind enough to know the necessity of

outward cheerfulness, I often withdrew to my chamber to vent my grief, or turn my condition in my mind, and examine by what means I might escape from perpetual mortification. At last my schemes and sorrows were interrupted by a sudden change of my relation's behaviour, who one day took an occasion when we were left together in a room, to bid me suffer myself no longer to be insulted, but assume the place which he always intended me to hold in the family. He assured me that his wife's preference of her own daughters should never hurt me : and, accompanying his professions with a purse of gold, ordered me to bespeak a rich suit at the mercer's, and to apply privately to him for money when I wanted it, and insinuate that my other friends supplied me, which he would take care to confirm.

'By this stratagem, which I did not then understand, he filled me with tenderness and gratitude, compelled me to repose on him as my only support, and produced a necessity of private conversation. He often appointed interviews at the house of an acquaintance, and sometimes called on me with a coach, and carried me abroad. My sense of his favour, and the desire of retaining it, disposed me to unlimited complaisance, and though I saw his kindness grow every day more fond, I did not suffer any suspicion to enter my thoughts. At last the wretch took advantage of the familiarity which he enjoyed as my relation, and the submission which he exacted as my benefactor, to complete the ruin of an orphan, whom his own promises had made indigent, whom his indulgence had melted, and his authority subdued.

'I know not why it should afford subject of exultation, to overpower on any terms the resolution, or surprise the caution of a girl; but of all the boasters that deck themselves in the spoils of innocence and beauty, they surely have the least pretensions to triumph, who submit to owe their success to some casual influence. They neither employ the graces of fancy, nor the force of understanding, in their attempts; they cannot please their vanity with the art of their approaches, the delicacy of their adulations, the elegance of their address, or the efficacy of their eloquence; nor applaud themselves as possessed of any qualities, by which affection is attracted. They surmount no obstacles, they defeat no rivals, but attack only those who cannot resist, and are often content to possess the body, without any solicitude to gain the heart.

'Many of these despicable wretches does my present acquaintance with infamy and wickedness enable me to number among the heroes of debauchery: reptiles whom their own servants would have despised, had they not been their servants, and with whom beggary would have disdained intercourse, had she not been allured by hopes of relief. Many of the beings which are now rioting in taverns, or shivering in the streets, have been corrupted not by arts of gallantry which stole gradually upon the affections and laid prudence asleep, but by the fear of losing benefits which were never intended, or of incurring resentment which they could not escape; some have been frighted by masters, and some awed by guardians into ruin.

'Our crime had its usual consequence, and he soon perceived that I could not long continue in his family. I was distracted at the thought of the reproach which I now believed inevitable. He comforted me with hopes of eluding all discovery, and often upbraided me with the anxiety, which perhaps none but himself saw in my countenance; but at last mingled his assurances of protection and maintenance with menaces of total desertion, if in the moments of pertur-

bation I should suffer his secret to escape, or endeavour to throw on him any part of my infamy.

'Thus passed the dismal hours till my retreat
could no longer be delayed. It was pretended that
my relations had sent for me to a distant county,
and I entered upon a state which shall be described
in my next letter.   I am, Sir, &c.

MISELLA.'

Nᵒ 171.   TUESDAY, NOVEMBER 5, 1751.

Tædet cæli convexa tueri.—VIRG.

Dark is the sun, and loathsome is the day.

'TO THE RAMBLER.

'SIR,

'MISELLA now sits down to continue her narrative.
I am convinced that nothing would more powerfully
preserve youth from irregularity, or guard inexperience from seduction, than a just description of the
condition into which the wanton plunges herself, and
therefore hope that my letter may be a sufficient antidote to my example.

'After the distraction, hesitation, and delays which
the timidity of guilt naturally produces, I was removed to lodgings in a distant part of the town,
under one of the characters commonly assumed upon
such occasions. Here being by my circumstances
condemned to solitude, I past most of my hours in
bitterness and anguish. The conversation of the
people with whom I was placed was not at all capable of engaging my attention, or dispossessing the
reigning ideas. The books which I carried to my
retreat were such as heightened my abhorrence of

myself; for I was not so far abandoned as to sink
voluntarily into corruption, or endeavour to conceal
from my own mind the enormity of my crime.

'My relation remitted none of his fondness, but
visited me so often, that I was sometimes afraid lest
his assiduity should expose him to suspicion. Whenever he came he found me weeping, and was therefore less delightfully entertained than he expected.
After frequent expostulations upon the unreasonable-
ness of my sorrow, and innumerable protestations of
everlasting regard, he at last found that I was more
affected with the loss of my innocence than the danger of my fame, and that he might not be disturbed
by my remorse, began to lull my conscience with the
opiates of irreligion. His arguments were such as
my course of life has since exposed me often to the
necessity of hearing, vulgar, empty, and fallacious;
yet they at first confounded me by their novelty,
filled me with doubt and perplexity, and interrupted
that peace which I began to feel from the sincerity
of my repentance, without substituting any other support. I listened a while to his impious gabble, but
its influence was soon overpowered by natural reason
and early education, and the convictions which this
new attempt gave me of his baseness completed my
abhorrence. I have heard of barbarians, who when
tempests drive ships upon their coast, decoy them to
the rocks that they may plunder their lading, and
have always thought that wretches thus merciless in
their depredations, ought to be destroyed by a general insurrection of all social beings; yet how light
is this guilt to the crime of him, who in the agita-
tions of remorse cuts away the anchor of piety, and
when he has drawn aside credulity from the paths
of virtue, hides the light of heaven which would direct her to return. I had hitherto considered him as a
man equally betrayed with myself by the concurrence

of appetite and opportunity; but I now saw with horror that he was contriving to perpetuate his gratification, and was desirous to fit me to his purpose by complete and radical corruption.

'To escape, however, was not yet in my power. I could support the expense of my condition, only by the continuance of his favour. He provided all that was necessary, and, in a few weeks, congratulated me upon my escape from the danger which we had both expected with so much anxiety. I then began to remind him of his promise to restore me with my fame uninjured to the world. He promised me in general terms, that nothing should be wanting which his power could add to my happiness, but forbore to release me from my confinement. I knew how much my reception in the world depended upon my speedy return, and was therefore outrageously impatient of his delays, which I now perceived to be only artifices of lewdness. He told me, at last, with an appearance of sorrow, that all hopes of restoration to my former state were for ever precluded; that chance had discovered my secret, and malice divulged it; and that nothing now remained, but to seek a retreat more private, where curiosity or hatred could never find us.

'The rage, anguish, and resentment, which I felt at this account are not to be expressed. I was in so much dread of reproach and infamy, which he represented as pursuing me with full cry, that I yielded myself implicitly to his disposal, and was removed, with a thousand studied precautions, through byways and dark passages, to another house, where I harassed him with perpetual solicitations for a small annuity, that might enable me to live in the country in obscurity and innocence.

'This demand he at first evaded with ardent professions, but in time appeared offended at my importunity and distrust ; and having one day endeavoured to soothe me with uncommon expressions of tenderness, when he found my discontent immovable, left me with some inarticulate murmurs of anger. I was pleased that he was at last roused to sensibility, and expecting that at his next visit he would comply with my request, lived with great tranquillity upon the money in my hands, and was so much pleased with this pause of persecution, that I did not reflect how much his absence had exceeded the usual intervals, till I was alarmed with the danger of wanting subsistence. I then suddenly contracted my expenses, but was unwilling to supplicate for assistance. Necessity, however, soon overcame my modesty or my pride, and I applied to him by a letter, but had no answer. I writ in terms more pressing, but without effect. I then sent an agent to inquire after him, who informed me that he had quitted his house, and was gone with his family to reside for some time upon his estate in Ireland.

'However shocked at this abrupt departure, I was yet unwilling to believe that he could wholly abandon me, and therefore, by the sale of my clothes, I supported myself, expecting that every post would bring me relief. Thus I passed seven months between hope and dejection, in a gradual approach to poverty and distress, emaciated with discontent, and bewildered with uncertainty. At last my landlady, after many hints of the necessity of a new lover, took the opportunity of my absence to search my boxes, and missing some of my apparel, seized the remainder for rent, and led me to the door.

' To remonstrate against legal cruelty was vain ; to supplicate obdurate brutality, was hopeless. I went away I knew not whither, and wandered about without any settled purpose, unacquainted with the usual expedients of misery, unqualified for laborious offices, afraid to meet an eye that had seen me before, and hopeless of relief from those who were strangers to my former condition. Night came on in the midst of my distraction, and I still continued to wander till the menaces of the watch obliged me to shelter myself in a covered passage.

'Next day I procured a lodging in the backward garret of a mean house, and employed my landlady to inquire for a service. My applications were generally rejected for want of a character. At length, I was received at a draper's; but when it was known to my mistress that I had only one gown, and that of silk, she was of opinion that I looked like a thief, and without warning hurried me away. I then tried to support myself by my needle; and, by my landlady's recommendation, obtained a little work from a shop, and for three weeks lived without repining; but when my punctuality had gained me so much reputation that I was trusted to make up a head of some value, one of my fellow-lodgers stole the lace, and I was obliged to fly from a prosecution.

'Thus driven again into the streets, I lived upon the least that could support me, and at night accommodated myself under pent-houses as well as I could. At length I became absolutely pennyless; and having strolled all day without sustenance, was, at the close of evening, accosted by an elderly man, with an invitation to a tavern. I refused him with hesitation; he seized me by the hand, and drew me into a neighbouring house, where, when he saw my face pale with hunger, and my eyes swelling with tears, he spurned me from him, and bade me cant and whine in some other place; he for his part would take care of his pockets.

'I still continued to stand in the way, having scarcely strength to walk farther, when another soon addressed me in the same manner. When he saw

the same tokens of calamity, he considered that I
might be obtained at a cheap rate, and therefore
quickly made overtures, which I had no longer firmness to reject. By this man I was maintained four
months in penurious wickedness, and then abandoned
to my former condition, from which I was delivered
by another keeper.

' In this abject state I have now passed four years,
the drudge of extortion and the sport of drunken-
ness; sometimes the property of one man, and sometimes the common prey of accidental lewdness; at
one time tricked up for sale by the mistress of a bro-
thel, at another begging in the streets to be relieved
from hunger by wickedness; without any hope in
the day but of finding some whom folly or excess
may expose to my allurements, and without any reflections at night, but such as guilt and terror impress upon me.

' If those who pass their days in plenty and security, could visit for an hour the dismal receptacles
to which the prostitute retires from her nocturnal excursions, and see the wretches that lie crowded together, mad with intemperance, ghastly with famine,
nauseous with filth, and noisome with disease; it
would not be easy for any degree of abhorrence to
harden them against compassion, or to repress the
desire which they must immediately feel to rescue
such numbers of human beings from a state so
dreadful.

' It is said that in France they annually evacuate
their streets, and ship their prostitutes and vaga-
bonds to their colonies. If the women that infest
this city had the same opportunity of escaping from
their miseries, I believe very little force would be
necessary; for who among them can dread any
change? Many of us indeed are wholly unqualified
for any but the most servile employments, and those

perhaps would require the care of a magistrate to hinder them from following the same practices in another country; but others are only precluded by infamy from reformation, and would gladly be delivered on any terms from the necessity of guilt and the tyranny of chance. No place but a populous city can afford opportunities for open prostitution, and where the eye of justice can attend to individuals, those who cannot be made good may be restrained from mischief. For my part, I should exult at the privilege of banishment, and think myself happy in any region that should restore me once again to honesty and peace.   I am, Sir, &c.

MISELLA.'

Nº 172. SATURDAY, NOVEMBER 9, 1751.

Sæpe rogare soles qualis sim, Prisce, futurus,
    Si fiam locuples, simque repentè potens.
Quemquam posse putas mores narrare futuros?
    Dic mihi, si fias tu leo, qualis eris.—MART.

Priscus, you've often ask'd me how I'd live,
Shou'd fate at once both wealth and honour give.
What soul his future conduct can foresee?
Tell me what sort of lion you wou'd be.—F. LEWIS.

NOTHING has been longer observed, than that a change of fortune causes a change of manners; and that it is difficult to conjecture, from the conduct of him whom we see in a low condition, how he would act, if wealth and power were put into his hands. But it is generally agreed, that few men are made better by affluence or exaltation; and that the powers of the mind, when they are unbound and expanded

by the sunshine of felicity, more frequently luxuriate
into follies, than blossom into goodness.

Many observations have concurred to establish
this opinion, and it is not likely soon to become ob-
solete, for want of new occasions to revive it. The
greater part of mankind are corrupt in every condition, and differ in high and in low stations only as
they have more or fewer opportunities of gratifying
their desires, or as they are more or less restrained
by human censures. Many vitiate their principles
in the acquisition of riches ; and who can wonder
that what is gained by fraud and extortion is enjoyed
with tyranny and excess ?

Yet I am willing to believe that the depravation of
the mind by external advantages, though certainly
not uncommon, yet approaches not so nearly to uni-
versality, as some have asserted in the bitterness of
resentment or that of declamation.

Whoever rises above those who once pleased
themselves with equality, will have many malevolent
gazers at his eminence. To gain sooner than others
that which all pursue with the same ardour, and to
which all imagine themselves entitled, will for ever
be a crime. When those who started with us in the
race of life, leave us so far behind, that we have
little hope to overtake them, we revenge our disappointment by remarks on the arts of supplantation
by which they gained the advantage, or on the folly
and arrogance with which they possess it. Of them,
whose rise we could not hinder, we solace ourselves
by prognosticating the fall.

It is impossible for human purity not to betray to
an eye thus sharpened by malignity, some stains
which lay concealed and unregarded, while none
thought it their interest to discover them ; nor can
the most circumspect attention, or steady rectitude,
escape blame from censors, who have no inclination

to approve. Riches therefore, perhaps, do not so often produce crimes as incite accusers.

The common charge against those who rise above their original condition, is that of pride. It is certain that success naturally confirms us in a favourable opinion of our own abilities. Scarce any man is willing to allot to accident, friendship, and a thousand causes, which concur in every event without human contrivance or interposition, the part which they may justly claim in his advancement. We rate ourselves by our fortune rather than our virtues, and exorbitant claims are quickly produced by imaginary merit. But captiousness and jealousy are likewise easily offended, and to him who studiously looks for an affront, every mode of behaviour will supply it; freedom will be rudeness, and reserve sullenness; mirth will be negligence, and seriousness formality; when he is received with ceremony, distance and respect are inculcated; if he is treated with familiarity, he concludes himself insulted by condescensions.

It must however be confessed, that as all sudden changes are dangerous, a quick transition from poverty to abundance can seldom be made with safety. He that has long lived within sight of pleasures which he could not reach, will need more than common moderation, not to lose his reason in unbounded riot, when they are first put into his power.

Every possession is endeared by novelty; every gratification is exaggerated by desire. It is difficult not to estimate what is lately gained above its real value; it is impossible not to annex greater happiness to that condition from which we are unwillingly excluded, than nature has qualified us to obtain. For this reason, the remote inheritor of an unexpected fortune, may be generally distinguished from those who are enriched in the common course of lineal descent, by his greater haste to enjoy his wealth, by the finery of his dress, the pomp of his equipage, the splendour of his furniture, and the luxury of his table.

A thousand things which familiarity discovers to be of little value, have power for a time to seize the imagination. A Virginian king, when the Europeans had fixed a lock on his door, was so delighted to find his subjects admitted or excluded with such facility, that it was from morning to evening his whole employment to turn the key. We, among whom locks and keys have been longer in use, are inclined to laugh at this American amusement; yet I doubt whether this paper will have a single reader that may not apply the story to himself, and recollect some hours of his life in which he has been equally overpowered by the transitory charms of trifling novelty.

Some indulgence is due to him whom a happy gale of fortune has suddenly transported into new regions, where unaccustomed lustre dazzles his eyes, and untasted delicacies solicit his appetite. Let him not be considered as lost in hopeless degeneracy, though he for a while forgets the regard due to others, to indulge the contemplation of himself, and in the extravagance of his first raptures expects that his eye should regulate the motions of all that approach him, and his opinion be received as decisive and oraculous. His intoxication will give way to time; the madness of joy will fume imperceptibly away; the sense of his insufficiency will soon return; he will remember that the co-operation of others is necessary to his happiness, and learn to conciliate their regard by reciprocal beneficence.

There is, at least, one consideration which ought to alleviate our censures of the powerful and rich.

To imagine them chargeable with all the guilt and
folly of their own actions, is to be very little acquainted with the world.

> De l'absolu pouvoir vous ignorez l'yuvresse,
> Et du lache flatteur la voix enchanteresse.

> Thou hast not known the giddy whirls of fate,
> Nor servile flatteries which enchant the great.

MISS A. W.

He that can do much good or harm, will not find
many whom ambition or cowardice will suffer to be
sincere. While we live upon the level with the rest
of mankind, we are reminded of our duty by the
admonitions of friends and reproaches of enemies;
but men who stand in the highest ranks of society,
seldom hear of their faults; if by any accident an
opprobrious clamour reaches their ears, flattery is
always at hand to pour in her opiates, to quiet conviction, and obtund remorse.

Favour is seldom gained but by conformity in vice.
Virtue can stand without assistance, and considers
herself as very little obliged by countenance and
approbation: but vice, spiritless and timorous, seeks
the shelter of crowds, and support of confederacy.
The sycophant, therefore, neglects the good qualities
of his patron, and employs all his art on his weaknesses and follies, regales his reigning vanity, or sti-
mulates his prevalent desire.

Virtue is sufficiently difficult with any circumstances, but the difficulty is increased when reproof
and advice are frighted away. In common life reason
and conscience have only the appetites and passions
to encounter; but in higher stations, they must oppose artifice and adulation. He, therefore, that
yields to such temptations, cannot give those who
look upon his miscarriage much reason for exultation, since few can justly presume that from the
same snare they should have been able to escape.

N° 173. TUESDAY, NOVEMBER 12, 1751.

Quò virtus, quò ferat error?—Hor.

Now say, where virtue stops, and vice begins?

As any action or posture, long continued, will distort and disfigure the limbs ; so the mind likewise is crippled and contracted by perpetual application to the same set of ideas. It is easy to guess the trade of an artisan by his knees, his fingers, or his shoulders; and there are few among men of the more liberal professions, whose minds do not carry the brand of their calling, or whose conversation does not quickly discover to what class of the community they belong.

These peculiarities have been of great use, in the general hostility which every part of mankind exercises against the rest, to furnish insults and sarcasms. Every art has its dialect, uncouth and ungrateful to all whom custom has not reconciled to its sound, and which therefore becomes ridiculous by a slight misapplication, or unnecessary repetition.

The general reproach with which ignorance revenges the superciliousness of learning, is that of pedantry ; a censure which every man incurs, who has at any time the misfortune to talk to those who cannot understand him, and by which the modest and timorous are sometimes frighted from the display of their acquisitions and the exertions of their powers.

The name of a pedant is so formidable to young men when they first sally from their colleges, and is so liberally scattered by those who mean to boast their elegance of education, easiness of manners, and knowledge of the world, that it seems to require particular consideration; since, perhaps, if it were once understood, many a heart might be freed from painful apprehensions, and many a tongue delivered from restraint.

Pedantry is the unseasonable ostentation of learning. It may be discovered either in the choice of a subject, or in the manner of treating it. He is undoubtedly guilty of pedantry, who, when he has made himself master of some abstruse and uncultivated part of knowledge, obtrudes his remarks and discoveries upon those whom he believes unable to judge of his proficiency, and from whom, as he cannot fear contradiction, he cannot properly expect applause.

To this error the student is sometimes betrayed by the natural recurrence of the mind to its common employment, by the pleasure which every man receives from the recollection of pleasing images, and the desire of dwelling upon topics, on which he knows himself able to speak with justness. But because we are seldom so far prejudiced in favour of each other, as to search out for palliations, this failure of politeness is imputed always to vanity; and the harmless collegiate, who perhaps intended entertainment and instruction, or at worst only spoke without sufficient reflection upon the character of his hearers, is censured as arrogant or overbearing, and eager to extend his renown, in contempt of the convenience of society and the laws of conversation.

All discourse of which others cannot partake, is not only an irksome usurpation of the time devoted to pleasure and entertainment, but, what never fails to excite very keen resentment, an insolent assertion of superiority, and a triumph over less enlightened understandings. The pedant is, therefore, not only heard with weariness, but malignity; and those who conceive themselves insulted by his knowledge, never fail to tell with acrimony how injudiciously it was exerted.

To avoid this dangerous imputation, scholars sometimes divest themselves with too much haste of their academical formality, and in their endeavours to accommodate their notions and their style to common conceptions, talk rather of any thing than of that which they understand, and sink into insipidity of sentiment and meanness of expression.

There prevails among men of letters an opinion, that all appearance of science is particularly hateful to women; and that, therefore, whoever desires to be well received in female assemblies, must qualify himself by a total rejection of all that is serious, rational, or important; must consider argument or criticism as perpetually interdicted; and devote all his attention to trifles, and all his eloquence to compliment.

Students often form their notions of the present generation from the writings of the past, and are not very early informed of those changes which the gradual diffusion of knowledge, or the sudden caprice of fashion, produces in the world. Whatever might be the state of female literature in the last century, there is now no longer any danger lest the scholar should want an adequate audience at the tea-table; and whoever thinks it necessary to regulate his conversation by antiquated rules will be rather despised for his futility than caressed for his politeness.

To talk intentionally in a manner above the comprehension of those whom we address, is unquestionably pedantry; but surely complaisance requires, that no man should, without proof, conclude his company incapable of following him to the highest elevation of his fancy, or the utmost extent of his knowledge. It is always safer to err in favour of

others than of ourselves, and therefore we seldom
hazard much by endeavouring to excel.

It ought at least to be the care of learning, when
she quits her exaltation, to descend with dignity.
Nothing is more despicable than the airiness and jocularity of a man bred to severe science and solitary
meditation. To trifle agreeably is a secret which
schools cannot impart; that gay negligence and vivacious levity, which charm down resistance wherever they appear, are never attainable by him who,
having spent his first years among the dust of libra-
ries, enters late into the gay world with an unpliant
attention and established habits.

It is observed in the panegyric on Fabricius the
mechanist, that, though forced by public employments into mingled conversation, he never lost the
modesty and seriousness of the convent, no drew
ridicule upon himself by an affected imitation of
fashionable life. To the same praise every man devoted to learning ought to aspire. If he attempts the
softer arts of pleasing, and endeavours to learn the
graceful bow and the familiar embrace, the insinuat-
ing accent and the general smile, he will lose the
respect due to the character of learning, without ar-
riving at the envied honour of doing any thing with
elegance and facility.

Theophrastus was discovered not to be a native of
Athens, by so strict an adherence to the Attic dialect,
as shewed that he had learned it not by custom, but
by rule. A man not early formed to habitual elegance, betrays in like manner the effects of his education, by an unnecessary anxiety of behaviour. It
is as possible to become pedantic by fear of pedantry, as to be troublesome by ill-timed civility. There
is no kind of impertinence more justly censurable,
than his who is always labouring to level thougths
to intellects higher than his own; who apologizes for

every word which his own narrowness of converse inclines him to think unusual; keeps the exuberance of his faculties under visible restraint; is solicitous to anticipate inquiries by needless explanations; and endeavours to shade his own abilities, lest weak eyes should be dazzled with their lustre.

Nᵒ 174. SATURDAY, NOVEMBER 15, 1751.

Fœnum habet in cornu, longè fuge; dummodò risum
Excutiat sibi, non hic cuiquam parcet amico.—Hor.

Yonder he drives—avoid that furious beast:
If he may have his jest, he never cares
At whose expense; nor friend nor patron spares.

FRANCIS.

'To the Rambler.

' MR. RAMBLER,

' The laws of social benevolence require, that every man should endeavour to assist others by his experience. He that has at last escaped into port from the fluctuations of chance and the gusts of opposition, ought to make some improvements in the chart of life, by marking the rocks on which he has been dashed, and the shallows where he has been stranded.

' The error into which I was betrayed, when custom first gave me up to my own direction, is very frequently incident to the quick, the sprightly, the fearless, and the gay; to all whose ardour hurries them into precipitate execution of their designs, and imprudent declaration of their opinions; who seldom count the cost of pleasure, or examine the distant consequences of any practice that flatters them with immediate gratification.

' I came forth into the crowded world with the usual juvenile ambition, and desired nothing beyond the title of a wit. Money I considered as below my care ; for I saw such multitudes grow rich without understanding, that I could not forbear to look on wealth as an acquisition easy to industry directed by genius, and therefore threw it aside as a secondary convenience, to be procured when my principal wish should be satisfied, and my claim to intellectual excellence universally acknowledged.

' With this view I regulated my behaviour in public, and exercised my meditations in solitude. My life was divided between the care of providing topics for the entertainment of my company, and that of collecting company worthy to be entertained : for I soon found, that wit, like every other power, has its boundaries ; that its success depends upon the aptitude of others to receive impressions ; and that as some bodies, indissoluble by heat, can set the furnace and crucible at defiance, there are minds upon which the rays of fancy may be pointed without effect, and which no fire of sentiment can agitate or exalt.

' It was, however, not long before I fitted myself with a set of companions who knew how to laugh, and to whom no other recommendation was necessary than the power of striking out a jest. Among those I fixed my residence, and for a time enjoyed the felicity of disturbing the neighbours every night with the obstreperous applause which my sallies forced from the audience. The reputation of our club every day increased, and as my flights and remarks were circulated by my admirers, every day brought new solicitations for admission into our society.

'To support this perpetual fund of merriment, I frequented every place of concourse, cultivated the acquaintance of all the fashionable race, and passed the day in a continual succession of visits, in which I collected a treasure of pleasantry for the expenses of the evening. Whatever error of conduct I could discover, whatever peculiarity of manner I could observe, whatever weakness was betrayed by confidence, whatever lapse was suffered by neglect, all was drawn together for the diversion of my wild companions, who, when they had been taught the art of ridicule, never failed to signalize themselves by a zealous imitation, and filled the town on the ensuing day with scandal and vexation, with merriment and shame.

'I can scarcely believe, when I recollect my own practice, that I could have been so far deluded with petty praise, as to divulge the secrets of trust, and to expose the levities of frankness; to waylay the walks of the cautious, and surprise the security of the thoughtless. Yet it is certain, that for many years I heard nothing but with design to tell it, and saw nothing with any other curiosity than after some failure that might furnish out a jest.

'My heart, indeed, acquits me of deliberate malignity, or interested insidiousness. I had no other purpose than to heighten the pleasure of laughter by communication, nor ever raised any pecuniary advantage from the calamities of others. I led weakness and negligence into difficulties, only that I might divert myself with their perplexities and distresses; and violated every law of friendship, with no other hope than that of gaining the reputation of smartness and waggery.

'I would not be understood to charge myself with any crimes of the atrocious or destructive kind. I never betrayed an heir to gamesters, or a girl to de-

bauchees; never intercepted the kindness of a patron, or sported away the reputation of innocence.
My delight was only in petty mischief and momentary
vexations, and my acuteness was employed not upon
fraud and oppression, which it had been meritorious
to detect, but upon harmless ignorance or absurdity,
prejudice or mistake.

' This inquiry I pursued with so much diligence
and sagacity, that I was able to relate, of every man
whom I knew, some blunder or miscarriage; to betray the most circumspect of my friends into follies,
by a judicious flattery of his predominant passion;
or expose him to contempt, by placing him in circumstances which put his prejudices into action,
brought to view his natural defects, or drew the attention of the company on his airs of affectation.

' The power had been possessed in vain if it had
never been exerted; and it was not my custom to
let any arts of jocularity remain unemployed. My
impatience of applause brought me always early to
the place of entertainment; and I seldom failed to
lay a scheme with the small knot that first gathered
round me, by which some of those whom we expected might be made subservient to our sport.
Every man has some favourite topic of conversation,
on which, by a feigned seriousness of attention, he
may be drawn to expatiate without end. Every man
has some habitual contortion of body, or established
mode of expression, which never fails to raise mirth
if it be pointed out to notice. By premonitions of
these particularities I secured our pleasantry. Our
companion entered with his usual gaiety, and began
to partake of our noisy cheerfulness, when the conversation was imperceptibly diverted to a subject
which pressed upon his tender part, and extorted
the expected shrug, the customary exclamation, or
the predicted remark. A general clamour of joy

then burst from all that were admitted to the stratagem. Our mirth was often increased by the triumph of him that occasioned it; for as we do not
hastily form conclusions against ourselves, seldom
any one suspected that he had exhilarated us otherwise than by his wit.

' You will hear, I believe with very little surprise,
that by this conduct I had in a short time united
mankind against me, and that every tongue was diligent in prevention or revenge. I soon perceived
myself regarded with malevolence or distrust, but
wondered what had been discovered in me either
terrible or hateful. I had invaded no man's property;
I had rivalled no man's claims; nor had ever engaged in any of those attempts which provoke the
jealousy of ambition or the rage of faction. I had
lived but to laugh, and make others laugh; and believed that I was loved by all who caressed, and favoured by all who applauded, me. I never imagined,
that he who, in the mirth of a nocturnal revel, concurred in ridiculing his friend, would consider, in a
cooler hour, that the same trick might be played
against himself; or that, even where there is no
sense of danger, the natural pride of human nature
rises against him, who by general censures lays
claim to general superiority.

' I was convinced, by a total desertion, of the impropriety of my conduct; every man avoided, and
cautioned others to avoid me. Wherever I came, I
found silence and dejection, coldness and terror.
No one would venture to speak, lest he should lay
himself open to unfavourable representations; the
company, however numerous, dropped off at my entrance upon various pretences; and if I retired to
avoid the shame of being left, I heard confidence
and mirth revive at my departure.

' If those whom I had thus offended, could have

contented themselves with repaying one insult for another, and kept up the war only by a reciprocation of sarcasms, they might have perhaps vexed, but would never much have hurt me; for no man heartily hates him at whom he can laugh. But these wounds which they give me as they fly, are without cure; this alarm which they spread by their solicitude to escape me, excludes me from all friendship and from all pleasure: I am condemned to pass a long interval of my life in solitude, as a man suspected of infection is refused admission into cities; and must linger in obscurity, till my conduct shall convince the world, that I may be approached without hazard.

I am, &c.   DICACULUS.'

Nº 175. TUESDAY, NOVEMBER 19, 1751.

Rari quippe boni; numero vix sunt totidem quot
Thebarum portæ, vel divitis ostia Nili.—Juv.

Good men are scarce, the just are thinly sown;
They thrive but ill, nor can they last when grown.
And should we count them, and our store compile;
Yet Thebes more gates could shew, more mouths the Nile.

NONE of the axioms of wisdom, which recommend the ancient sages of veneration, seems to have required less extent of knowledge, or perspicacity of penetration, than the remark of Bias, that οἱ πλέονες, κακοί, *the majority are wicked.*

The depravity of mankind is so easily discoverable, that nothing but the desert or the cell can exclude it from notice. The knowledge of crimes intrudes uncalled and undesired. They whom their abstraction from common occurrences hinders from seeing iniquity, will quickly have their attention awakened by feeling it. Even he who ventures not into the world, may learn its corruption in his closet. For what are treatises of morality, but persuasives to the practice of duties, for which no arguments would be necessary, but that we are continually tempted to violate or neglect them? What are all the records of history, but narratives of successive villanies, of treason and usurpations, massacres and wars?

But perhaps, the excellence of aphorisms consists not so much in the expression of some rare or abstruse sentiment, as in the comprehension of some obvious and useful truth in a few words. We frequently fall into error and folly, not because the true principles of action are not known, but because, for a time, they are not remembered; and he may therefore be justly numbered among the benefactors of mankind, who contracts the great rules of life into short sentences, that may be easily impressed on the memory, and taught by frequent recollection to recur habitually to the mind.

However those who have passed through half the life of man, may now wonder that any should require to be cautioned against corruption, they will find that they have themselves purchased their conviction by many disappointments and vexations, which an earlier knowledge would have spared them; and may see, on every side, some entangling themselves in perplexities, and some sinking into ruin, by ignorance or neglect of the maxim of Bias.

Every day sends out, in quest of pleasure and distinction, some heir fondled in ignorance, and flattered into pride. He comes forth with all the confidence of a spirit unacquainted with superiors, and all the benevolence of a mind not yet irritated by opposition, alarmed by fraud, or imbittered by cruelty. He loves all, because he imagines himself the universal favourite. Every exchange of salutation produces new acquaintance, and every acquaintance kindles into friendship.

Every season brings a new flight of beauties into the world who have hitherto heard only of their own charms, and imagine that the heart feels no passion but that of love. They are soon surrounded by admirers whom they credit, because they tell them only what is heard of with delight. Whoever gazes upon them is a lover; and whoever forces a sigh is pining in despair.

He surely is a useful monitor, who inculcates to these thoughtless strangers that the *majority are wicked*; who informs them that the train which wealth and beauty draw after them, is lured only by the scent of prey; and that, perhaps, among all those who crowd about them with professions and flatteries, there is not one who does not hope for some opportunity to devour or betray them, to glut himself by their destruction, or to share their spoils with a stronger savage.

Virtue presented singly to the imagination or the reason, is so well recommended by its own graces, and so strongly supported by arguments, that a good man wonders how any can be bad; and they who are ignorant of the force of passion and interest, who never observed the arts of seduction, the contagion of example, the gradual descent from one crime to another, or the insensible depravation of the principles, by loose conversation, naturally expect to find integrity in every bosom, and veracity on every tongue.

It is indeed impossible not to hear from those who have lived longer, of wrongs and falsehoods, of violence and circumvention; but such narratives are commonly regarded by the young, the heady, and the confident, as nothing more than the murmurs of peevishness, or the dreams of dotage; and notwithstanding all the documents of hoary wisdom, we commonly plunge into the world fearless and credulous, without any foresight of danger, or apprehension of deceit.

I have remarked, in a former paper, that credulity is the common failing of unexperienced virtue; and that he who is spontaneously suspicious, may be justly charged with radical corruption; for if he has not known the prevalence of dishonesty by information, nor had time to observe it with his own eyes, whence can he take his measures of judgment but from himself?

They who best deserve to escape the snares of artifice, are most likely to be entangled. He that endeavours to live for the good of others, must always be exposed to the arts of them who live only for themselves, unless he is taught by timely precepts the caution required in common transactions, and shewn at a distance at the pitfalls of treachery.

To youth, therefore, it should be carefully inculcated, that to enter the road of life without caution or reserve, in expectation of general fidelity and justice, is to launch into the wide ocean without the instruments of steerage, and to hope that every wind will be prosperous, and that every coast will afford a harbour.

To enumerate the various motives to deceit and injury, would be to count all the desires that prevail among the sons of men; since there is no ambition however petty, no wish however absurd, that by indulgence will not be enabled to overpower the influence of virtue. Many there are who openly and almost professedly regulate all their conduct by their love of money: who have no reason for action or forbearance, for compliance or refusal, than that they hope to gain more by one than by the other. These are indeed the meanest and cruellest of human beings, a race with whom, as with some pestiferous animals, the whole creation seems to be at war; but who, however detested or scorned, long continue to add heap to heap, and when they have reduced one to beggary, are still permitted to fasten on another.

Others, yet less rationally wicked, pass their lives in mischief, because they cannot bear the sight of success, and mark out every man for hatred, whose fame or fortune they believe increasing.

Many, who have not advanced to these degrees of guilt, are yet wholly unqualified for friendship, and unable to maintain any constant or regular course of kindness. Happiness may be destroyed not only by union with the man who is apparently the slave of interest, but with him whom a wild opinion of the dignity of perseverance, in whatever cause, disposes to pursue every injury with unwearied and perpetual resentment; with him whose vanity inclines him to consider every man as a rival in every pretension; with him whose airy negligence puts his friend's affairs or secrets in continual hazard, and who thinks his forgetfulness of others excused by his inattention to himself; and with him whose inconstancy ranges without any settled rule of choice through varieties of friendship, and who adopts and dismisses favourites by the sudden impulse of caprice.

Thus numerous are the dangers to which the converse of mankind exposes us, and which can be avoided only by prudent distrust. He, therefore, that remembering this salutary maxim learns early to withhold his fondness from fair appearances, will have reason to pay some honours to Bias of Priene, who enabled him to become wise without the cost of experience.

Nº 176.   SATURDAY, NOVEMBER 23, 1751.

——Naso suspendis adunco.——Hor.

On me you turn the nose.——

There are many vexatious accidents and uneasy situations which raise little compassion for the sufferer, and which no man but those whom they immediately distress, can regard with seriousness. Petty mischiefs that have no influence on futurity, nor extend their effects to the rest of life, are always seen with a kind of malicious pleasure. A mistake or embarrassment which for the present moment fills the face with blushes, and the mind with confusion, will have no other effect upon those who observe it than that of convulsing them with irresistible laughter. Some circumstances of misery are so powerfully ridiculous, that neither kindness nor duty can withstand them; they bear down love, interest, and reverence, and force the friend, the dependant, or the child, to give way to instantaneous motions of merriment.

Among the principal of comic calamities, may be reckoned the pain which an author, not yet hardened into insensibility, feels at the onset of a furious critic, whose age, rank, or fortune, gives him confidence to speak without reserve; who heaps one objection upon another, and obtrudes his remarks, and enforces his corrections, without tenderness or awe.

The author full of the importance of his work, and anxious for the justification of every syllable, starts and kindles at the slightest attack; the critic, eager to establish his superiority, triumphing in every discovery of failure, and zealous to impress the cogency of his arguments, pursues him from line to line, without cessation or remorse. The critic, who hazards little, proceeds with vehemence, impetuosity, and fearlessness : the author, whose quiet and fame, and life and immortality, are involved in the controversy, tries every art of subterfuge and defence ; maintains modestly what he resolves never to yield, and yields unwillingly what cannot be maintained. The critic's purpose is to conquer, the author only hopes to escape ; the critic therefore knits his brow and raises his voice, and rejoices whenever he perceives any tokens of pain excited by the pressure of his assertions, or the point of his sarcasms. The author, whose endeavour is at once to mollify and elude his persecutor, composes his features and softens his accents, breaks the force of assault by retreat, and rather steps aside than flies or advances.

As it very seldom happens that the rage of extemporary criticism inflicts fatal or lasting wounds, I know not that the laws of benevolence entitle this distress to much sympathy. The diversion of baiting an author has the sanction of all ages and nations, and is more lawful than the sport of teasing other animals, because, for the most part, he comes voluntarily to the stake, furnished, as he imagines, by the patron powers of literature, with resistless weapons, and impenetrable armour, with the mail of the boar of Erymanth, and the paws of the lion of Nemea.

But the works of genius are sometimes produced by other motives than vanity ; and he whom necessity or duty enforces to write is not always so well satisfied with himself, as not to be discouraged by censorious impudence. It may therefore be necessary to consider how they whom publication lays open to the insults of such as their obscurity secures against reprisals, may extricate themselves from unexpected encounters.

Vida, a man of considerable skill in the politics of literature, directs his pupil wholly to abandon his defence, and even when he can irrefragably refute all objections, to suffer tamely the exultations of his antagonist.

This rule may perhaps be just, when advice is asked and severity solicited, because no man tells his opinion so freely as when he imagines it received with implicit veneration; and critics ought never to be consulted, but while errors may yet be rectified or insipidity suppressed. But when the book has once been dismissed into the world, and can be no more retouched, I know not whether a very different conduct should not be prescribed, and whether firmness and spirit may not sometimes be of use to over-power arrogance and repel brutality. Softness, diffidence, and moderation, will often be mistaken for imbecility and dejection; they lure cowardice to the attack by the hopes of easy victory, and it will soon be found that he whom every man thinks he can conquer, shall never be at peace.

The animadversions of critics are commonly such as may easily provoke the sedatest writer, to some quickness of resentment and asperity of reply. A man who by long consideration has familiarized a subject to his own mind, carefully surveyed the series of his thoughts, and planned all the parts of his composition into a regular dependance on each other, will often start at the sinistrous interpretations, or absurd remarks, of haste or ignorance, and wonder by what infatuation they have been led away from the obvious sense, and upon what peculiar principles of judgment they decide against him.

The eye of the intellect, like that of the body, is not equally perfect in all, nor equally adapted in any to all objects; the end of criticism is to supply its defects; rules are the instruments of mental vision,

which may indeed assist our faculties when properly
used, but produce confusion and obscurity by unskilful application.

Some seem always to read with the microscope of
criticism, and employ their whole attention upon minute elegance, or faults scarcely visible to common
observation. The dissonance of a syllable, the recurrence of the same sound, the repetition of a particle, the smallest deviation from propriety, the
slightest defect in construction or arrangement, swell
before their eyes into enormities. As they discern
with great exactness, they comprehend but a narrow
compass, and know nothing of the justness of the
design, the general spirit of the performance, the artifice of connexion, or the harmony of the parts;
they never conceive how small a proportion that
which they are busy in contemplating bears to the
whole, or how the petty inaccuracies with which they
are offended, are absorbed and lost in general excellence.

Others are furnished by criticism with a telescope.
They see with great clearness whatever is too remote
to be discovered by the rest of mankind, but are totally blind to all that lies immediately before them.
They discover in every passage some secret meaning,
some remote allusion, some artful allegory, or some
occult imitation which no other reader ever suspected; but they have no perception of the cogency of
arguments, the force of pathetic sentiments, the various colours of diction, or the flowery embellishments of fancy; of all that engages the attention of
others, they are totally insensible, while they pry into
worlds of conjecture, and amuse themselves with
phantoms in the clouds.

In criticism, as in every other art, we fail sometimes by our weakness, but more frequently by our
fault. We are sometimes bewildered by ignorance,

and sometimes by prejudice, but we seldom deviate
far from the right, but when we deliver ourselves up
to the direction of vanity.

N° 177. TUESDAY, NOVEMBER 26, 1751.

Turpe est difficiles habere nugas.—MART.

Those things which now seem frivolous and slight,
Will be of serious consequence to you,
When they have made you once ridiculous.—ROSCOMMON.

'TO THE RAMBLER.

' SIR,

' WHEN I was, at the usual time, about to enter upon
the profession to which my friends had destined me,
being summoned, by the death of my father, into the
country, I found myself master of an unexpected
sum of money, and of an estate which, though not
large, was, in my opinion, sufficient to support me in
a condition far preferable to the fatigue, dependance,
and uncertainty of any gainful occupation. I therefore resolved to devote the rest of my life wholly to
curiosity, and without any confinement of my excursions, or termination of my views, to wander over
the boundless regions of general knowledge.

' This scheme of life seemed pregnant with inexhaustible variety, and therefore I could not forbear
to congratulate myself upon the wisdom of my choice.
I furnished a large room with all conveniences for
study ; collected books of every kind ; quitted every
science at the first perception of disgust ; returned to

it again as soon as my former ardour happened to revive; and having no rival to depress me by comparison, nor any critic to alarm me with objections, I spent day after day in profound tranquillity, with only so much complaisance in my own improvements, as served to excite and animate my application.

'Thus I lived for some years with complete acquiescence in my own plan of conduct, rising early to read, and dividing the latter part of the day between economy, exercise, and reflection. But in time I began to find my mind contracted and stiffened by solitude. My ease and elegance was sensibly impaired; I was no longer able to accommodate myself with readiness to the accidental current of conversation, my notions grew particular and parodoxical, and my phraseology formal and unfashionable; I spoke, on common occasions, the language of books. My quickness of apprehension, and celerity of reply, had entirely deserted me: when I delivered my opinion, or detailed my knowledge, I was bewildered by an unseasonable interrogatory, disconcerted by any slight opposition, and overwhelmed and lost in dejection, when the smallest advantage was gained against me in dispute. I became decisive and dogmatical, impatient of contradiction, perpetually jealous of my character, insolent to such as acknowledged my superiority, and sullen and malignant to all who refused to receive my dictates.

'This I soon discovered to be one of those intellectual diseases which a wise man should make haste to cure. I therefore resolved for a time to shut my books, and learn again the art of conversation; to defecate and clear my mind by brisker motions and stronger impulses; and to unite myself once more to the living generation.

'For this purpose I hasted to London, and entreated

one of my academical acquaintances to introduce me
into some of the little societies of literature, which are
formed in taverns and coffee-houses. He was pleased
with an opportunity of shewing me to his friends, and
soon obtained me admission among a select company of curious men, who met once a week to exhilarate their studies and compare their acquisitions.

'The eldest and most venerable of this society was
Hirsutus, who, after the first civilities of my reception, found means to introduce the mention of his
favourite studies, by a severe censure of those who
want the due regard for their native country. He
informed me, that he had early withdrawn his attention from foreign trifles, and that since he begun to
addict his mind to serious and manly studies, he had
very carefully amassed all the English books that
were printed in the black character. This search he
had pursued so diligently, that he was able to shew
the deficiencies of the best catalogues. He had long
since completed his Caxton, had three sheets of Tre-
veris unknown to the antiquaries, and wanted to a
perfect Pynson but two volumes, of which one was promised him as a legacy by its present possessor, and
the other he was resolved to buy, at whatever price,
when Quisquilius's library should be sold. Hirsutus
had no other reason for the valuing or slighting a
book, than that it was printed in the Roman or the
Gothic letter, nor any ideas but such as his favourite
volumes had supplied; when he was serious he ex-
patiated on the narratives of Johan de Trevisa, and
when he was merry, regaled us with a quotation from
the "Shippe of Foles."

'While I was listening to this hoary student, Fer-
ratus entered in a hurry, and informed us with the
abruptness of ecstasy, that his set of halfpence was
now complete; he had just received in a handful of

change, the piece that he had so long been seeking, and could now defy mankind to outgo his collection of English copper.

'Chartophylax then observed how fatally human sagacity was sometimes baffled, and how often the most valuable discoveries are made by chance. He had employed himself and his emissaries seven years at great expense, to perfect his series of Gazettes, but had long wanted a single paper, which, when he despaired of obtaining it, was sent him wrapped round a parcel of tobacco.

'Cantilenus turned all his thoughts upon old ballads, for he considered them as the genuine records of the national taste. He offered to shew me a copy of "The Children in the Wood," which he firmly believed to be of the first edition, and by the help of which, the text might be freed from several corruptions, if this age of barbarity had any claim to such favours from him.

'Many were admitted into this society as inferior members, because they had collected old prints and neglected pamphlets, or possessed some fragment of antiquity, as the seal of an ancient corporation, the charter of a religious house, the genealogy of a family extinct, or a letter written in the reign of Elizabeth.

'Every one of these virtuosoes looked on all his associates as wretches of depraved taste and narrow notions. Their conversation was, therefore, fretful and waspish, their behaviour brutal, their merriment bluntly sarcastic, and their seriousness gloomy and suspicious. They were totally ignorant of all that passes, or has lately passed, in the world; unable to discuss any question of religious, political, or military knowledge; equally strangers to science and politer learning, and without any wish to improve their minds, or any other pleasure than that of displaying rarities, of which they would not suffer others to make the proper use.

' Hirsutus graciously informed me, that the number of their society was limited, but that I might sometimes attend as an auditor. I was pleased to find myself in no danger of an honour, which I could not have willingly accepted, nor gracefully refused, and left them without any intention of returning, for I soon found, that the suppression of those habits with which I was vitiated, required association with men very different from this solemn race.

I am, Sir, &c.
VIVACULUS.'

It is natural to feel grief or indignation, when any thing, necessary or useful, is wantonly wasted or negligently destroyed; and therefore my correspondent cannot be blamed for looking with uneasiness on the waste of life. Leisure and curiosity might soon make great advances in useful knowledge, were they not diverted by minute emulation and laborious trifles. It may, however, somewhat mollify his anger to reflect, that perhaps none of the assembly which he describes, was capable of any nobler employment, and that he who does his best, however little, is always to be distinguished from him who does nothing. Whatever busies the mind without corrupting it, has at least this use, that it rescues the day from idleness, and he that is never idle will not often be vicious.

Nº 178. SATURDAY, NOVEMBER 30, 1751.

Pars sanitatis velle sanari fuit. —SENECA.

To yield to remedies is half the cure.

PYTHAGORAS is reported to have required from those whom he instructed in philosophy a probationary silence of five years. Whether this prohibition of speech extended to all the parts of this time, as seems generally to be supposed, or was to be observed only in the school or in the presence of their master, as is more probable, it was sufficient to discover the pupil's disposition ; to try whether he was willing to pay the price of learning, or whether he was one of those whose ardour was rather violent than lasting, and who expected to grow wise on other terms than those of patience and obedience.

Many of the blessings universally desired, are very frequently wanted, because most men, when they should labour, content themselves to complain, and rather linger in a state in which they cannot be at rest, than improve their condition by vigour and resolution.

Providence has fixed the limits of human enjoyment by immoveable boundaries, and has set different gratifications at such a distance from each other, that no art or power can bring them together. This great law it is the business of every rational being to understand, that life may not pass away in an attempt to make contradictions consistent, to combine opposite qualities, and to unite things which the nature of their being must always keep asunder.

Of two objects tempting at a distance on contrary sides, it is impossible to approach one but by receding from the other ; by long deliberation and di-

latory projects, they may be both lost, but can never
be both gained. It is, therefore, necessary to compare them, and when we have determined the preference, to withdraw our eyes and our thoughts at once
from that which reason directs us to reject. This is
more necessary, if that which we are forsaking has
the power of delighting the senses, or firing the
fancy. He that once turns aside to the allurements
of unlawful pleasure, can have no security that he
shall ever regain the paths of virtue.

The philosophic goddess of Boethius, having related the story of Orpheus, who, when he had recovered his wife from the dominions of death, lost her
again by looking back upon her in the confines of
light, concludes with a very elegant and forcible application. "Whoever you are that endeavour to
elevate your minds to the illuminations of Heaven,
consider yourselves as represented in this fable; for
he that is once so far overcome as to turn back his
eyes towards the infernal caverns, loses at first sight
all that influence which attracted him on high."

> Vos hæc fabula respicit,
> Quicunque in superum diem
> Mentem ducere quæritis.
> Nam qui Tartareum in specus
> Victus lumina flexerit,
> Quidquid præcipuum trahit,
> Perdit, dum videt inferos.

It may be observed in general that the future is
purchased by the present. It is not possible to secure distant or permanent happiness but by the forbearance of some immediate gratification. This is
so evidently true with regard to the whole of our
existence, that all the precepts of theology have no
other tendency than to enforce the life of faith; a
life regulated not by our senses but our belief; a life
in which pleasures are to be refused for fear of in-

visible punishments, and calamities sometimes to be sought, and always endured, in hope of rewards that shall be obtained in another state.

Even if we take into our view only that particle of our duration which is terminated by the grave, it will be found that we cannot enjoy one part of life beyond the common limitations of pleasure, but by anticipating some of the satisfaction which should exhilarate the following years. The heat of youth may spread happiness into wild luxuriance, but the radical vigour requisite to make it perennial is exhausted, and all that can be hoped afterward is languor and sterility.

The reigning error of mankind is, that we are not content with the conditions on which the goods of life are granted. No man is insensible of the value of knowledge, the advantages of health, or the convenience of plenty, but every day shews us those on whom the conviction is without effect.

Knowledge is praised and desired by multitudes whom her charms could never rouse from the couch of sloth; whom the faintest invitation of pleasure draws away from their studies; to whom any other method of wearing out the day is more eligible than the use of books, and who are more easily engaged by any conversation, than such as may rectify their notions or enlarge their comprehension.

Every man that has felt pain, knows how little all other comforts can gladden him to whom health is denied. Yet who is there does not sometimes hazard it for the enjoyment of an hour? All assemblies of jollity, all places of public entertainment, exhibit examples of strength wasting in riot, and beauty withering in irregularity; nor is it easy to enter a house in which part of the family is not groaning in repentance of past intemperance, and part admitting disease by negligence, or soliciting it by luxury.

There is no pleasure which men of every age and sect have more generally agreed to mention with contempt, than the gratifications of the palate, an entertainment so far removed from intellectual happiness, that scarcely the most shameless of the sensual herd have dared to defend it : yet even to this, the lowest of our delights, to this, though neither quick nor lasting, is health with all its activity and sprightliness daily sacrificed ; and for this are half the miseries endured which urge impatience to call on death.

The whole world is put in motion by the wish for riches, and the dread of poverty. Who, then, would not imagine that such conduct as will inevitably destroy what all are thus labouring to acquire, must generally be avoided? That he who spends more than he receives, must in time become indigent, cannot be doubted; but how evident soever this consequence may appear, the spendthrift moves in the whirl of pleasures with too much rapidity to keep it before his eyes, and in the intoxication of gaiety, grows every day poorer without any such sense of approaching ruin as is sufficient to wake him into caution.

Many complaints are made of the misery of life ; and indeed it must be confessed that we are subject to calamities by which the good and bad, the diligent and slothful, the vigilant and heedless, are equally afflicted. But surely, though some indulgence may be allowed to groans extorted by inevitable misery, no man has a right to repine at evils which, against warning, against experience, he deliberately and leisurely brings upon his own head; or to consider himself as debarred from happiness by such obstacles as resolution may break, or dexterity may put aside.

Great numbers who quarrel with their condition

have wanted not the power but the will to obtain a
better state. They have never contemplated the difference between good and evil sufficiently to quicken
aversion or invigorate desire; they have indulged a
drowsy thoughtlessness or giddy lenity; have committed the balance of choice to the management of
caprice; and when they have long accustomed themselves to receive all that chance offered them, without examination, lament at last that they find themselves deceived.

Nº 179.　TUESDAY, DECEMBER 3, 1751.

Perpetuo risu pulmonem agitare solebat.—Juv.

Democritus would feed his spleen, and shake
His sides and shoulders till he felt them ake.—Dryden.

'Every man,' says Tully, ' has two characters;
one, which he partakes with all mankind, and by
which he is distinguished from brute animals; another, which discriminates him from the rest of his
own species, and impresses on him a manner and
temper peculiar to himself; this particular character,
if it be not repugnant to the laws of general humanity, it is always his business to cultivate and preserve.'

Every hour furnishes some confirmation of Tully's
precept. It seldom happens, that an assembly of
pleasure is so happily selected, but that some one
finds admission, with whom the rest are deservedly
offended; and it will appear, on a close inspection,
that scarce any man becomes eminently disagreeable
but by a departure from his real character, and an

attempt at something for which nature or education have left him unqualified.

Ignorance or dulness have indeed no power of affording delight, but they never give disgust except when they assume the dignity of knowledge, or ape the sprightliness of wit. Awkwardness and inelegance have none of those attractions by which ease and politeness take possession of the heart; but ridicule and censure seldom rise against them, unless they appear associated with that confidence which belongs only to long acquaintance with the modes of life, and to consciousness of unfailing propriety of behaviour. Deformity itself is regarded with tenderness rather than aversion, when it does not attempt to deceive the sight by dress and decoration, and to seize, upon fictitious claims, the prerogatives of beauty.

He that stands to contemplate the crowds that fill the streets of a populous city, will see many passengers whose air and motion it will be difficult to behold without contempt and laughter; but if he examines what are the appearances that thus powerfully excite his risibility, he will find among them neither poverty nor disease, nor any involuntary or painful defect. The disposition to derision and insult is awakened by the softness of foppery, the swell of insolence, the liveliness of levity, or the solemnity of grandeur; by the sprightly tip, the stately stalk, the formal strut, and the lofty mien; by gestures intended to catch the eye, and by looks elaborately formed as evidences of importance.

It has, I think, been sometimes urged in favour of affectation, that it is only a mistake of the means to a good end, and that the intention with which it is practised is always to please. If all attempts to innovate the constitutional or habitual character have really proceeded from public spirit and love of others, the world has hitherto been sufficiently ungrateful, since no return but scorn has yet been made to the most difficult of all enterprises, a contest with nature; nor has any pity been shewn to the fatigues of labour which never succeeded, and the uneasiness of disguise, by which nothing was concealed.

It seems therefore to be determined by the general suffrage of mankind, that he who decks himself in adscititious qualities rather purposes to command applause than impart pleasure; and he is therefore treated as a man who by an unreasonable ambition usurps the place in society to which he has no right. Praise is seldom paid with willingness even to incontestable merit, and it can be no wonder that he who calls it without desert is repulsed with universal indignation.

Affectation naturally counterfeits those excellences which are placed at the greatest distance from possibility of attainment. We are conscious of our own defects, and eagerly endeavour to supply them by artificial excellence; nor would such efforts be wholly without excuse, were they not often excited by ornamental trifles, which he that thus anxiously struggles for the reputation of possessing them, would not have been known to want, had not his industry quickened observation.

Gelasimus passed the first part of his life in academical privacy, and rural retirement, without any other conversation than that of scholars, grave, studious, and abstracted as himself. He cultivated the mathematical sciences with indefatigable diligence, discovered many useful theorems, discussed with great accuracy the resistance of fluids, and, though his priority was not generally acknowledged, was the first who fully explained all the properties of the catenarian curve.

Learning, when it rises to eminence, will be observed in time, whatever mists may happen to surround it. Gelasimus, in his forty-ninth year, was distinguished by those who have the rewards of knowledge in their hands, and called out to display his acquisitions for the honour of his country, and add dignity by his presence to philosophical assemblies. As he did not suspect his unfitness for common affairs, he felt no reluctance to obey the invitation, and what he did not feel he had yet too much honesty to feign. He entered into the world as a larger and more populous college, where his performances would be more public, and his renown farther extended; and imagined that he should find his reputation universally prevalent, and the influence of learning every where the same.

His merit introduced him to splendid tables and elegant acquaintance; but he did not find himself always qualified to join in the conversation. He was distressed by civilities, which he knew not how to repay, and entangled in many ceremonial perplexities, from which his books and diagrams could not extricate him. He was sometimes unluckily engaged in disputes with ladies, with whom algebraic axioms had no great weight, and saw many whose favour and esteem he could not but desire, to whom he was very little recommended by his theories of the tides, or his approximations to the quadrature of the circle.

Gelasimus did not want penetration to discover, that no charm was more generally irresistible than that of easy facetiousness and flowing hilarity. He saw that diversion was more frequently welcome than improvement, that authority and seriousness were rather feared than loved, and that the grave scholar was a kind of imperious ally, hastily dismissed when his assistance was no longer necessary. He came to a sudden resolution of throwing off those cumbrous ornaments of learning, which hindered his reception, and commenced a man of wit and jocularity. Utterly unacquainted with every topic of merriment, ignorant of the modes and follies, the vices and virtues of mankind, and unfurnished with any ideas but such as Pappus and Archimedes had given him, he began to silence all inquiries with a jest instead of a solution, extended his face with a grin, which he mistook for a smile, and in the place of a scientific discourse, retailed in a new language, formed between the college and the tavern, the intelligence of the newspaper.

Laughter, he knew was a token of alacrity; and, therefore, whatever he said or heard, he was careful not to fail in that great duty of a wit. If he asked or told the hour of the day, if he complained of heat or cold, stirred the fire, or filled the glass, removed his chair, or snuffed the candle, he always found some occasion to laugh. The jest was indeed a secret to all but himself; but habitual confidence in his own discernment hindered him from suspecting any weakness or mistake. He wondered that his wit was so little understood, but expected that his audience would comprehend it by degrees, and persisted all his life to shew by gross buffoonery, how little the strongest faculties can perform beyond the limits of their own province.

Nº 180. SATURDAY, DECEMBER 7, 1751.

Ταῦτ' εἰδὼς, σοφὸς ἴσθι· μάτην δ' Ἐπίκουρον ἔασον,
Ποῦ τὸ κενὸν, ζητεῖν, καὶ τίνες αἱ μόναδες.——AUTOMEDON.

On life, on morals, be thy thoughts employ'd;
Leave to the schools their atoms and their void.

IT is somewhere related by Le Clerc, that a wealthy trader of good understanding, having the common ambition to breed his son a scholar, carried him to a university, resolving to use his own judgment in the choice of a tutor. He had been taught, by whatever intelligence, the nearest way to the heart of an academic, and at his arrival entertained all who came about him with such profusion, that the professors were lured by the smell of his table from their books, and flocked round him with all the cringes of awkward complaisance. This eagerness answered the merchant's purpose; he glutted them with delicacies, and softened them with caresses, till he prevailed upon one after another to open his bosom, and make a discovery of his competitions, jealousies, and resentments. Having thus learned each man's character, partly from himself, and partly from his acquaintance, he resolved to find some other education for his son, and went away convinced, that a scholastic life has no other tendency than to vitiate the morals and contract the understanding; nor would he afterward hear with patience the praises of the ancient authors, being persuaded that scholars of all ages must have been the same, and that Xenophon and Cicero were professors of some former university and therefore mean and selfish, ignorant and servile, like those whom he had lately visited and forsaken.

Envy, curiosity, and a sense of the imperfection of our present state, incline us to estimate the advantages which are in the possession of others, above their real value. Every one must have remarked, what powers and prerogatives the vulgar imagine to be conferred by learning. A man of science is expected to excel the unlettered and unenlightened even on occasions where literature is of no use, and among weak minds, loses part of his reverence, by discovering no superiority in those parts of life, in which all are unavoidably equal; as when a monarch makes a progress to the remoter provinces, the rustics are said sometimes to wonder that they find him of the same size with themselves.

These demands of prejudice and folly can never be satisfied; and therefore many of the imputations which learning suffers from disappointed ignorance, are without reproach. But there are some failures to which men of study are peculiarly exposed. Every condition has its disadvantages. The circle of knowledge is too wide for the most active and diligent intellect, and while science is pursued, other accomplishments are neglected; as a small garrison must leave one part of an extensive fortress naked when an alarm calls them to another.

The learned, however, might generally support their dignity with more success, if they suffered not themselves to be misled by the desire of superfluous attainments. Raphael, in return to Adam's inquiries into the courses of the stars and the revolutions of heaven, counsels him to withdraw his mind from idle speculations, and employ his faculties upon nearer and more interesting objects, the survey of his own life, the subjection of his passions, the knowledge of duties which must daily be performed, and the detection of dangers which must daily be incurred.

This angelic counsel every man of letters should always have before him. He that devotes himself to retired study, naturally sinks from omission to forgetfulness of social duties; he must be therefore sometimes awakened, and recalled to the general condition of mankind.

I am far from any intention to limit curiosity, or confine the labours of learning to arts of immediate and necessary use. It is only from the various essays of experimental industry, and the vague excursions of minds set upon discovery, that any advancement of knowledge can be expected; and though many must be disappointed in their labours, yet they are not to be charged with having spent their time in vain; their example contributed to inspire emulation, and their miscarriage taught others the way to success.

But the distant hope of being one day useful or eminent, ought not to mislead us too far from that study, which is equally requisite to the great and mean, to the celebrated and obscure; the art of moderating the desires, of repressing the appetites; and of conciliating or retaining the favour of mankind.

No man can imagine the course of his own life or the conduct of the world around him, unworthy his attention; yet among the sons of learning many seem to have thought of every thing rather than of themselves, and to have observed every thing but what passes before their eyes; many who toil through the intricacy of complicated systems, are insuperably embarrassed with the least perplexity in common affairs; many who compare the actions, and ascertain the characters of ancient heroes, let their own days glide away without examination, and suffer vicious habits to encroach upon their minds without resistance or detection.

The most frequent reproach of the scholastic race is the want of fortitude, not martial but philosophic. Men bred in shades and silence, taught to immure themselves at sunset, and accustomed to no other weapon than syllogism, may be allowed to feel terror at personal danger, and to be disconcerted by tumult and alarm. But why should he whose life is spent in contemplation, and whose business is only to discover truth, be unable to rectify the fallacies of imagination, or contend successfully against prejudice and passion? To what end has he read and meditated, if he gives up his understanding to false appearances, and suffers himself to be enslaved by fear of evils to which only folly or vanity can expose him, or elated by advantages to which, as they are equally conferred upon the good and bad, no real dignity is annexed?

Such, however, is the state of the world, that the most obsequious of the slaves of pride, the most rapturous of the gazers upon wealth, the most officious of the whisperers of greatness, are collected from seminaries appropriated to the study of wisdom and of virtue, where it was intended that appetite should learn to be content with little, and that hope should aspire only to honours which no human power can give or take away.

The student, when he comes forth into the world, instead of congratulating himself upon his exemption from the errors of those whose opinions have been formed by accident or custom, and who live without any certain principles of conduct, is commonly in haste to mingle with the multitude, and shew his sprightliness and ductility by an expeditious compliance with fashions or vices. The first smile of a man whose fortune gives him power to reward his dependants, commonly enchants him beyond resistance; the glare of equipage, the sweets of luxury, the liberality of general promises, the softness of habitual affability, fill his imagination; and he soon ceases to have any other wish than to be well received, or any measure of right and wrong but the opinion of his patron.

A man flattered and obeyed, learns to exact grosser adulation and enjoin lower submission. Neither our virtues nor vices are all our own. If there were no cowardice, there would be little insolence; pride cannot rise to any great degree, but by the concurrence of blandishment or the sufferance of tameness. The wretch who would shrink and crouch before one that should dart his eye upon him with the spirit of

natural equality, becomes capricious and tyrannical
when he sees himself approached with a downcast
look, and hears the soft address of awe and servility. To those who are willing to purchase favour by
cringes and compliance, is to be imputed the haughtiness that leaves nothing to be hoped by firmness
and integrity.

If, instead of wandering after the meteors of philosophy, which fill the world with splendour for a
while, and then sink and are forgotten, the candidates of learning fixed their eyes upon the permanent
lustre of moral and religious truth, they would find
a more certain direction to happiness. A little
plausibility of discourse, and acquaintance with unnecessary speculations, is dearly purchased, when it
excludes those instructions which fortify the heart
with resolution, and exalt the spirit to independence.

N° 181.   TUESDAY, DECEMBER 10, 1751.

―――Neu fluitem dubiæ spe pendulus horæ.―Hor.

Nor let me float in fortune's pow'r,
Dependant on the future hour.―Francis.

'To the Rambler.

'Sir,

'As I have passed much of life in disquiet and suspense, and lost many opportunities of advantage by
a passion which I have reason to believe prevalent
in different degrees over a great part of mankind, I
cannot but think myself well qualified to warn those
who are yet uncaptivated, of the danger which they
incur by placing themselves within its influence.

'I served an apprenticeship to a linen-draper, with uncommon reputation for diligence and fidelity; and at the age of three-and-twenty opened a shop for myself with a large stock, and such credit among all the merchants, who were acquainted with my master, that I could command whatever was imported curious or valuable. For five years I proceeded with success proportionate to close application and untainted integrity; was a daring bidder at every sale; always paid my notes before they were due; and advanced so fast in commercial reputation, that I was proverbially marked out as the model of young traders, and every one expected that a few years would make me an alderman.

'In this course of even prosperity, I was one day persuaded to buy a ticket in the lottery. The sum was inconsiderable, part was to be repaid though fortune might fail to favour me, and therefore my established maxims of frugality did not restrain me from so trifling an experiment. The ticket lay almost forgotten till the time at which every man's fate was to be determined; nor did the affair even then seem of any importance, till I discovered by the public papers that the number next to mine had conferred the great prize.

'My heart leaped at the thought of such an approach to sudden riches, which I considered myself, however contrarily to the laws of computation, as having missed by a single chance; and I could not forbear to revolve the consequences which such a bounteous allotment would have produced, if it had happened to me. This dream of felicity, by degrees, took possession of my imagination. The great delight of my solitary hours was to purchase an estate, and form plantations with money which once might have been mine, and I never met my friends but I spoiled all their merriment by perpetual complaints of my ill luck.

'At length another lottery was opened, and I had now so heated my imagination with the prospect of a prize, that I should have pressed among the first purchasers, had not my ardour been withheld by deliberation upon the probability of success from one ticket rather than another. I hesitated long between even and odd; considered the square and cubic numbers through the lottery; examined all those to which good luck had been hitherto annexed; and at last fixed upon one, which, by some secret relation to the events of my life, I thought predestined to make me happy. Delay in great affairs is often mischievous; the ticket was sold, and its possessor could not be found.

'I returned to my conjectures, and after many arts of prognostication, fixed upon another chance, but with less confidence. Never did captive, heir, or lover, feel so much vexation from the slow pace of time, as I suffered between the purchase of my ticket and the distribution of the prizes. I solaced my uneasiness as well as I could, by frequent contemplations of approaching happiness; when the sun arose I knew it would set, and congratulated myself at night that I was so much nearer to my wishes. At last the day came, my ticket appeared, and rewarded all my care and sagacity with a despicable prize of fifty pounds.

'My friends, who honestly rejoiced upon my success, were very coldly received; I hid myself a fortnight in the country, that my chagrin might fume away without observation, and then returning to my shop, began to listen after another lottery.

'With the news of a lottery I was soon gratified, and having now found the vanity of conjecture and inefficacy of computation, I resolved to take the prize by violence, and therefore bought forty tickets, not omitting however to divide them between the even and odd numbers, that I might not miss the lucky class. Many conclusions did I form, and many experiments did I try, to determine from which of those tickets I might most reasonably expect riches. At last, being unable to satisfy myself by any modes of reasoning, I wrote the numbers upon dice, and allotted five hours every day to the amusement of throwing them in a garret; and examining the event by an exact register, found, on the evening before the lottery was drawn, that one of my numbers had been turned up five times more than any of the rest in three hundred and thirty thousand throws.

'This experiment was fallacious; the first day presented the hopeful ticket, a detestable blank. The rest came out with different fortune, and in conclusion I lost thirty pounds by this great adventure.

'I had now wholly changed the cast of my behaviour and the conduct of my life. The shop was for the most part abandoned to my servants, and if I entered it, my thoughts were so engrossed by my tickets, that I scarcely heard or answered a question, but considered every customer as an intruder upon my meditations, whom I was in haste to dispatch. I mistook the price of my goods, committed blunders in my bills, forgot to file my receipts, and neglected to regulate my books. My acquaintances by degrees began to fall away; but I perceived the decline of my business with little emotion, because whatever deficience there might be in my gains I expected the next lottery to supply.

'Miscarriage naturally produces diffidence; I began now to seek assistance against ill luck, by an alliance with those that had been more successful.

I inquired diligently at what office any prize had
been sold, that I might purchase of a propitious
vender; solicited those who had been fortunate in
former lotteries, to partake with me in my new tickets;
and whenever I met with one that had in any event
of his life been eminently prosperous, I invited him
to take a larger share. I had, by this rule of conduct, so diffused my interest, that I had a fourth
part of fifteen tickets, an eighth of forty, and a sixteenth of ninety.

'I waited for the decision of my fate with my former palpitations, and looked upon the business of
my trade with the usual neglect. The wheel at last
was turned, and its revolutions brought me a long
succession of sorrows and disappointments. I indeed often partook of a small prize, and the loss of
one day was generally balanced by the gain of the
next; but my desires yet remained unsatisfied, and
when one of my chances had failed, all my expectation was suspended on those which remained yet un-
determined. At last a prize of five thousand pounds
was proclaimed; I caught fire at the cry, and inquiring the number, found it to be one of my own
tickets, which I had divided among those on whose
luck I depended, and of which I had retained only
a sixteenth part.

'You will easily judge with what detestation of
himself, a man thus intent upon gain reflected that
he had sold a prize that was once in his possession.
It was to no purpose, that I represented to my mind
the impossibility of recalling the past, or the folly of
condemning an act, which only its event, an event
which no human intelligence could foresee, proved
to be wrong. The prize which, though put in my
hands, had been suffered to slip from me, filled me
with anguish; and knowing that complaint would

only expose me to ridicule, I gave myself up silently to grief, and lost by degrees my appetite and my rest.

'My indisposition soon became visible; I was visited by my friends, and among them by Eumathes, a clergyman, whose piety and learning gave him such an ascendant over me, that I could not refuse to open my heart. "There are," said he, "few minds sufficiently firm to be trusted in the hands of chance. Whoever finds himself inclined to anticipate futurity, and exalt possibility to certainty, should avoid every kind of casual adventure, since his grief must be always proportionate to his hope. You have long wasted that time, which, by a proper application, would have certainly, though moderately, increased your fortune, in a laborious and anxious pursuit of a species of gain, which no labour or anxiety, no art or expedient, can secure or promote. You are now fretting away your life in repentance of an act, against which repentance can give no caution, but to avoid the occasion of committing it. Rouse from this lazy dream of fortuitous riches, which, if obtained, you could scarcely have enjoyed, because they could confer no consciousness of desert; return to rational and manly industry, and consider the mere gift of luck as below the care of a wise man."

N⁰ 182.   SATURDAY, DECEMBER 14, 1751.

——Dives qui fieri vult,
Et citò vult fieri.—JUVENAL.

The lust of wealth can never bear delay.

IT has been observed in a late paper, that we are unreasonably desirous to separate the goods of life from

those evils which Providence has connected with
them, and to catch advantages without paying the
price at which they are offered us. Every man wishes
to be rich, but very few have the powers necessary
to raise a sudden fortune, either by new discoveries,
or by superiority of skill in any necessary employment; and among lower understandings many want
the firmness and industry requisite to regular gain
and gradual acquisitions.

From the hope of enjoying affluence by methods
more compendious than those of labour, and more
generally practicable than those of genius, proceeds
the common inclination of experiment and hazard,
and that willingness to snatch all opportunities of
growing rich by chance, which, when it has once
taken possession of the mind, is seldom driven out
either by time or argument, but continues to waste
life in perpetual delusion, and generally ends in
wretchedness and want.

The folly of untimely exultation and visionary prosperity, is by no means peculiar to the purchasers of
tickets; there are multitudes whose life is nothing
but a continual lottery; who are always within a few
months of plenty and happiness, and how often soever they are mocked with blanks, expect a prize
from the next adventure.

Among the most resolute and ardent of the votaries of chance, may be numbered the mortals whose
hope is to raise themselves by a wealthy match; who
lay out all their industry on the assiduities of courtship, and sleep and wake with no other ideas than of
treats, compliments, guardians, and rivals.

One of the most indefatigable of this class, is my
old friend Leviculus, whom I have never known for
thirty years without some matrimonial project of advantage. Leviculus was bred under a merchant,
and by the graces of his person, the sprightliness of

his prattle, and the neatness of his dress, so much enamoured his master's second daughter, a girl of sixteen, that she declared her resolution to have no other husband. Her father, after having chidden her for undutifulness, consented to the match, not much to the satisfaction of Leviculus, who was sufficiently elated with this conquest to think himself entitled to a larger fortune. He was, however, soon rid of his perplexity, for his mistress died before their marriage.

He was now so well satisfied with his own accomplishments, that he determined to commence fortune-hunter; and when his apprenticeship expired, instead of beginning, as was expected, to walk the exchange with a face of importance, or associating himself with those who were most eminent for their knowledge of the stocks, he at once threw off the solemnity of the counting-house, equipped himself with a modish wig, listened to wits in coffee-houses, passed his evenings behind the scenes in the theatres, learned the names of beauties of quality, hummed the last stanzas of fashionable songs, talked familiarly of high play, boasted his achievements upon drawers and coachmen, was often brought to his lodgings at midnight in a chair, told with negligence and jocularity of bilking a taylor, and now and then let fly a shrewd jest at a sober citizen.

Thus furnished with irresistible artillery, he turned his batteries upon the female world, and in the first warmth of self-approbation, proposed no less than the possession of riches and beauty united. He therefore paid his civilities to Flavilla, the only daughter of a wealthy shopkeeper, who not being accustomed to amorous blandishments or respectful addresses, was delighted with the novelty of love, and easily suffered him to conduct her to the play, and to meet her where she visited. Leviculus did

not doubt but her father, however offended by a
clandestine marriage, would soon be reconciled by
the tears of his daughter and the merit of his son-
in-law, and was in haste to conclude the affair. But
the lady liked better to be courted than married, and
kept him three years in uncertainty and attendance.
At last she fell in love with a young ensign at a ball,
and having danced with him all night, married him
in the morning.

Leviculus, to avoid the ridicule of his companions,
took a journey to a small estate in the country,
where, after his usual inquiries concerning the
nymphs in the neighbourhood, he found it proper to
fall in love with Altilia, a maiden lady, twenty years
older than himself, for whose favour fifteen nephews
and nieces were in perpetual contention. They ho-
vered round her with such jealous officiousness, as
scarcely left a moment vacant for a lover. Leviculus, nevertheless, discovered his passion in a letter,
and Altilia could not withstand the pleasure of
hearing vows and sighs, and flatteries and protestations. She admitted his visits, enjoyed, for five years,
the happiness of keeping all her expectants in perpetual alarms, and amused herself with the various
stratagems which were practised to disengage her
affections. Sometimes she was advised with great
earnestness to travel for her health, and sometimes to
keep her brother's house. Many stories were spread
to the disadvantage of Leviculus, by which she commonly seemed affected for a time, but took care soon
afterward to express her conviction of their falsehood. But being at last satiated with this ludicrous
tyranny, she told her lover, when he pressed for the
reward of his services, that she was very sensible of
his merit, but was resolved not to impoverish an ancient family.

He then returned to the town, and soon after his

arrival became acquainted with Latronia, a lady distinguished by the elegance of her equipage and the regularity of her conduct. Her wealth was evident in her magnificence, and her prudence in her economy; and therefore Leviculus, who had scarcely confidence to solicit her favour, readily acquitted fortune of her former debts, when he found himself distinguished by her with such marks of preference as a woman of modesty is allowed to give. He now grew bolder, and ventured to breathe out his impatience before her. She heard him without resentment, in time permitted him to hope for happiness, and at last fixed the nuptial day, without any distrustful reserve of pin-money, or sordid stipulations for jointure and settlements.

Leviculus was triumphing on the eve of marriage, when he heard on the stairs the voice of Latronia's maid, whom frequent bribes had secured in his service. She soon burst into his room, and told him that she could not suffer him to be longer deceived; that her mistress was now spending the last payment of her fortune, and was only supported in her expense by the credit of his estate. Leviculus shuddered to see himself so near a precipice, and found that he was indebted for his escape to the resentment of the maid, who, having assisted Latronia to gain the conquest, quarrelled with her at last about the plunder.

Leviculus was now hopeless and disconsolate, till one Sunday he saw a lady in the Mall, whom her dress declared a widow, and whom, by the jolting prance of her gait, and the broad resplendence of her countenance, he guessed to have lately buried some prosperous citizen. He followed her home, and found her to be no less than the relict of Prune the grocer, who having no children had bequeathed to her all his debts and dues, and his estates real and personal. No formality was necessary in addressing Madam Prune, and therefore Leviculus went next morning without an introductor. His declaration was received with a loud laugh; she then collected her countenance, wondered at his impudence, asked if he knew to whom he was talking, then shewed him the door, and again laughed to find him confused. Leviculus discovered that this coarseness was nothing more than the coquetry of Cornhill, and next day returned to the attack. He soon grew familiar to her dialect, and in a few weeks heard, without any emotion, hints of gay clothes with empty pockets; concurred in many sage remarks on the regard due to people of property; and agreed with her in detestation of the ladies at the other end of the town, who pinched their bellies to buy fine laces, and then pretended to laugh at the city.

He sometimes presumed to mention marriage; but was always answered with a slap, a hoot, and a flounce. At last he began to press her closer, and thought himself more favourably received; but going one morning, with a resolution to trifle no longer, he found her gone to church with a young journeyman from the neighbouring shop, of whom she had become enamoured at her window.

In these, and a thousand intermediate adventures, has Leviculus spent his time, till he has now grown gray with age, fatigue, and disappointment. He begins at last to find that success is not to be expected, and being unfit for any employment that might improve his fortune, and unfurnished with any arts that might amuse his leisure, is condemned to wear out a tasteless life in narratives which few will hear, and complaints which none will pity.

Nº 183.   TUESDAY, DECEMBER 17, 1751.

> Nulla fides regni sociis, omnisque potestas
> Impatiens consortis erit.—LUCAN.
>
> No faith of partnership dominion owns;
> Still discord hovers o'er divided thrones.

THE hostility perpetually exercised between one man and another, is caused by the desire of many for that which only few can possess. Every man would be rich, powerful, and famous; yet fame, power, and riches, are only the names of relative conditions, which imply the obscurity, dependance, and poverty of greater numbers.

This universal and incessant competition produces injury and malice by two motives, interest and envy; the prospect of adding to our possessions what we can take from others, and the hope of alleviating the sense of our disparity by lessening others, though we gain nothing to ourselves.

Of these two malignant and destructive powers, it seems probable at the first view, that interest has the strongest and most extensive influence. It is easy to conceive that opportunities to seize what has been long wanted may excite desires almost irresistible; but surely the same eagerness cannot be kindled by an accidental power of destroying that which gives happiness to another. It must be more natural to rob for gain, than to ravage only for mischief.

Yet I am inclined to believe that the great law of mutual benevolence is oftener violated by envy than by interest, and that most of the misery which the defamation of blameless actions, or the obstruction of honest endeavours, brings upon the world, is inflicted by men that propose no advantage to themselves but the satisfaction of poisoning the banquet which they cannot taste, and blasting the harvest which they have no right to reap.

Interest can diffuse itself but to a narrow compass. The number is never large of those who can hope to fill the posts of degraded power, catch the fragments of shattered fortune, or succeed to the honours of depreciated beauty. But the empire of envy has no limits, as it requires to its influence very little help from external circumstances. Envy may always be produced by idleness and pride, and in what place will they not be found?

Interest requires some qualities not universally bestowed. The ruin of another will produce no profit to him who has not discernment to mark his advantage, courage to seize, and activity to pursue it; but the cold malignity of envy may be exerted in a torpid and quiescent state, amidst the gloom of stupidity, in the coverts of cowardice. He that falls by the attacks of interest, is torn by hungry tigers; he may discover and resist his enemies. He that perishes in the ambushes of envy, is destroyed by unknown and invisible assailants, and dies like a man suffocated by a poisonous vapour, without knowledge of his danger or possibility of contest.

Interest is seldom pursued but at some hazard. He that hopes to gain much, has commonly something to lose, and when he ventures to attack superiority, if he fails to conquer, is irrecoverably crushed. But envy may act without expense or danger. To spread suspicion, to invent calumnies, to propagate scandal, requires neither labour nor courage. It is easy for the author of a lie, however malignant, to escape detection, and infamy needs very little industry to assist its circulation.

Envy is almost the only vice which is practicable at all times, and in every place; the only passion which can never lie quiet for want of irritation : its effects therefore are every where discoverable, and its attempts always to be dreaded.

It is impossible to mention a name which any advantageous distinction has made eminent, but some latent animosity will burst out. The wealthy trader, however he may abstract himself from public affairs, will never want those who hint, with Shylock, that ships are but boards. The beauty, adorned only with the unambitious graces of innocence and modesty, provokes, whenever she appears, a thousand murmurs of detraction. The genius, even when he endeavours only to entertain or instruct, yet suffers persecution from innumerable critics, whose acrimony is excited merely by the pain of seeing others pleased, and of hearing applauses which another enjoys.

The frequency of envy makes it so familiar, that it escapes our notice ; nor do we often reflect upon its turpitude or malignity, till we happen to feel its influence. When he that has given no provocation to malice, but by attempting to excel, finds himself pursued by multitudes whom he never saw, with all the implacability of personal resentment ; when he perceives clamour and malice let loose upon him as a public enemy, and incited by every stratagem of defamation ; when he hears the misfortunes of his family, or the follies of his youth, exposed to the world, and every failure of conduct, or defect of nature, aggravated and ridiculed ; he then learns to abhor those artifices at which he only laughed before, and discovers how much the happiness of life would be advanced by the eradication of envy from the human heart.

Envy is, indeed, a stubborn weed of the mind, and seldom yields to the culture of philosophy. There are, however, considerations, which if carefully im-

planted and diligently propagated, might in time
overpower and repress it, since no one can nurse it
for the sake of pleasure, as its effects are only shame,
anguish, and perturbation.

It is above all other vices inconsistent with the
character of a social being, because it sacrifices truth
and kindness to very weak temptations. He that
plunders a wealthy neighbour gains as much as he
takes away, and may improve his own condition in
the same proportion as he impairs another's; but he
that blasts a flourishing reputation, must be content
with a small dividend of additional fame, so small as
can afford very little consolation to balance the guilt
by which it is obtained.

I have hitherto avoided that dangerous and empi-
rical morality, which cures one vice by means of another. But envy is so base and detestable, so vile
in its original, and so pernicious in its effects, that the
predominance of almost any other quality is to be
preferred. It is one of those lawless enemies of society, against which poisoned arrows may honestly
be used. Let it therefore be constantly remembered,
that whoever envies another confesses his superiority,
and let those be reformed by their pride who have
lost their virtue.

It is no slight aggravation of the injuries which
envy incites, that they are committed against those
who have given no intentional provocation; and
the sufferer is often marked out for ruin, not because
he has failed in any duty, but because he has dared
to do more than was required.

Almost every other crime is practised by the help
of some quality which might have produced esteem
or love, if it had been well employed; but envy is
mere unmixed and genuine evil; it pursues a hateful evil by despicable means, and desires not so much
its own happiness as another's misery. To avoid

depravity like this, it is not necessary that any one should aspire to heroism or sanctity, but only that he should resolve not to quit the rank which nature assigns him, and wish to maintain the dignity of a human being.

<hr>

N° 184. SATURDAY, DECEMBER 21, 1751.

> Permittes ipsis expendere numinibus, quid
> Conveniat nobis, rebusque sit utile nostris.—Juv.

> Intrust thy fortune to the pow'rs above ;
> Leave them to manage for thee, and to grant
> What their unerring wisdom sees thee want.—Dryden.

As every scheme of life, so every form of writing, has its advantages and inconveniences, though not mingled in the same proportions. The writer of essays escapes many embarrassments to which a large work would have exposed him ; he seldom harasses his reason with long trains of consequences, dims his eyes with the perusal of antiquated volumes, or burdens his memory with great accumulations of preparatory knowledge. A careless glance upon a favourite author, or transient survey of the varieties of life, is sufficient to supply the first hint or seminal idea, which, enlarged by the gradual accretion of matter stored in the mind, is by the warmth of fancy easily expanded into flowers, and sometimes ripened into fruit.

The most frequent difficulty by which the authors of these petty compositions are distressed, arises from the perpetual demand of novelty and change. The compiler of a system of science lays his invention at rest, and employs only his judgment, the fa-

culty exerted with least fatigue. Even the relator
of feigned adventures, when once the principal characters are established, and the great events regularly connected, finds incidents and episodes crowd-
ing upon his mind; every change opens new views,
and the latter part of the story grows without labour
out of the former. But he that attempts to entertain
his reader with unconnected pieces, finds the irk-
someness of his task rather increased than lessened
by every production. The day calls afresh upon him
for a new topic, and he is again obliged to choose,
without any principle to regulate his choice.

It is indeed true, that there is seldom any necessity of looking far, or inquiring long, for a proper
subject, every diversity of art or nature, every public
blessing or calamity, every domestic pain or gratification, every sally of caprice, blunder of absurdity,
or stratagem of affectation, may supply matter to him
whose only rule is to avoid uniformity. But it often
happens, that the judgment is distracted with boundless multiplicity, the imagination ranges from one
design to another, and the hours pass imperceptibly
away, till the composition can be no longer delayed,
and necessity enforces the use of those thoughts
which then happen to be at hand. The mind rejoicing at deliverance on any terms from perplexity and
suspense, applies herself vigorously to the work before her, collects embellishments and illustrations,
and sometimes finishes, with great elegance and happiness, what in a state of ease and leisure she never
had begun.

It is not commonly observed, how much, even of
actions considered as particularly subject to choice,
is to be attributed to accident, or some cause out of
our own power, by whatever name it be distinguished.
To close tedious deliberations with hasty resolves,
and after long consultations with reason to refer the

question to caprice, is by no means peculiar to the essayist. Let him that peruses this paper review the series of his life, and inquire how he was placed in his present condition. He will find that of the good or ill which he has experienced, a great part came unexpected without any visible gradations of approach; that every event has been influenced by causes acting without his intervention; and that whenever he pretended to the prerogative of foresight, he was mortified with new conviction of the shortness of his views.

The busy, the ambitious, the inconstant, and the adventurous, may be said to throw themselves by design into the arms of fortune, and voluntarily to quit the power of governing themselves; they engage in a course of life in which little can be ascertained by previous measures; nor is it any wonder that their time is past between elation and despondency, hope and disappointment.

Some there are who appear to walk the road of life with more circumspection, and make no step till they think themselves secure from the hazard of a precipice; when neither pleasure nor profit can tempt them from the beaten path; who refuse to climb lest they should fall, or to run lest they should stumble, and move slowly forward without any compliance with those passions by which the heady and vehement are seduced and betrayed.

Yet even the timorous prudence of this judicious class is far from exempting them from the dominion of chance, a subtle and insidious power, who will intrude upon privacy and embarrass caution. No course of life is so prescribed and limited, but that many actions must result from arbitrary election. Every one must form the general plan of his conduct by his own reflections; he must resolve whether he will endeavour at riches or at content; whether he will exercise private or public virtues: whether he will labour for the general benefit of mankind, or contract his beneficence to his family and his dependants.

This question has long exercised the schools of philosophy, but remains yet undecided; and what hope is there that a young man, unacquainted with the arguments on either side, should determine his own destiny otherwise than by chance?

When chance has given him a partner of his bed, whom he prefers to all other women, without any proof of superior desert, chance must again direct him in the education of his children; for, who was ever able to convince himself by arguments, that he had chosen for his son that mode of instruction to which his understanding was best adapted, or by which he would most easily be made wise or virtuous?

Whoever shall inquire by what motive he was determined on these important occasions, will find them such as his pride will scarcely suffer him to confess; some sudden ardour of desire, some uncertain glimpse of advantage, some petty competition, some inaccurate conclusion, or some example implicitly reverenced. Such are often the first causes of our resolves; for it is necessary to act, but impossible to know the consequences of action, or to discuss all the reasons which offer themselves on every part to inquisitiveness and solicitude.

Since life itself is uncertain, nothing which has life for its basis can boast much stability. Yet this is but a small part of our perplexity. We set out on a tempestuous sea in quest of some port, where we expect to find rest, but where we are not sure of admission; we are not only in danger of sinking in the way, but of being misled by meteors mistaken for stars, of being driven from our course by the changes of the wind, and of losing it by unskilful steerage; yet it sometimes happens, that cross winds blow us to a safer coast, that meteors draw us aside from whirlpools, and that negligence or error contributes to our escape from mischiefs, to which a direct course would have exposed us. Of those that, by precipitate conclusions, involve themselves in calamities without guilt, very few, however they may reproach themselves, can be certain that other measures would have been more successful.

In this state of universal uncertainty, where a thousand dangers hover about us, and none can tell whether the good that he pursues is not evil in disguise, or whether the next step will lead him to safety or destruction, nothing can afford any rational tranquillity, but the conviction that, however we amuse ourselves with unideal sounds, nothing in reality is governed by chance, but that the universe is under the perpetual superintendence of him who created it; that our being is in the hands of omnipotent goodness, by whom what appears casual to us, is directed for ends ultimately kind and merciful; and that nothing can finally hurt him who debars not himself from the divine favour.

N° 185.　TUESDAY, DECEMBER 24, 1751.

'At vindicta bonum vitâ jucundius ipsâ,'
Nempè hoc indocti.——
Chrysippus non dicit idem, nec mite Thaletis
Ingenium, dulcique senex vicinus Hymetto,
Qui partem acceptæ sæva inter vincla cicutæ
Accusatori nollet dare.——Quippè minuti
Semper, et infirmi est animi, exiguique voluptas
Ultio.　　　　　　　　　　　　Juv.

But O! revenge is sweet,
Thus think the crowd; who, eager to engage,
Take quickly fire, and kindle into rage.
Not so mild Thales nor Chrysippus thought,
Nor that good man, who drank the pois'nous draught
With mind serene; and could not wish to see
His vile accuser drink as deep as he:
Exalted Socrates! divinely brave!
Injur'd he fell, and dying he forgave,
Too noble for revenge; which still we find
The weakest frailty of a feeble mind.—DRYDEN.

No vicious dispositions of the mind more obstinately resist both the counsels of philosophy and the injunctions of religion, than those which are complicated with an opinion of dignity; and which we cannot dismiss without leaving in the hands of opposition some advantage iniquitously obtained, or suffering from our own prejudices some imputation of pusillanimity.

For this reason scarcely any law of our Redeemer is more openly transgressed, or more industriously evaded, than that by which he commands his followers to forgive injuries, and prohibits, under the sanction of eternal misery, the gratification of the desire which every man feels to return pain upon him that inflicts it. Many who could have conquered their anger are unable to combat pride, and pursue offences to extremity of vengeance, lest they should be insulted by the triumph of an enemy.

But certainly no precept could better become him, at whose birth *peace* was proclaimed *to the earth*. For, what would so soon destroy all the order of society, and deform life with violence and ravage, as a permission to every one to judge his own cause, and to apportion his own recompense for imagined injuries?

It is difficult for a man of the strictest justice not to favour himself too much, in the calmest moments of solitary meditation. Every one wishes for the distinctions for which thousands are wishing at the same time, in their own opinion, with better claims. He that, when his reason operates in its full force, can thus, by the mere prevalence of self-love, prefer himself to his fellow-beings, is very unlikely to judge equitably when his passions are agitated by a sense of wrong, and his attention wholly engrossed by pain, interest, or danger. Whoever arrogates to himself the right of vengeance, shews how little he is qualified to decide his own claims, since he certainly demands what he would think unfit to be granted to another.

Nothing is more apparent than that, however injured or however provoked, some must at last be contented to forgive. For it can never be hoped, that he who first commits an injury, will contentedly acquiesce in the penalty required: the same haughtiness of contempt, or vehemence of desire, that prompts the act of injustice, will more strongly incite its justification; and resentment can never so exactly balance the punishment with the fault, but there will remain an overplus of vengeance which even he who condemns his first action will think himself entitled to retaliate. What then can ensue but a continual exacerbation of hatred, and unextinguishable feud, an incessant reciprocation of mischief, a mutual vigilance to entrap, and eagerness to destroy?

Since then the imaginary right of vengeance must be at last remitted, because it is impossible to live in perpetual hostility, and equally impossible, that of two enemies, either should first think himself obliged by justice to submission, it is surely eligible to forgive early. Every passion is more easily subdued before it has been long accustomed to possession of the heart; every idea is obliterated with less difficulty, as it has been more slightly impressed, and less frequently renewed. He who has often brooded over his wrongs, pleased himself with schemes of malignity, and glutted his pride with the fancied supplications of humbled enmity, will not easily open his bosom to amity and reconciliation, or indulge the gentle sentiments of benevolence and peace.

It is easiest to forgive, while there is yet little to be forgiven. A single injury may soon be dismissed from the memory; but a long succession of ill offices by degrees associates itself with every idea, a long contest involves so many circumstances, that every place and action will recall it to the mind, and fresh remembrance of vexation must still enkindle rage and irritate revenge.

A wise man will make haste to forgive, because he knows the true value of time, and will not suffer it to pass away in unnecessary pain. He that willingly suffers the corrosions of inveterate hatred, and gives up his days and nights to the gloom of malice and perturbations of stratagem, cannot surely be said to consult his ease. Resentment is a union of sorrow with malignity, a combination of a passion which all endeavour to avoid, with a passion which all concur to detest. The man who retires to meditate mischief, and to exasperate his own rage; whose thoughts are employed only on means of distress and contrivances of ruin; whose mind never pauses from the remembrance of his own sufferings, but to indulge some hope of enjoying the calamities of another, may justly be numbered among the most miserable of human beings, among those who are guilty without reward, who have neither the gladness of prosperity nor the calm of innocence.

Whoever considers the weakness both of himself and others, will not long want persuasives to forgiveness. We know not to what degree of malignity any injury is to be imputed; or how much its guilt, if we were to inspect the mind of him that committed it, would be extenuated by mistake, precipitance, or negligence; we cannot be certain how much more we feel than was intended to be inflicted, or how much we increase the mischief to ourselves by voluntary aggravations. We may charge to design the effects of accident; we may think the blow violent only because we have made ourselves delicate and tender; we are on every side in danger of error and of guilt, which we are certain to avoid only by speedy forgiveness.

From this pacific and harmless temper, thus propitious to others and ourselves, to domestic tranquillity and to social happiness, no man is withheld but by pride, by the fear of being insulted by his adversary, or despised by the world.

It may be laid down as an unfailing and universal axiom, that 'all pride is abject and mean.' It is always an ignorant, lazy, or cowardly acquiescence in a false appearance of excellence, and proceeds not from consciousness of our attainments, but insensibility of our wants.

Nothing can be great which is not right. Nothing which reason condemns can be suitable to the dignity of the human mind. To be driven by external motives from the path which our own heart approves, to give way to any thing but conviction, to suffer the opinion of others to rule our choice or overpower our resolves, is to submit, tamely to the lowest and most ignominious slavery, and to resign the right of directing our own lives.

The utmost excellence at which humanity can arrive, is a constant and determinate pursuit of virtue, without regard to present dangers or advantages; a continual reference of every action to the divine will; an habitual appeal to everlasting justice; and an unvaried elevation of the intellectual eye to the reward which perseverance only can obtain. But that pride which many, who presume to boast of generous sentiments, allow to regulate their measures, has nothing nobler in view than the approbation of men, of beings whose superiority we are under no obligation to acknowledge, and who, when we have courted them with the utmost assiduity, can confer no valuable or permanent reward; of beings, who ignorantly judge of what they do not understand, or partially determine what they never have examined; and whose sentence is therefore of no weight till it has received the ratification of our own conscience.

He that can descend to bribe suffrages like these at the price of his innocence; he that can suffer the delight of such acclamations to withhold his attention from the commands of the universal Sovereign, has little reason to congratulate himself upon the greatness of his mind: whenever he awakes to seriousness and reflection, he must become despicable in his own eyes, and shrink with shame from the remembrance of his cowardice and folly.

Of him that hopes to be forgiven, it is indispensably required that he forgive. It is therefore superfluous to urge any other motive. On this great duty eternity is suspended, and to him that refuses to practise it, the throne of mercy is inaccessible, and the SAVIOUR of the world has been born in vain.

Nᵒ 186. SATURDAY, DECEMBER 28, 1751.

Pone me, pigris ubi nulla campis
  Arbor æstivâ recreatur aurâ——
Dulce ridentem Lalagen amabo,
        Dulce loquentem.—Hor.

Place me where never summer breeze
Unbinds the glebe, or warms the trees:
Where ever lowering clouds appear,
And angry Jove deforms th' inclement year:
Love and the nymph shall charm my toils,
The nymph, who sweetly speaks and sweetly smiles.

                                    Francis.

Of the happiness and misery of our present state,
part arises from our sensations, and part from our
opinions; part is distributed by nature, and part is
in a great measure apportioned by ourselves. Positive pleasure we cannot always obtain, and positive
pain we often cannot remove. No man can give
to his own plantations the fragrance of the Indian
groves; nor will any precepts of philosophy enable
him to withdraw his attention from wounds or diseases. But the negative infelicity which proceeds,
not from the pressure of suffering, but the absence
of enjoyments, will always yield to the remedies of
reason.

One of the great arts of escaping superfluous uneasiness, is to free our minds from the habit of comparing our condition with that of others on whom
the blessings of life are more bountifully bestowed,
or with imaginary states of delight and security, perhaps unattainable by mortals. Few are placed in a
situation so gloomy and distressful, as not to see
every day beings yet more forlorn and miserable,

from whom they may learn to rejoice in their own lot.

No inconvenience is less superable by art or diligence than the inclemency of climates, and therefore none affords more proper exercise for this philosophical abstraction. A native of England, pinched with the frosts of December, may lessen his affection for his own country, by suffering his imagination to wander in the vales of Asia, and sport among woods that are always green, and streams that always murmur; but if he turns his thoughts towards the polar regions, and considers the nations to whom a great portion of the year is darkness, and who are condemned to pass weeks and months amidst mountains of snow, he will soon recover his tranquillity, and while he stirs his fire, or throws his cloak about him, reflect how much he owes to Providence, that he is not placed in Greenland or Siberia.

The barrenness of the earth and the severity of the skies in these dreary countries, are such as might be expected to confine the mind wholly to the contemplation of necessity and distress, so that the care of escaping death from cold and hunger, should leave no room for those passions which, in lands of plenty, influence conduct or diversify characters; the summer should be spent wholly in providing for the winter, and the winter in longing for the summer.

Yet learned curiosity is known to have found its way into those abodes of poverty and gloom: Lapland and Iceland have their historians, their critics, and their poets; and love, that extends his dominion wherever humanity can be found, perhaps exerts the same power in the Greenlander's hut as in the palaces of eastern monarchs.

In one of the large caves to which the families of Greenland retire together, to pass the cold months, and which may be termed their villages or cities, a youth and maid, who came from different parts of the country, were so much distinguished for their beauty that they were called by the rest of the inhabitants Anningait and Ajut, from a supposed resemblance to their ancestors of the same names, who had been transformed of old into the sun and moon.

Anningait for some time heard the praises of Ajut with little emotion, but at last, by frequent interviews, became sensible of her charms, and first made a discovery of his affection, by inviting her with her parents to a feast, where he placed before Ajut the tail of a whale. Ajut seemed not much delighted by this gallantry; yet, however, from that time, was observed rarely to appear, but in a vest made of the skin of a white deer; she used frequently to renew the black die upon her hands and forehead, to adorn her sleeves with coral and shells, and to braid her hair with great exactness.

The elegance of her dress, and the judicious disposition of her ornaments, had such an effect upon Anningait that he could no longer be restrained from a declaration of his love. He therefore composed a poem in her praise, in which, among other heroic and tender sentiments, he protested, that 'She was beautiful as the vernal willow, and fragrant as thyme upon the mountains; that her fingers were white as the teeth of the morse, and her smile grateful as the dissolution of the ice; that he would pursue her, though she should pass the snows of the midland cliffs, or seek shelter in the caves of the eastern cannibals; that he would tear her from the embraces of the genius of the rocks, snatch her from the paws of Amaroc, and rescue her from the ravine of Hafgufa.' He concluded with a wish, that 'whoever shall attempt to hinder his union with Ajut, might be buried without his bow, and that in the land of souls his skull might serve for no other use than to catch the droppings of the starry lamps.'

This ode being universally applauded, it was expected that Ajut would soon yield to such fervour and accomplishments; but Ajut, with the natural haughtiness of beauty, expected all the forms of courtship; and before she would confess herself conquered, the sun returned, the ice broke, and the season of labour called all to their employments.

Anningait and Ajut, for a time, always went out in the same boat, and divided whatever was caught. Anningait, in the sight of his mistress, lost no opportunity of signalizing his courage; he attacked the sea-horses on the ice; pursued the seals into the water; and leaped upon the back of the whale, while he was yet struggling with the remains of life. Nor was his diligence less to accumulate all that could be necessary to make winter comfortable: he dried the roe of fishes and the flesh of seals; he entrapped deer and foxes, and dressed their skins to adorn his bride; he feasted her with eggs from the rocks, and strewed her tent with flowers.

It happened that a tempest drove the fish to a distant part of the coast, before Anningait had completed his store; he therefore entreated Ajut that she would at last grant him her hand, and accompany him to that part of the country whither he was now summoned by necessity. Ajut thought him not yet entitled to such condescension, but proposed, as a trial of his constancy, that he should return at the end of summer to the cavern where their acquaintance commenced, and there expect the reward of his assiduities. 'O virgin, beautiful as the sun shining on the water, consider,' said Anningait, 'what thou hast required. How easily may my return be precluded by a sudden frost or unexpected fogs; then must the night be past without my Ajut. We live not, my fair, in those fabled countries, which lying strangers so wantonly describe; where the whole year is divided into short days and nights; where the same habitation serves for summer and winter; where they raise houses in rows above the ground; dwell together from year to year, with flocks of tame animals grazing in the fields about them; can travel at any time from one place to another, through ways inclosed with trees, or over walls raised upon the inland waters; and direct their course through wide countries by the sight of green hills or scattered buildings. Even in summer, we have no means of crossing the mountains, whose snows are never dissolved; nor can remove to any distant residence, but in our boats coasting the bays. Consider, Ajut; a few summer-days, and a few winter nights, and the life of man is at an end. Night is the time of ease and festivity, of revels and gaiety; but what will be the flaming lamp, the delicious seal, or the soft oil, without the smile of Ajut?'

The eloquence of Anningait was vain; the maid continued inexorable, and they parted with ardent promises to meet again before the night of winter.

N° 187. TUESDAY, DECEMBER 31, 1751.

> Non illum nostri possunt mutare labores,
> Non si frigoribus mediis Hebrumque bibamus,
> Sithoniasque nives hiemis subeamus aquosæ,——
> Omnia vincit amor.—VIRGIL.

> Love alters not for us his hard decrees,
> Not tho' beneath the Thracian clime we freeze,
> Or the mild bliss of temperate skies forego,
> And in mid winter tread Sithonian snow :——
> Love conquers all.—— DRYDEN.

ANNINGAIT, however discomposed by the dilatory coyness of Ajut, was yet resolved to omit no tokens of amorous respect; and therefore presented her at his departure with the skins of seven white fawns, of five swans, and eleven seals, with three marble lamps, ten vessels of seal oil, and a large kettle of brass, which he had purchased from a ship, at the price of half a whale, and two horns of sea-unicorns.

Ajut was so much affected by the fondness of her lover, or so much overpowered by his magnificence, that she followed him to the sea-side; and, when she saw him enter the boat, wished aloud that he might return with plenty of skins and oil; that neither the mermaids might snatch him into the deeps, nor the spirits of the rocks confine him in their caverns.

She stood a while to gaze upon the departing vessel, and then returning to her hut, silent and dejected, laid aside, from that hour, her white deer skin, suffered her hair to spread unbraided on her shoulders, and forbore to mix in the dances of the maidens. She endeavoured to divert her thoughts by continual application to feminine employments, gathered moss for the winter lamps, and dried grass to line the boots of Anningait. Of the skins which he had bestowed upon her, she made a fishing-coat, a small boat, and tent, all of exquisite manufacture; and while she was thus busied, solaced her labours with a song, in which she prayed, ' that her lover might have hands stronger than the paws of the bear, and feet swifter than the feet of the rein-deer, that his dart might never err, and that his boat might never leak; that he might never stumble on the ice, nor faint in the water; that the seal might rush on his harpoon, and the wounded whale might dash the waves in vain.'

The large boats in which the Greenlanders transport their families, are always rowed by women; for a man will not debase himself by work which requires neither skill nor courage. Anningait was therefore exposed by idleness to the ravages of passion. He went thrice to the stern of the boat, with an intent to leap into the water, and swim back to his mistress; but recollecting the misery which they must endure in the winter, without oil for the lamp, or skins for the bed, he resolved to employ the weeks of absence in provision for a night of plenty and felicity. He then composed his emotions as he could, and expressed in wild numbers and uncouth images, his hopes, his sorrows, and his fears. ' O life,' says he, ' frail and uncertain! where shall wretched man find thy resemblance but in ice floating on the ocean? It towers on high, it sparkles from afar, while the storms drive and the waters beat it, the sun melts it above, and the rocks shatter it below. What art thou, deceitful pleasure! but a sudden blaze streaming from the north, which plays a moment on the eye, mocks the traveller with the hopes of light, and then vanishes for ever? What, love, art thou but a whirlpool, which we approach without knowledge of our danger, drawn on by imperceptible degrees, till we have lost all power of resistance and escape? Till

I fixed my eyes on the graces of Ajut, while I had not yet called her to the banquet, I was careless as the sleeping morse, I was merry as the singers in the stars. Why, Ajut, did I gaze upon thy graces? why, my fair, did I call thee to the banquet? Yet, be faithful, my love, remember Anningait, and meet my return with the smile of virginity. I will chase the deer, I will subdue the whale, resistless as the frost of darkness, and unwearied as the summer's sun. In a few weeks I shall return prosperous and wealthy; then shall the roefish and the porpoise feast thy kindred; the fox and hare shall cover thy couch, the tough hide of the seal shall shelter thee from cold, and the fat of the whale illuminate thy dwelling.'

Anningait having with these sentiments consoled his grief and animated his industry, found that they had now coasted the headland, and saw the whales spouting at a distance. He therefore placed himself in his fishing-boat, called his associates to their several employments, plied his oar and harpoon with incredible courage and dexterity; and, by dividing his time between the chase and fishery, suspended the miseries of absence and suspicion.

Ajut, in the mean time, notwithstanding her neglected dress, happened, as she was drying some skins in the sun, to catch the eye of Norngsuk, on his return from hunting. Norngsuk was of birth truly illustrious. His mother had died in childbirth, and his father, the most expert fisher of Greenland, had perished by too close pursuit of the whale. His dignity was equalled by his riches; he was master of four men's and two women's boats, had ninety tubs of oil in his winter habitation, and five-and-twenty seals buried in the snow against the season of darkness. When he saw the beauty of Ajut, he immediately threw over her the skin of a deer that he had taken, and soon after presented her with a branch of coral. Ajut refused his gifts, and determined to admit no lover in the place of Anningait.

Norngsuk, thus rejected, had recourse to stratagem. He knew that Ajut would consult an Angekkok, or diviner, concerning the fate of her lover, and the felicity of her future life. He therefore applied himself to the most celebrated Angekkok of that part of the country, and by a present of two seals and a marble kettle obtained a promise, that when Ajut should consult him, he would declare that her lover was in the land of souls. Ajut in a short time brought him a coat made by herself, and inquired what events were to befal her, with assurances of a much larger reward at the return of Anningait, if the prediction should flatter her desires. The Angekkok knew the way to riches, and foretold that Anningait, having already caught two whales, would soon return home with a large boat laden with provisions.

This prognostication she was ordered to keep secret; and Norngsuk depending upon his artifice, renewed his addresses with greater confidence; but finding his suit still unsuccessful, applied himself to her parents with gifts and promises. The wealth of Greenland is too powerful for the virtue of a Greenlander; they forgot the merit and presents of Anningait, and decreed Ajut to the embraces of Norngsuk. She entreated; she remonstrated; she wept, and raved: but finding riches irresistible, fled away into the uplands, and lived in a cave upon such berries as she could gather, and the birds or hares which she had the fortune to ensnare, taking care, at an hour when she was not likely to be found, to view the sea every day, that her lover might not miss her at his return.

At last she saw the great boat in which Anningait had departed, stealing slow and heavy laden along the coast. She ran with all the impatience of affection to catch her lover in her arms, and relate her constancy and sufferings. When the company reached the land, they informed her, that Anningait, after the fishery was ended, being unable to support the slow passage of the vessel of carriage, had set out before them in his fishing-boat, and they expected at their arrival to have found him on shore.

Ajut, distracted at this intelligence, was about to fly into the hills, without knowing why, though she was now in the hands of her parents who forced her back to their own hut, and endeavoured to comfort her ; but when at last they retired to rest, Ajut went down to the beach ; where finding a fishing-boat, she entered it without hesitation, and telling those who wondered at her rashness, that she was going in search of Anningait, rowed away with great swiftness, and was seen no more.

The fate of these lovers gave occasion to various fictions and conjectures. Some are of opinion, that they were changed into stars ; others imagine that Anningait was seized in his passage by the genius of the rocks, and that Ajut was transformed into a mermaid, and still continues to seek her lover in the deserts of the sea. But the general persuasion is, that they are both in that part of the land of souls where the sun never sets, where oil is always fresh, and provisions always warm. The virgins sometimes throw a thimble and a needle into the bay, from which the hapless maid departed ; and when a Greenlander would praise any couple for virtuous affection, he declares that they love like Anningait and Ajut.

Nº 188. SATURDAY, JANUARY 4, 1751.

——Si te colo, Sexte, non amabo.—MART.

The more I honour thee, the less I love.

NONE of the desires dictated by vanity is more general, or less blamable, than that of being distinguished for the arts of conversation. Other accomplishments may be possessed without opportunity of
exerting them, or wanted without danger that the
defect can often be remarked; but as no man can
live otherwise than in an hermitage, without hourly
pleasure or vexation, from the fondness or neglect of
those about him, the faculty of giving pleasure is of
continual use. Few are more frequently envied than
those who have the power of enforcing attention wherever they come, whose entrance is considered as a
promise of felicity, and whose departure is lamented,
like the recess of the sun from northern climates, as
a privation of all that enlivens fancy or inspirits
gaiety.

It is apparent that to excellence in this valuable
art, some peculiar qualifications are necessary; for
every one's experience will inform him, that the pleasure which men are able to give in conversation,
holds no stated proportion to their knowledge or
their virtue. Many find their way to the tables and
the parties of those who never consider them as of
the least importance in any other place; we have all,
at one time or other, been content to love those whom
we could not esteem, and been persuaded to try the
dangerous experiment of admitting him for a companion whom we knew to be too ignorant for a coun-
sellor, and too treacherous for a friend.

I question whether some abatement of character is not necessary to general acceptance. Few spend their time with much satisfaction under the eye of incontestable superiority; and, therefore, among those whose presence is courted at assemblies of jollity, there are seldom found men eminently distinguished for powers or acquisitions. The wit whose vivacity condemns slower tongues to silence, the scholar whose knowledge allows no man to fancy that he instructs him, the critic who suffers no fallacy to pass undetected, and the reasoner who condemns the idle to thought, and the negligent to attention, are generally praised and feared, reverenced and avoided.

He that would please must rarely aim at such excellence as depresses his hearers in their own opinion, or debars them from the hope of contributing reciprocally to the entertainment of the company. Merriment, extorted by sallies of imagination, sprightliness of remark, or quickness of reply, is too often what the Latins call, the Sardinian laughter, a distortion of the face without gladness of heart.

For this reason, no style of conversation is more extensively acceptable than the narrative. He who has stored his memory with slight anecdotes, private incidents, and personal peculiarities, seldom fails to find his audience favourable. Almost every man listens with eagerness to contemporary history; for almost every man has some real or imaginary connexion with a celebrated character; some desire to advance or oppose a rising name. Vanity often cooperates with curiosity. He that is a hearer in one place, qualifies himself to become a speaker in another; for though he cannot comprehend a series of argument, or transport the volatile spirit of wit without evaporation, yet he thinks himself able to treasure up the various incidents of a story, and pleases his hopes with the information which he shall give to some inferior society.

Narratives are for the most part heard without envy, because they are not supposed to imply any intellectual qualities above the common rate. To be acquainted with facts not yet echoed by plebeian mouths, may happen to one man as well as to another; and to relate them when they are known, has in appearance so little difficulty, that every one concludes himself equal to the task.

But it is not easy, and in some situations of life not possible, to accumulate such a stock of materials as may support the expense of continual narration; and it frequently happens, that they who attempt this method of ingratiating themselves, please only at the first interview; and, for want of new supplies of intelligence, wear out their stories by continual repetition.

There would be, therefore, little hope of obtaining the praise of a good companion, were it not to be gained by more compendious methods; but such is the kindness of mankind to all, except those who aspire to real merit and rational dignity, that every understanding may find some way to excite benevolence; and whoever is not envied may learn the art of procuring love. We are willing to be pleased, but are not willing to admire; we favour the mirth or officiousness that solicits our regard, but oppose the worth or spirit that enforces it.

The first place among those that please, because they desire only to please, is due to the *merry fellow*, whose laugh is loud, and whose voice is strong; who is ready to echo every jest with obstreperous approbation, and countenance every frolic with vociferations of applause. It is not necessary to a merry fellow to have in himself any fund of jocularity, or force of conception; it is sufficient that he always appears in the highest exaltation of gladness; for the greater part of mankind are gay or serious by infection, and follow without resistance the attraction of example.

Next to the merry fellow is the *good-natured man*, a being generally without benevolence, or any other virtue, than such as indolence and insensibility confer. The characteristic of a good-natured man is to bear a joke; to sit unmoved and unaffected amidst noise and turbulence, profaneness and obscenity; to hear every tale without contradiction; to endure insult without reply; and to follow the stream of folly, whatever course it shall happen to take. The good-natured man is commonly the darling of the petty wits, with whom they exercise themselves in the rudiments of raillery; for he never takes advantage of failings, nor disconcerts a puny satirist with unexpected sarcasms; but while the glass continues to circulate, contentedly bears the expense of uninterrupted laughter, and retires rejoicing at his own importance.

The *modest man* is a companion of a yet lower rank, whose only power of giving pleasure is not to interrupt it. The modest man satisfies himself with peaceful silence, which all his companions are candid enough to consider as proceeding not from inability to speak, but willingness to hear.

Many, without being able to attain any general character of excellence, have some single art of entertainment, which serves them as a passport through the world. One I have known for fifteen years the darling of a weekly club, because every night precisely at eleven, he begins his favourite song, and during the vocal performance, by corresponding motions of his hand, chalks out a giant upon the wall. Another has endeared himself to a long succession of acquaintances by sitting among them with his wig reversed; another by contriving to smut the nose of any stranger who was to be initiated in the club; another by purring like a cat, and then pretending to be frighted; and another by yelping like a hound, and calling to the drawers to drive out the dog.

Such are the arts by which cheerfulness is promoted, and sometimes friendship established; arts, which those who despise them should not rigorously blame, except when they are practised at the expense of innocence; for it is always necessary to be loved, but not always necessary to be reverenced.

Nº 189. TUESDAY, JANUARY 7, 1752.

Quòd tam grande sophos clamat tibi turba togata,
Non tu, Pomponi, cæna diserta tua est.—MART.

Resounding plaudits thro' the crowd have rung;
Thy treat is eloquent, and not thy tongue.—F. LEWIS.

THE world scarcely affords opportunities of making any observation more frequently, than on false claims to commendation. Almost every man wastes part of his life in attempts to display qualities which he does not possess, and to gain applauses which he cannot keep; so that scarcely can two persons casually meet, but one is offended or diverted by the ostentation of the other.

Of these pretenders it is fit to distinguish those who endeavour to deceive from them who are deceived; those who by designed impostures promote their interest or gratify their pride, from them who mean only to force into regard their latent excellences and neglected virtues; who believe themselves qualified to instruct or please, and therefore invite the notice of mankind.

The artful and fraudulent usurpers of distinction deserve greater severities than ridicule and contempt, since they are seldom content with empty praise, but are instigated by passions more pernicious than vanity. They consider the reputation which they endeavour to establish as necessary to the accomplishment of some subsequent design, and value praise only as it may conduce to the success of avarice or ambition.

The commercial world is very frequently put into confusion by the bankruptcy of merchants, that assumed the splendour of wealth only to obtain the privilege of trading with the stock of other men, and of contracting debts which nothing but lucky casualties could enable them to pay; till after having supported their appearance a while by tumultuary magnificence of boundless traffic, they sink at once, and drag down into poverty those whom their equipages had induced to trust them.

Among wretches that place their happiness in the favour of the great, of beings whom only high titles or large estates set above themselves, nothing is more common than to boast of confidence which they do not enjoy; to sell promises which they know their interest unable to perform; and to reimburse the tribute which they pay to an imperious master, from the contributions of meaner dependants, whom they can amuse with tales of their influence, and hopes of their solicitation.

Even among some, too thoughtless and volatile for avarice or ambition, may be found a species of falsehood more detestable than the levee or exchange can shew. There are men that boast of debaucheries, of which they never had address to be guilty; ruin, by lewd tales, the characters of women to whom they are scarcely known, or by whom they have been rejected; destroy in a drunken frolic the happiness of families; blast the bloom of beauty, and intercept the reward of virtue.

Other artifices of falsehood, though utterly unworthy of an ingenuous mind, are not yet to be ranked with flagitious enormities, nor is it necessary to incite sanguinary justice against them, since they may be adequately punished by detection and laughter. The traveller who describes cities which he has never seen; the squire who, at his return from London, tells of his intimacy with nobles, to whom he has only bowed in the Park or coffee-house; the author who entertains his admirers with stories of the assistance which he gives to wits of a higher rank; the city dame who talks of her visits at great houses, where she happens to know the cook-maid, are surely such harmless animals as truth herself may be content to despise without desiring to hurt them. But of the multitudes who struggle in vain for distinction and display their own merits only to feel more acutely the sting of neglect, a great part are wholly innocent of deceit, and are betrayed, by infatuation and credulity, to that scorn with which the universal love of praise incites us all to drive feeble competitors out of our way.

Few men survey themselves with so much severity, as not to admit prejudices in their own favour, which an artful flatterer may gradually strengthen, till wishes for a particular qualification are improved to hopes of attainment, and hopes of attainment to belief of possession. Such flatterers every one will find, who has power to reward their assiduities. Wherever there is wealth, there will be dependance and expectation, and wherever there is dependance, there will be an emulation of servility.

Many of the follies which provoke general censure, are the effects of such vanity as, however it might have wantoned in the imagination, would

scarcely have dared the public eye, had it not been
animated and imboldened by flattery. Whatever
difficulty there may be in the knowledge of ourselves, scarcely any one fails to suspect his own imperfections, till he is elevated by others to confidence. We are almost all naturally modest and
timorous; but fear and shame are uneasy sensations,
and whosoever helps to remove them is received with
kindness.

Turpicula was the heiress of a large estate, and
having lost her mother in her infancy, was committed
to a governess whom misfortunes had reduced to
suppleness and humility. The fondness of Turpicula's father would not suffer him to trust her at a
public school, but he hired domestic teachers, and
bestowed on her all the accomplishments that wealth
could purchase. But how many things are necessary to happiness which money cannot obtain!
Thus secluded from all with whom she might converse on terms of equality, she heard none of those
intimations of her defects, which envy, petulance, or
anger, produce among children, where they are not
afraid of telling what they think.

Turpicula saw nothing but obsequiousness, and
heard nothing but commendations. None are so
little acquainted with the heart, as not to know that
woman's first wish is to be handsome, and that con-
sequently the readiest method of obtaining her kindness is to praise her beauty. Turpicula had a dis-
torted shape and a dark complexion; yet when the
impudence of adulation had ventured to tell her of
the commanding dignity of her motion, and the soft
enchantment of her smile, she was easily convinced,
that she was the delight or torment of every eye, and
that all who gazed upon her felt the fire of envy or
love. She therefore neglected the culture of an understanding which might have supplied the defects

of her form, and applied all her care to the decoration of her person; for she considered that more could judge of beauty than of wit, and was, like the rest of human beings, in haste to be admired. The desire of conquests naturally led her to the lists in which beauty signalizes her power. She glittered at court, fluttered in the park, and talked aloud in the front-box: but, after a thousand experiments of her charms, was at last convinced that she had been flattered, and that her glass was honester than her maid.

Nᵒ 190. SATURDAY, JANUARY 11, 1752.

> Ploravere suis non respondere favorem
> Speratum meritis.—HOR.

> Henry and Alfred——
> Clos'd their long glories with a sigh, to find
> Th' unwilling gratitude of base mankind.—POPE.

AMONG the emirs and viziers, the sons of valour and of wisdom, that stand at the corners of the Indian throne, to assist the councils or conduct the wars of the posterity of Timur, the first place was long held by Morad the son of Hanuth. Morad having signalized himself in many battles and sieges, was rewarded with the government of a province, from which the fame of his wisdom and moderation was wafted to the pinnacles of Agra, by the prayers of those whom his administration made happy. The emperor called him into his presence, and gave into his hand the keys of riches and the sabre of command. The voice of Morad was heard from the cliffs of Taurus to the Indian ocean, every tongue faultered in his presence, and every eye was cast down before him.

Morad lived many years in prosperity ; every day increased his wealth and extended his influence. The sages repeated his maxims, the captains of thousands waited his commands. Competition withdrew into the cavern of envy, and discontent trembled at her own murmurs. But human greatness is short and transitory, as the odour of incense in the fire. The sun grew weary of gilding the palaces of Morad, the clouds of sorrow gathered round his head, and the tempest of hatred roared about his dwelling.

Morad saw ruin hastily approaching. The first that forsook him were his poets ; their example was followed by all those whom he had rewarded for contributing to his pleasures, and only a few, whose virtue had entitled them to favour, were now to be seen in his hall or chambers. He felt his danger, and prostrated himself at the foot of the throne. His accusers were confident and loud, his friends stood contented with frigid neutrality, and the voice of truth was overborne by clamour. He was divested of his power, deprived of his acquisitions, and condemned to pass the rest of his life on his hereditary estate.

Morad had been so long accustomed to crowds and business, supplicants and flattery, that he knew not how to fill up his hours in solitude ; he saw with regret the sun rise to force on his eye a new day for which he had no use; and envied the savage that wanders in the desert, because he has no time vacant from the calls of nature, but is always chasing his prey, or sleeping in his den.

His discontent in time vitiated his constitution, and a slow disease seized upon him. He refused physic, neglected exercise, and lay down on his couch peevish and restless, rather afraid to die than desirous to live. His domestics, for a time, redoubled their assiduities; but finding that no officiousness could soothe, nor exactness satisfy, they soon gave way to negligence and sloth, and he that once commanded nations, often languished in his chamber without an attendant.

In this melancholy state he commanded messengers to recall his eldest son Abouzaid from the army. Abouzaid was alarmed at the account of his father's sickness, and hasted by long journeys to his place of residence. Morad was yet living, and felt his strength return at the embraces of his son, then commanding him to sit down at his bed-side, 'Abouzaid,' says he, ' thy father has no more to hope or fear from the inhabitants of the earth, the cold hand of the angel of death is now upon him, and the voracious grave is howling for his prey. Hear therefore the precepts of ancient experience ; let not my last instructions issue forth in vain. Thou hast seen me happy and calamitous, thou hast beheld my exaltation and my fall. My power is in the hands of my enemies, my treasures have rewarded my accusers ; but my inheritance the clemency of the emperor has spared, and my wisdom his anger could not take away. Cast thine eyes round thee, and whatever thou beholdest will in a few hours be thine; apply thine ear to my dictates, and these possessions will promote thine happiness. Aspire not to public honours, enter not the palaces of kings ; thy wealth will set thee above insult, let thy moderation keep thee below envy. Content thyself with private dignity, diffuse thy riches among thy friends, let every day extend thy beneficence, and suffer not thy heart to be at rest till thou art loved by all to whom thou art known. In the height of my power, I said to defamation, Who will hear thee ? and to artifice, What canst thou perform ? But, my son, despise not thou the malice of the weakest, remember that venom supplies the want of strength, and that the lion may perish by the puncture of an asp.'

Morad expired in a few hours. Abouzaid, after the months of mourning, determined to regulate his conduct by his father's precepts, and cultivate the love of mankind by every art of kindness, and endearment. He wisely considered that domestic happiness was first to be secured, and that none have so much power of doing good or hurt, as those who are present in the hour of negligence, hear the burst of thoughtless merriment, and observe the starts of unguarded passion. He therefore augmented the pay of all his attendants, and requited every exertion of uncommon diligence by supernumerary gratuities. While he congratulated himself upon the fidelity and affection of his family, he was in the night alarmed with robbers, who, being pursued and taken, declared that they had been admitted by one of his servants; the servant immediately confessed that he unbarred the door, because another not more worthy of confidence was intrusted with the keys.

Abouzaid was thus convinced that a dependant could not easily be made a friend; and that while many were soliciting for the first rank of favour, all those would be alienated whom he disappointed. He therefore resolved to associate with a few equal companions, selected from among the chief men of the province. With these he lived happily for a time, till familiarity set them free from restraint, and every man thought himself at liberty to indulge his own caprice and advance his own opinions. They then disturbed each other with contrariety of inclinations and difference of sentiments, and Abouzaid was necessitated to offend one party by concurrence, or both by indifference.

He afterward determined to avoid a close union

with beings so discordant in their nature, and to diffuse himself in a large circle. He practised the smile of universal courtesy, and invited all to his table, but admitted none to his retirements. Many who had been rejected in his choice of friendship now refused to accept his acquaintance; and of those whom plenty and magnificence drew to his table, every one pressed forward towards intimacy, thought himself overlooked in the crowd, and murmured because he was not distinguished above the rest. By degrees all made advances, and all resented repulse. The table was then covered with delicacies in vain; the music sounded in empty rooms; and Abouzaid was left to form in solitude some new scheme of pleasure or security.

Resolving now to try the force of gratitude, he inquired for men of science, whose merit was obscured by poverty. His house was soon crowded with poets, sculptors, painters, and designers, who wantoned in unexperienced plenty, and employed their powers in celebration of their patron. But in a short time they forgot the distress from which they had been rescued, and began to consider their deliverer as a wretch of narrow capacity, who was growing great by works which he could not perform, and whom they overpaid by condescending to accept his bounties. Abouzaid heard their murmurs and dismissed them, and from that hour continued blind to colours, and deaf to panegyric.

As the sons of art departed, muttering threats of perpetual infamy, Abouzaid, who stood at the gate, called to him Hamet the poet. 'Hamet,' said he, 'thy ingratitude has put an end to my hopes and experiments: I have now learned the vanity of those labours that wish to be rewarded by human benevolence; I shall henceforth do good and avoid evil, without respect to the opinion of men; and resolve

to solicit only the approbation of that Being whom
alone we are sure to please by endeavouring to please
him.'

N° 191. TUESDAY, JANUARY 14, 1752.

Cereus in vitium flecti, monitoribus asper.—Hor.

The youth——
Yielding like wax, th' impressive folly bears;
Rough to reproof, and slow to future cares.—Francis.

' To the Rambler.

' DEAR MR. RAMBLER,

' I HAVE been four days confined to my chamber by
a cold, which has already kept me from three plays,
nine sales, five shows, and six card-tables, and put
me seventeen visits behind-hand ; and the doctor
tells my mamma, that if I fret and cry, it will settle
in my head, and I shall not be fit to be seen these
six weeks. But, dear Mr. Rambler, how can I help
it ? At this very time Melissa is dancing with the
prettiest gentleman ;—she will breakfast with him
to-morrow, and then run to two auctions, and hear
compliments, and have presents ; then she will be
drest and visit, and get a ticket to the play ; then go
to cards and win, and come home with two flambeaus
before her chair. Dear Mr. Rambler, who can bear it?

'My aunt has just brought me a bundle of your
papers for my amusement. She says, you are a philosopher and will teach me to moderate my desires,
and look upon the world with indifference. But, dear
Sir, I do not wish, nor intend to moderate my desires,
nor can I think it proper to look upon the world with
indifference, till the world looks with indifference on

me. I have been forced, however, to sit this morning a whole quarter of an hour with your paper before my face; but just as my aunt came in, Phyllida had brought me a letter from Mr. Trip, which I put within the leaves, and read about *absence* and *inconsolableness*, and *ardour*, and *irresistible passion*, and *eternal constancy*, while my aunt imagined that I was puzzling myself with your philosophy, and often cried out, when she saw me look confused, "If there is any word that you do not understand, child, I will explain it."

‘ Dear soul! how old people that think themselves wise may be imposed upon. But it is fit that they should take their turn, for I am sure, while they can keep poor girls close in the nursery, they tyrannize over us in a very shameful manner, and fill our imaginations with tales of terror, only to make us live in quiet subjection, and fancy that we can never be safe but by their protection.

‘ I have a mamma and two aunts, who have all been formerly celebrated for wit and beauty, and are still generally admired by those that value themselves upon their understanding, and love to talk of vice and virtue, nature and simplicity, and beauty and propriety; but if there was not some hope of meeting me, scarcely a creature would come near them that wears a fashionable coat. These ladies, Mr. Rambler, have had me under their government fifteen years and a half, and have all that time been endeavouring to deceive me by such representations of life as I now find not to be true; but I know not whether I ought to impute them to ignorance or malice, as it is possible the world may be much changed since they mingled in general conversation.

‘ Being desirous that I should love books, they told me, that nothing but knowledge could make me an agreeable companion to men of sense, or qualify me to distinguish the superficial glitter of vanity from the solid merit of understanding; and that a habit of reading would enable me to fill up the vacuities of life without the help of silly or dangerous amusements, and preserve me from the snares of idleness and the inroads of temptation.

‘ But their principal intention was to make me afraid of men; in which they succeeded so well for a time, that I durst not look in their faces, or be left alone with them in a parlour; for they made me fancy, that no man ever spoke but to deceive, or looked but to allure; that the girl who suffered him that had once squeezed her hand, to approach her a second time, was on the brink of ruin; and that she who answered a billet without consulting her relations, gave love such power over her, that she would certainly become either poor or infamous.

‘ From the time that my leading-strings were taken off, I scarce heard any mention of my beauty but from the milliner, the mantua-maker, and my own maid; for my mamma never said more, when she heard me commended, but, “The girl is very well,” and then endeavoured to divert my attention by some inquiry after my needle or my book.

‘ It is now three months since I have been suffered to pay and receive visits, to dance at public assemblies, to have a place kept for me in the boxes, and to play at Lady Racket's rout; and you may easily imagine what I think of those who so long cheated me with false expectations, disturbed me with fictitious terrors, and concealed from me all that I have found to make the happiness of woman.

‘ I am so far from perceiving the usefulness or necessity of books, that if I had not dropped all pretensions to learning, I should have lost Mr. Trip, whom I once frighted into another box, by retailing some of Dryden's remarks upon a tragedy; for Mr.

Trip declares that he hates nothing like hard words, and I am sure there is not a better partner to be found; his very walk is a dance. I have talked once or twice among ladies about principles and ideas, but they put their fans before their faces, and told me I was too wise for them, who for their part never pretended to read any thing but the play-bill, and then asked me the price of my best head.

'Those vacancies of time which are to be filled up with books, I have never yet obtained; for consider, Mr. Rambler, I go to bed late, and therefore cannot rise early; as soon as I am up, I dress for the gardens; then walk in the park; then always go to some sale or show, or entertainment at the little theatre; then must be dressed for dinner; then must pay my visits; then walk in the park; then hurry to the play; and from thence to the card-table. This is the general course of the day, when there happens nothing extraordinary; but sometimes I ramble into the country, and come back again to a ball; sometimes I am engaged for a whole day and part of the night. If, at any time, I can gain an hour by not being at home, I have so many things to do, so many orders to give to the milliner, so many alterations to make in my clothes, so many visitants' names to read over, so many invitations to accept or refuse, so many cards to write, and so many fashions to consider, that I am lost in confusion, forced at last to let in company or step into my chair, and leave half my affairs to the direction of my maid.

'This is the round of my day; and when shall I either stop my course, or so change it as to want a book? I suppose it cannot be imagined that any of these diversions will soon be at an end. There will always be gardens, and a park, and auctions, and shows, and playhouses, and cards; visits will always be paid, and clothes always be worn; and how can I have time unemployed on my hands?

But I am most at a loss to guess for what purpose
they related such tragic stories of the cruelty, per-
fidy, and artifices of men, who, if they ever were so
malicious and destructive, have certainly now reformed their manners. I have not, since my entrance
into the world, found one who does not profess himself devoted to my service, and ready to live or die,
as I shall command him. They are so far from intending to hurt me, that their only contention is, who
shall be allowed most closely to attend, and most
frequently to treat me; when different places of entertainment, or schemes of pleasure are mentioned,
I can see the eye sparkle and the cheek glow of him
whose proposals obtain my approbation: he then
leads me off in triumph, adores my condescension,
and congratulates himself that he has lived to the
hour of felicity. Are these, Mr. Rambler, creatures
to be feared? Is it likely that any injury will be
done me by those who can enjoy life only while I favour them with my presence?

‘ As little reason can I yet find to suspect them of
stratagems and fraud. When I play at cards they
never take advantage of my mistakes, nor exact from
me a rigorous observation of the game. Even Mr.
Shuffle, a grave gentleman, who has daughters older
than myself, plays with me so negligently, that I am
sometimes inclined to believe he loses his money by
design, and yet he is so fond of play, that he says,
he will one day take me to his house in the country,
that we may try by ourselves who can conquer. I
have not yet promised him; but when the town grows
a little empty, I shall think upon it, for I want some
trinkets, like Letitia's, to my watch. I do not doubt
my luck, but must study some means of amusing my
relations.

‘ For all these distinctions I find myself indebted
to that beauty which I was never suffered to hear
praised, and of which, therefore, I did not before

know the full value. This concealment was certainly an intentional fraud, for my aunts have eyes like other people, and I am every day told, that nothing but blindness can escape the influence of my charms. Their whole account of that world which they pretend to know so well, has been only one fiction entangled with another; and though the modes of life obliged me to continue some appearances of respect, I cannot think that they, who have been so clearly detected in ignorance or imposture, have any right to the esteem, veneration, or obedience of,

Sir, yours,   BELLARIA.

Nº 192. SATURDAY, JANUARY 18, 1752.

Γένος, οὐδὲν εἰς ἔρωτα·
Σοφίη, τρόπος πατεῖται.
Μόνον ἄργυρον βλέπουσιν.
Ἀπόλοιτο πρῶτος αὐτὸς
Ὁ τὸν ἄργυρον φιλήσας.
Διὰ τοῦτον οὐκ ἀδελφός,
Διὰ τοῦτον οὐ τοκῆες·
Πόλεμοι, φόνοι δι' αὐτόν.
Τὸ δὲ χεῖρον, ὀλλύμεσθα
Διὰ τοῦτον οἱ φιλοῦντες.—ANACREON.

Vain the noblest birth would prove,
Nor worth nor wit avail in love ;
'Tis gold alone succeeds—by gold
The venal sex is bought and sold.
Accurs'd be he who first of yore
Discover'd the pernicious ore!
This sets a brother's heart on fire,
And arms the son against the sire,
And what, alas ! is worse than all,
To this the lover owes his fall.—F. LEWIS.

' TO THE RAMBLER.

' SIR,

' I AM the son of a gentleman, whose ancestors, for many ages, held the first rank in the country ; till at

last one of them, too desirous of popularity, set his
house open, kept a table covered with continual profusion, and distributed his beef and ale to such as
chose rather to live upon the folly of others than their
own labour, with such thoughtless liberality, that he
left a third part of his estate mortgaged. His suc-
cessor, a man of spirit, scorned to impair his dignity by parsimonious retrenchments, or to admit,
by a sale of his lands, and participation of the rights
of his manor; he therefore made another mortgage to pay the interest of the former, and pleased
himself with the reflection, that his son would have
the hereditary estate without the diminution of an
acre.

' Nearly resembling this was the practice of my
wise progenitors for many ages. Every man boasted
the antiquity of his family, resolved to support the
dignity of his birth, and lived in splendour and
plenty at the expense of his heir, who, sometimes by
a wealthy marriage, and sometimes by lucky legacies,
discharged part of the incumbrances, and thought
himself entitled to contract new debts, and to leave
to his children the same inheritance of embarrassment and distress.

' Thus the estate perpetually decayed; the woods
were felled by one, the park ploughed by another,
the fishery let to farmers by a third; at last the old
hall was pulled down to spare the cost of reparation,
and part of the materials sold to build a small house
with the rest. We are now openly degraded from
our original rank, and my father's brother was allowed with less reluctance to serve an apprenticeship,
though we never reconciled ourselves heartily to the
sound of a haberdasher, but always talked of ware-
houses and a merchant, and when the wind happened
to blow loud, affected to pity the hazards of commerce, and to sympathize with the solicitude of my
poor uncle, who had the true retailer's terror of ad-

venture, and never exposed himself or his property to any wider water than the Thames.

' In time, however, by continual profit and small expenses, he grew rich, and began to turn his thoughts towards rank. He hung the arms of the family over his parlour chimney; pointed at a chariot decorated only with a cipher; became of opinion that money could not make a gentleman; resented the petulance of upstarts; told stories of Alderman Puff's grandfather the porter; wondered that there was no better method of regulating precedence; wished for some dress peculiar to men of fashion; and when his servant presented a letter, always inquired whether it came from his brother the esquire.

' My father was careful to send him game by every carrier, which, though the conveyance often cost more than the value, was well received, because it gave him an opportunity of calling his friends together, describing the beauty of his brother's seat, and lamenting his own folly, whom no remonstrances could withhold from polluting his fingers with a shop-book.

' The little presents which we sent were always returned with great munificence. He was desirous of being the second founder of his family, and could not bear that we should be any longer outshone by those whom we considered as climbers upon our ruins, and usurpers of our fortune. He furnished our house with all the elegance of fashionable expense and was careful to conceal his bounties, lest the poverty of his family should be suspected.

' At length it happened that, by misconduct like our own, a large estate, which had been purchased from us, was again exposed to the best bidder. My uncle, delighted with an opportunity of reinstating the family in their possessions, came down with treasures scarcely to be imagined in a place where commerce has not made large sums familiar, and at once drove all the competitors away, expedited the writings, and took possession. He now considered himself as superior to trade, disposed of his stock, and as soon as he had settled his economy, began to shew his rural sovereignty by breaking the hedges of his tenants in hunting, and seizing the guns or nets of those whose fortunes did not qualify them for sportsmen. He soon afterward solicited the office of sheriff, from which all his neighbours were glad to be reprieved, but which he regarded as a resumption of ancestorial claims, and a kind of restoration to blood after the attainder of a trade.

' My uncle, whose mind was so filled with this change of his condition, that he found no want of domestic entertainment, declared himself too old to marry, and resolved to let the newly-purchased estate fall into the regular channel of inheritance. I was therefore considered as heir-apparent, and courted with officiousness and caresses, by the gentlemen who had hitherto coldly allowed me that rank which they could not refuse, depressed me with studied neglect, and irritated me with ambiguous insults.

' I felt not much pleasure from the civilities for which I knew myself indebted to my uncle's industry, till by one of the invitations which every day now brought me, I was induced to spend a week with Lucius, whose daughter Flavilla I had often seen and admired like others, without any thought of nearer approaches. The inequality which had hitherto kept me at a distance being now levelled, I was received with every evidence of respect; Lucius told me the fortune which he intended for his favourite daughter, many odd accidents obliged us to be often together without company, and I soon began to find that they were spreading for me the nets of matrimony.

'Flavilla was all softness and complaisance. I, who had been excluded by a narrow fortune from much acquaintance with the world, and never been honoured before with the notice of so fine a lady, was easily enamoured. Lucius either perceived my passion, or Flavilla betrayed it; care was taken that our private meetings should be less frequent, and my charmer confessed by her eyes how much pain she suffered from our restraint. I renewed my visit upon every pretence, but was not allowed one interview without witness; at last I declared my passion to Lucius, who received me as a lover worthy of his daughter, and told me that nothing was wanting to his consent, but that my uncle should settle his estate upon me. I objected the indecency of encroaching on his life, and the danger of provoking him by such an unseasonable demand. Lucius seemed not to think decency of much importance, but admitted the danger of displeasing, and concluded that as he was now old and sickly, we might, without any inconvenience, wait for his death.

'With this resolution I was better contented, as it procured me the company of Flavilla, in which the days passed away amidst continual rapture; but in time I began to be ashamed of sitting idle, in expectation of growing rich by the death of my benefactor, and proposed to Lucius many schemes of raising my own fortune by such assistance as I knew my uncle willing to give me. Lucius, afraid lest I should change my affection in absence, diverted me from my design by dissuasives to which my passion easily listened. At last my uncle died, and considering himself as neglected by me, from the time that Flavilla took possession of my heart, left his estate to my younger brother, who was always hovering about his bed, and relating stories of my pranks and extravagance, my contempt of the commercial dialect, and my impatience to be selling stock.

'My condition was soon known, and I was no longer admitted by the father of Flavilla. I repeated the protestations of regard, which had been formerly returned with so much ardour, in a letter which she received privately, but returned by her father's footman. Contempt has driven out my love, and I am content to have purchased, by the loss of fortune, an escape from a harpy, who has joined the artifices of age to the allurements of youth. I am now going to pursue my former projects with a legacy which my uncle bequeathed me, and if I succeed, shall expect to hear of the repentance of Flavilla.

I am, Sir, yours, &c.

CONSTANTIUS.'

Nº 193.   TUESDAY, JANUARY 21, 1752.

Laudis amore tumes? sunt certa piacula, quæ te
Ter purè lecto poterunt recreare libello.—HOR.

Or art thou vain? books yield a certain spell,
To stop thy tumour; you shall cease to swell,
When you have read them thrice, and studied well.
                                        CREECH.

WHATEVER is universally desired, will be sought by industry and artifice, by merit and crimes, by means good and bad, rational and absurd, according to the prevalence of virtue or vice, of wisdom or folly. Some will always mistake the degree of their own desert, and some will desire that others may mistake it.

The cunning will have recourse to stratagem, and the powerful to violence, for the attainment of their wishes; some will stoop to theft, and others venture upon plunder.

Praise is so pleasing to the mind of man, that it is the orginal motive of almost all our actions. The desire of commendation, as of every thing else, is varied indeed by innumerable differences of temper, capacity, and knowledge; some have no higher wish than for the applause of a club; some expect the acclamations of a county; and some have hoped to fill the mouths of all ages and nations with their names. Every man pants for the highest eminence within his views; none, however mean, ever sinks below the hope of being distinguished by his fellow beings, and very few have by magnanimity or piety been so raised above it, as to act wholly without regard to censure or opinion.

To be praised, therefore, every man resolves; but resolutions will not execute themselves. That which all think too parsimoniously distributed to their own claims, they will not gratuitously squander upon others, and some expedient must be tried, by which praise may be gained before it can be enjoyed.

Among the innumerable bidders for praise, some are willing to purchase at the highest rate, and offer ease and health, fortune and life. Yet even of these only a small part have gained what they so earnestly desired; the student wastes away in meditation, and the soldier perishes on the ramparts; but unless some accidental advantage co-operates with merit, neither perseverance nor adventure attract attention, and learning and bravery sink into the grave, without honour or remembrance.

But ambition and vanity generally expect to be gratified on easier terms. It has been long observed, that what is procured by skill or labour to the first possessor, may be afterward transferred for money; and that the man of wealth may partake all the acquisitions of courage without hazard, and all the products of industry without fatigue. It was easily discovered, that riches would obtain praise among other conveniences, and that he whose pride was unluckily associated with laziness, ignorance, or cowardice, needed only to pay the hire of a panegyrist, and he might be regaled with periodical eulogies; might determine, at leisure, what virtue or science he would be pleased to appropriate, and be lulled in the evening with soothing serenades, or waked in the morning by sprightly gratulations.

The happiness which mortals receive from the celebration of beneficence which never relieved, eloquence which never persuaded, or elegance which never pleased, ought not to be envied or disturbed, when they are known honestly to pay for their entertainment. But there are unmerciful exactors of adulation, who withhold the wages of venality; retain their encomiast from year to year by general promises and ambiguous blandishments; and when he has run through the whole compass of flattery, dismiss him with contempt, because his vein of fiction is exhausted.

A continual feast of commendation is only to be obtained by merit or by wealth; many are therefore obliged to content themselves with single morsels, and recompense the infrequency of their enjoyment by excess and riot, whenever fortune sets the banquet before them. Hunger is never delicate; they who are seldom gorged to the full with praise, may be safely fed with gross compliments; for the appetite must be satisfied before it is disgusted.

It is easy to find the moment at which vanity is eager for sustenance, and all that impudence or servility can offer will be well received. When any one

complains of the want of what he is known to possess in an uncommon degree, he certainly waits with
impatience to be contradicted. When the trader
pretends anxiety about the payment of his bills, or
the beauty remarks how frightfully she looks, then
is the lucky moment to talk of riches or of charms,
of the death of lovers, or the honour of a merchant.

Others there are yet more open and artless, who,
instead of suborning a flatterer, are content to supply
his place, and, as some animals impregnate themselves, swell with the praises which they hear from
their own tongues. *Rectè is dicitur laudare sese,
cui nemo alius contigit laudator.* ' It is right,' says
Erasmus, ' that he whom no one else will commend,
should bestow commendations on himself.' Of all
the sons of vanity, these are surely the happiest and
greatest; for, what is greatness or happiness but independence on external influences, exemption from
hope or fear, and the power of supplying every want
from the common stores of nature, which can neither be exhausted nor prohibited? Such is the wise
man of the stoics; such is the divinity of the epicu-
reans; and such is the flatterer of himself. Every
other enjoyment malice may destroy; every other
panegyric envy may withhold; but no human power
can deprive the boaster of his own encomiums. Infamy may hiss, or contempt may growl, the hirelings
of the great may follow fortune, and the votaries of
truth may attend on virtue; but his pleasures still
remain the same; he can always listen with rapture
to himself, and leaves those who dare not repose
upon their own attestation, to be elated or depressed
by chance, and toil on in the hopeless task of fixing
caprice and propitiating malice.

This art of happiness has been long practised by
periodical writers, with little apparent violation of
decency. When we think our excellences overlooked

by the world, or desire to recall the attention of the
public to some particular performance, we sit down
with great composure and write a letter to ourselves.
The correspondent, whose character we assume, always addresses us with the deference due to a superior intelligence; proposes his doubts with a proper
sense of his own inability; offers an objection with
trembling diffidence; and at last has no other pretensions to our notice than his profundity of respect,
and sincerity of admiration, his submission to our
dictates, and zeal for our success. To such a reader
it is impossible to refuse regard, nor can it easily be
imagined with how much alacrity we snatch up the
pen which indignation or despair had condemned to
inactivity, when we find such candour and judgment
yet remaining in the world.

A letter of this kind I had lately the honour of
perusing, in which, though some of the periods were
negligently closed, and some expressions of familiarity were used, which I thought might teach others
to address me with too little reverence, I was so much
delighted with the passages in which mention was
made of universal learning—unbounded genius—
soul of Homer, Pythagoras, and Plato—solidity of
thought—accuracy of distinction—elegance of combination—vigour of fancy—strength of reason—and
regularity of composition—that I had once determined to lay it before the public. Three times I
sent it to the printer, and three times I fetched it
back. My modesty was on the point of yielding,
when, reflecting that I was about to waste panegyrics
on myself, which might be more profitably reserved
for my patron, I locked it up for a better hour, in
compliance with the farmer's principle, who never
eats at home what he can carry to the market.

N° 194. SATURDAY, JANUARY 25, 1752.

Si damnosa senem juvat alea, ludit et hæres
Bullatus, parvoque eadem quatit arma fritillo.—Juv.

If gaming does an aged sire entice,
Then my young master swiftly learns the vice,
And shakes in hanging sleeves the little box and dice.
            J. Dryden, jun.

'To the Rambler.

'Sir,

'That vanity which keeps every man important in his own eyes, inclines me to believe that neither you nor your readers have yet forgotten the name of Eumathes, who sent you a few months ago an account of his arrival at London with a young nobleman his pupil. I shall therefore continue my narrative without preface or recapitulation.

'My pupil, in a very short time, by his mother's countenance and direction, accomplished himself with all those qualifications which constitute puerile politeness. He became in a few days a perfect master of his hat, which with a careless nicety he could put off or on, without any need to adjust it by a second motion. This was not attained but by frequent consultations with his dancing-master, and constant practice before the glass, for he had some rustic habits to overcome; but, what will not time and industry perform? A fortnight more furnished him with all the airs and forms of familiar and respectful salutation, from the clap on the shoulder to the humble bow; he practises the stare of strangeness, and the smile of condescension, the solemnity of promise, and the graciousness of encouragement, as if he had been nursed at a levee; and pronounces with no less propriety than his father, the monosyllables of coldness, and sonorous periods of respectful profession.

'He immediately lost the reserve and timidity which solitude and study are apt to impress upon the most courtly genius; was able to enter a crowded room with airy civility; to meet the glances of a hundred eyes without perturbation; and address those whom he never saw before with ease and confidence. In less than a month his mother declared her satisfaction at his proficiency by a triumphant observation, that she believed *nothing would make him blush.*

'The silence with which I was contented to hear my pupil's praises, gave the lady reason to suspect me not much delighted with his acquisitions: but she attributed my discontent to the diminution of my influence, and my fears of losing the patronage of the family; and though she thinks favourably of my learning and morals, she considers me as wholly unacquainted with the customs of the polite part of mankind; and therefore not qualified to form the manners of a young nobleman, or communicate the knowledge of the world. This knowledge she comprises in the rules of visiting, the history of the present hour, an early intelligence of the change of fashions, an extensive acquaintance with the names and faces of persons of rank, and a frequent appearance in places of resort.

'All this my pupil pursues with great application. He is twice a-day in the Mall, where he studies the dress of every man splendid enough to attract his notice, and never comes home without some observation upon sleeves, button-holes, and embroidery. At his return from the theatre, he can give an account of the gallantries, glances, whispers, smiles, sighs, flirts, and blushes, of every box, so much to his mother's satisfaction, that when I attempted to resume my character, by inquiring his opinion of the sentiments and diction of the tragedy, she at once repressed my criticism, by telling me, *that she hoped he did not go to lose his time in attending to the creatures on the stage.*

'But his acuteness was most eminently signalized at the masquerade, where he discovered his acquaintance through their disguises, with such wonderful facility, as has afforded the family an inexhaustible topic of conversation. Every new visitor is informed how one was detected by his gait, and another by the swing of his arms, a third by the toss of his head, and another by his favourite phrase; nor can you doubt but these performances receive their just applause, and a genius thus hastening to maturity is promoted by every art of cultivation.

'Such have been his endeavours, and such his assistances, that every trace of literature was soon obliterated. He has changed his language with his dress, and instead of endeavouring at purity or propriety, has no other care than to catch the reigning phrase and current exclamation, till by copying whatever is peculiar in the talk of all those whose birth or fortune entitle them to imitation, he has collected every fashionable barbarism of the present winter, and speaks a dialect not to be understood among those who form their style by poring upon authors.

'To this copiousness of ideas and felicity of language, he has joined such eagerness to lead the conversation, that he is celebrated among the ladies as the prettiest gentleman that the age can boast of, except that some who love to talk themselves think him too forward, and others lament that, with so much wit and knowledge, he is not taller.

'His mother listens to his observations with her eye sparkling and her heart beating, and can scarcely contain in the most numerous assemblies, the ex-

pectations which she has formed for his future eminence. Women, by whatever fate, always judge ab-
surdly on the intellects of boys. The vivacity and
confidence which attract female admiration, are seldom produced in the early part of life, but by ignorance at least, if not by stupidity; for they proceed
not from confidence of right, but fearlessness of
wrong. Whoever has a clear apprehension, must
have quick sensibility, and where he has no sufficient
reason to trust his own judgment, will proceed with
doubt and caution, because he perpetually dreads the
disgrace of error. The pain of miscarriage is naturally proportionate to the desire of excellence; and,
therefore, till men are hardened by long familiarity
with reproach, or have attained, by frequent struggles, the art of suppressing their emotions, diffidence
is found the inseparable associate of understanding.

'But so little distrust has my pupil of his own
abilities, that he has for some time professed himself
a wit, and tortures his imagination on all occasions
for burlesque and jocularity. How he supports a
character which, perhaps, no man ever assumed without repentance, may be easily conjectured. Wit,
you know, is the unexpected copulation of ideas, the
discovery of some occult relation between images in
appearance remote from each other; an effusion of
wit, therefore, presupposes an accumulation of knowledge; a memory stored with notions, which the
imagination may cull out to compose new assem-
blages. Whatever may be the native vigour of the
mind, she can never form any combinations from few
ideas, as many changes can never be rung upon a few
bells. Accident may indeed sometimes produce a
lucky parallel or a striking contrast; but these gifts
of chance are not frequent, and he that has nothing
of his own, and yet condemns himself to needless
expenses, must live upon loans or theft.

'The indulgence which his youth has hitherto obtained, and the respect which his rank secures, have hitherto supplied the want of intellectual qualifications; and he imagines that all admire who applaud, and that all who laugh are pleased. He therefore returns every day to the charge with increase of courage, though not of strength, and practises all the tricks by which wit is counterfeited. He lays trains for a quibble; he contrives blunders for his footman; he adapts old stories to present characters; he mistakes the question, that he may return a smart answer; he anticipates the argument, that he may plausibly object; when he has nothing to reply, he repeats the last words of his antagonist, then says, "your humble servant," and concludes with a laugh of triumph.

'These mistakes I have honestly attempted to correct: but, what can be expected from reason, unsupported by fashion, splendour, or authority? He hears me indeed, or appears to hear me, but is soon rescued from the lecture by more pleasing avocations; and shows, diversions, and caresses, drive my precepts from his remembrance.

'He at last imagines himself qualified to enter the world, and has met with adventures in his first sally, which I shall, by your paper, communicate to the public.　　　I am, &c.　　　EUMATHES.'

Nᵒ 195. TUESDAY, JANUARY 28, 1752.

> ——————Nescit equo rudis
>   Hærere ingenuus puer,
> Venarique timet ; ludere doctior
>   Seu Græco jubeas trocho,
>   Seu malis vetitâ legibus aleâ.—Hor.

> Nor knows our youth of noblest race,
>   To mount the manag'd steed, or urge the chsae ;
> More skill'd in the mean arts of vice,
>   The whirling troque, or law-forbidden dice.—Francis.

To the Rambler.

'SIR,

'FAVOURS of every kind are doubled when they are speedily conferred. This is particularly true of the gratification of curiosity; he that long delays a story, and suffers his auditor to torment himself with expectation, will seldom be able to recompense the uneasiness, or equal the hope which he suffers to be raised.

'For this reason, I have already sent you the continuation of my pupil's history, which, though it contains no events very uncommon, may be of use to young men who are in too much haste to trust their own prudence, and quit the wing of protection before they are able to shift for themselves.

'When he first settled in London, he was so much bewildered in the enormous extent of the town, so confounded by incessant noise, and crowds, and hurry, and so terrified by rural narratives of the arts of sharpers, the rudeness of the populace, malignity of porters, and treachery of coachmen, that he was afraid to go beyond the door without an attendant, and imagined his life in danger if he was obliged to pass the streets at night in any vehicle but his mother's chair.

thought him too much a man to be any longer confined to his book, and he therefore begins his travels to-morrow under a French governor.

I am, Sir, &c.   EUMATHES.'

N° 196.   SATURDAY, FEBRUARY 1, 1752.

Multa ferunt anni venientes commoda secum,
    Multa recedentes adimunt.——— Hor.

The blessings flowing in with life's full tide,
    Down with our ebb of life decreasing glide.—Francis.

BAXTER, in the narrative of his own life, has enumerated several opinions, which though he thought them evident and incontestable at his first entrance into the world, time and experience disposed him to change.

Whoever reviews the state of his own mind from the dawn of manhood to its decline, and considers what he pursued or dreaded, slighted or esteemed, at different periods of his age, will have no reason to imagine such changes of sentiment peculiar to any station of character. Every man, however careless and inattentive, has conviction forced upon him : the lectures of time obtrude themselves upon the most unwilling or dissipated auditor : and, by comparing our past with our present thoughts, we perceive that we have changed our minds, though perhaps we cannot discover when the alteration happened, or by what causes it was produced.

This revolution of sentiments occasions a perpetual contest between the old and young. They who imagine themselves entitled to veneration by the prerogative of longer life, are inclined to treat the notions of

those whose conduct they superintend with superciliousness and contempt, for want of considering that
the future and the past have different appearances;
that the disproportion will always be great between
expectation and enjoyment, between new possession
and satiety; that the truth of many maxims of age,
gives too little pleasure to be allowed till it is felt;
and that the miseries of life would be increased beyond all human power of endurance, if we were to
enter the world with the same opinions as we carry
from it.

We naturally indulge those ideas that please us.
Hope will predominate in every mind, till it has been
suppressed by frequent disappointments. The youth
has not yet discovered how many evils are continually
hovering about us, and when he is set free from the
shackles of discipline, looks abroad into the world
with rapture; he sees an elysian region open before
him, so variegated with beauty, and so stored with
pleasure, that his care is rather to accumulate good,
than to shun evil; he stands distracted by different
forms of delight, and has no other doubt, than which
path to follow of those which all lead equally to the
bowers of happiness.

He who has seen only the superficies of life believes
every thing to be what it appears, and rarely suspects
that external splendour conceals any latent sorrow
or vexation. He never imagines that there may be
greatness without safety, affluence without content,
jollity without friendship, and solitude without peace.
He fancies himself permitted to cull the blessings of
every condition, and to leave its inconveniences to
the idle and the ignorant. He is inclined to believe no
man miserable but by his own fault, and seldom looks
with much pity upon failings or miscarriages, because he thinks them willingly admitted, or negligently incurred.

It is impossible without pity and contempt, to hear a youth of generous sentiments and warm imagination, declaring in the moment of openness and confidence his designs and expectations; because long life is possible, he considers it as certain, and therefore promises himself all the changes of happiness, and provides gratifications for every desire. He is, for a time, to give himself wholly to frolic and diversion, to range the world in search of pleasure, to delight every eye, to gain every heart, and to be celebrated equally for his pleasing levities and solid attainments, his deep reflections and his sparkling repartees. He then elevates his views to nobler enjoyments, and finds all the scattered excellences of the female world united in a woman, who prefers his addresses to wealth and titles; he is afterward to engage in business, to dissipate difficulty, and overpower opposition; to climb by the mere force of merit to fame and greatness; and reward all those who countenanced his rise, or paid due regard to his early excellence. At last he will retire in peace and honour; contract his views to domestic pleasures; form the manners of children like himself; observe how every year expands the beauty of his daughters, and how his sons catch ardour from their father's history; he will give laws to the neighbourhood; dictate axioms to posterity; and leave the world an example of wisdom and of happiness.

With hopes like these, he sallies jocund into life; to little purpose is he told, that the condition of humanity admits no pure and unmingled happiness; that the exuberant gaiety of youth ends in poverty or disease; that uncommon qualifications and contrarieties of excellence produce envy equally with applause; that, whatever admiration and fondness may promise him, he must marry a wife like the wives of others, with some virtues and some faults, and be as often disgusted by her vices, as delighted by her elegance; that if he adventures into the circle of action, he must expect to encounter men as artful, as daring, as resolute as himself; that of his children, some may be deformed, and others vicious; some may disgrace him by their follies, some offend him by their insolence, and some exhaust him by their profusion. He hears all this with obstinate incredulity, and wonders by what malignity old age is influenced, that it cannot forbear to fill his ears with predictions of misery.

Among other pleasing errors of young minds, is the opinion of their own importance. He that has not yet remarked, how little attention his contemporaries can spare from their own affairs, conceives al eyes turned upon himself, and imagines every one that approaches him to be an enemy or a follower, an admirer or a spy. He therefore considers his fame as involved in the event of every action. Many of the virtues and vices of youth proceed from this quick sense of reputation. This it is that gives firmness and constancy, fidelity and disinterestedness, and it is this that kindles resentment for slight injuries, and dictates all the principles of sanguinary honour.

But as time brings him forward into the world, he soon discovers that he only shares fame or reproach with innumerable partners; that he is left unmarked in the obscurity of the crowd; and that what he does, whether good or bad, soon gives way to new objects of regard. He then easily sets himself free from the anxieties of reputation, and considers praise or censure as a transient breath, which, while he hears it, is passing away, without any lasting mischief or advantage.

In youth it is common to measure right and wrong by the opinion of the world, and in age to act without any measure but interest, and to lose shame without substituting virtue.

Such is the condition of life, that something is always wanting to happiness. In youth, we have warm hopes, which are soon blasted by rashness and negligence, and great designs which are defeated by inexperience. In age, we have knowledge and prudence, without spirit to exert, or motives to prompt them; we are able to plan schemes, and regulate measures, but have not time remaining to bring them to completion.

Nº 197. TUESDAY, FEBRUARY 4, 1752.

Cujus vulturis hoc erit cadaver?—MART.

Say, to what vulture's share this carcass falls?—F. Lewis.

'To the Rambler.

'SIR,

'I belong to an order of mankind, considerable at least for their number, to which your notice has never been formally extended, though equally entitled to regard with those triflers, who have hitherto supplied you with topics of amusement or instruction. I am, Mr. Rambler, a legacy-hunter; and as every man is willing to think well of the tribe in which his name is registered, you will forgive my vanity if I remind you that the legacy-hunter, however degraded by an ill-compounded appellation in our barbarous language, was known, as I am told, in ancient Rome, by the sonorous titles of *Captator* and *Hæredipeta*.

' My father was an attorney in the country, who married his master's daughter in hopes of a fortune which he did not obtain, having been, as he afterward discovered, chosen by her only because she had no better offer, and was afraid of service. I was the first offspring of a marriage thus reciprocally fraudulent, and therefore could not be expected to inherit much dignity or generosity, and if I had them not from nature, was not likely ever to attain them; for in the years which I spent at home, I never heard any reason for action or forbearance, but that we should gain money or lose it; nor was taught any other style of commendation, than that Mr. Sneaker is a warm man, Mr. Gripe has done his business, and needs care for nobody.

'My parents, though otherwise not great philosophers, knew the force of early education, and took care that the blank of my understanding should be filled with impressions of the value of money. My mother used, upon all occasions, to inculcate some salutary axioms, such as might incite me *to keep what I had, and get what I could;* she informed me that we were in a world, where *all must catch that catch can;* and as I grew up, stored my memory with deeper observations; restrained me from the usual puerile expenses by remarking that *many a little made a mickle;* and, when I envied the finery of any of my neighbours, told me, that *Brag was a good dog, but Holdfast was a better.*

'I was soon sagacious enough to discover that I was not born to great wealth; and, having heard no other name for happiness, was sometimes inclined to repine at my condition. But my mother always relieved me, by saying, that there was money enough in the family, that *it was good to be of kin to means,* that I had nothing to do but to please my friends, and I might come to hold up my head with the best squire in the country.

'These splendid expectations arose from our alliance to three persons of considerable fortune. My mother's aunt had attended on a lady, who, when she died, rewarded her officiousness and fidelity with a large legacy, My father had two relations, of whom one had broken his indentures and run to sea, from whence, after an absence of thirty years, he returned with ten thousand pounds; and the other had lured an heiress out of a window, who dying of her first child, had left him her estate, on which he lived without any other care than to collect his rents, and preserve from poachers that game which he could not kill himself.

' These hoarders of money were visited and courted by all who had any pretence to approach them, and received presents and compliments from cousins who could scarcely tell the degree of their relation. But we had peculiar advantages which encouraged us to hope, that we should by degrees supplant our competitors. My father, by his profession, made himself necessary in their affairs; for the sailor and the chambermaid, he inquired out mortgages and securities, and wrote bonds and contracts; and had endeared himself to the old woman, who once rashly lent a hundred pounds without consulting him, by informing her, that her debtor was on the point of bankruptcy, and posting so expeditiously with an execution, that all the other creditors were defrauded.

' To the squire he was a kind of steward, and had distinguished himself in his office by his address in raising the rents, his inflexibility in distressing the tardy tenants, and his acuteness in setting the parish free from burdensome inhabitants, by shifting them off to some other settlement.

' Business made frequent attendance necessary; trust soon produced intimacy; and success gave a claim to kindness; so that we had opportunity to practise all the arts of flattery and endearment. My mother, who could not support the thoughts of losing any thing, determined that all their fortunes should centre in me; and, in the prosecution of her schemes, took care to inform me, that "nothing cost less than good words," and "that it is comfortable to leap into an estate which another has got."

'She trained me by these precepts to the utmost ductility of obedience, and the closest attention to profit. At an age when other boys are sporting in the fields, or murmuring in the school, I was contriving some new method of paying my court; inquiring the age of my future benefactors; or considering how I should employ their legacies.

'If our eagerness of money could have been satisfied with the possessions of any one of my relations, they might perhaps have been obtained; but as it was impossible to be always present with all three, our competitors were busy to efface any trace of affection which we might have left behind; and since there was not, on any part, such superiority of merit as could enforce a constant and unshaken preference, whoever was the last that flattered or obliged, had, for a time, the ascendant.

'My relations maintained a regular exchange of courtesy, took care to miss no occasion of condolence or congratulation, and sent presents at stated times, but had in their hearts not much esteem for one another. The seaman looked with contempt upon the squire as a milk-sop and a landman, who had lived without knowing the points of the compass, or seeing any part of the world beyond the county-town; and whenever they met, would talk of longitude and latitude, and circles and tropics, would scarcely tell him the hour without some mention of the horizon and meridian, nor shew him the news without detecting his ignorance of the situation of other countries.

'The squire considered the sailor as a rude uncultivated savage, with little more of human than
his form, and diverted himself with his ignorance
of all common objects and affairs; when he could
persuade him to go into the field, he always exposed
him to the sportsmen, by sending him to look for
game in improper places; and once prevailed upon
him to be present at the races, only that he might
shew the gentlemen how a sailor sat upon a horse.

'The old gentlewoman thought herself wiser than
both, for she lived with no servant but a maid, and
saved her money. The others were indeed sufficiently frugal; but the squire could not live without
dogs and horses, and the sailor never suffered the
day to pass but over a bowl of punch, to which, as
he was not critical in the choice of his company,
every man was welcome that could roar out a catch,
or tell a story.

'All these, however, I was to please: an arduous
task; but what will not youth and avarice undertake? I had an unresisting suppleness of temper,
and an unsatiable wish for riches; I was perpetually
instigated by the ambition of my parents, and assisted occasionally by their instructions. What
these advantages enabled me to perform, shall be
told in the next letter of,

Yours, &c.   CAPTATOR.'

No 198. SATURDAY, FEBRUARY 8, 1752.

Nil mihi das vivus, dicis post fata daturum;
  Si non insanis, scis, Maro, quid cupiam.—MART.

You've told me, Maro, whilst you live,
You'd not a single penny give,
But that whene'er you chance to die,
You'd leave a handsome legacy:
You must be mad beyond redress,
If my next wish you cannot guess.—F. LEWIS.

'TO THE RAMBLER.

'SIR,

'YOU, who must have observed the inclination which almost every man, however inactive or insignificant, discovers of representing his life as distinguished by extraordinary events, will not wonder that Captator thinks his narrative important enough to be continued. Nothing is more common than for those to tease their companions with their history, who have neither done nor suffered any thing that can excite curiosity or afford instruction.

'As I was taught to flatter with the first essays of speech, and had very early lost every other passion in the desire of money, I began my pursuit with omens of success; for I divided my officiousness so judiciously among my relations, that I was equally the favourite of all. When any of them entered the door, I went to welcome him with raptures; when he went away, I hung down my head, and sometimes entreated to go with him with so much importunity, that I very narrowly escaped a consent which I dreaded in my heart. When at an annual entertainment they were all together, I had a harder task; but plied them so impartially with caresses, that none could charge me with neglect; and when they were wearied with my fondness and civilities, I was always dismissed with money to buy play-things.

' Life cannot be kept at a stand; the years of innocence and prattle were soon at an end, and other qualifications were necessary to recommend me to continuance of kindness. It luckily happened that none of my friends had high notions of book-learning. The sailor hated to see tall boys shut up in a school, when they might more properly be seeing the world, and making their fortunes; and was of opinion, that when the first rules of arithmetic were known, all that was necessary to make a man complete might be learned on ship-board. The squire only insisted, that so much scholarship was indispensably necessary, as might confer ability to draw a lease and read the court-hands; and the old chambermaid declared loudly her contempt of books, and her opinion that they only took the head off the main chance.

' To unite, as well as we could, all their systems, I was bred at home. Each was taught to believe, that I followed his directions, and I gained likewise, as my mother observed, this advantage, that I was always in the way; for she had known many favourite children sent to schools or academies, and forgotten.

' As I grew fitter to be trusted to my own discretion, I was often dispatched upon various pretences to visit my relations, with directions from my parents how to ingratiate myself, and drive away competitors.

' I was, from my infancy, considered by the sailor as a promising genius, because I liked punch better than wine; and I took care to improve this prepossession by continual inquiries about the art of navigation, the degree of heat and cold in different cli-

mates, the profits of trade, and the dangers of ship-
wreck. I admired the courage of the seamen, and
gained his heart by importuning him for a recital of
his adventures, and a sight of his foreign curiosities.
I listened with an appearance of close attention to
stories which I could already repeat, and at the close
never failed to express my resolution to visit distant
countries, and my contempt of the cowards and
drones that spend all their lives in their native parish; though I had in reality no desire of any thing
but money, nor ever felt the stimulations of curiosity
or ardour of adventure, but would contentedly have
passed the years of Nestor in receiving rents and
lending upon mortgages.

' The squire I was able to please with less hypo-
crisy, for I really thought it pleasant enough to kill
the game and eat it. Some arts of falsehood, however, the hunger of gold persuaded me to practise,
by which, though no other mischief was produced,
the purity of my thoughts was vitiated, and the reverence for truth gradually destroyed. I sometimes
purchased fish, and pretended to have caught them;
I hired the countrymen to shew me partridges, and
then gave my uncle intelligence of their haunt; I
learned the seats of hares at night, and discovered
them in the morning with sagacity that raised the
wonder and envy of old sportsmen. One only obstruction to the advancement of my reputation I
could never fully surmount; I was naturally a cow-
ard, and was therefore always left shamefully behind, when there was a necessity to leap a hedge, to
swim a river, or force the horses to their utmost
speed; but as these exigencies did not frequently
happen, I maintained my honour with sufficient success, and was never left out of a hunting party.

' The old chambermaid was not so certainly, nor so
easily pleased, for she had no predominant passion

but avarice, and was therefore cold and inaccessible.
She had no conception of any virtue in a young man
but that of saving his money. When she heard of
my exploits in the field, she would shake her head,
inquire how much I should be the richer for all my
performances, and lament that such sums should be
spent upon dogs and horses. If the sailor told her
of my inclination to travel, she was sure there was no
place like England, and could not imagine why any
man that can live in his own country should leave it.
This sullen and frigid being I found means however
to propitiate, by frequent commendations of frugality, and perpetual care to avoid expense.

'From the sailor was our first and most considerable expectation; for he was richer than the chambermaid, and older than the squire. He was so
awkward and bashful among women, that we concluded him secure from matrimony; and the noisy
fondness with which he used to welcome me to his
house, made us imagine that he would look out for
no other heir, and that we had nothing to do but wait
patiently for his death. But in the midst of our triumph, my uncle saluted us one morning with a cry of
transport, and clapping his hand hard on my shoulder,
told me, I was a happy fellow to have a friend like
him in the world, for he came to fit me out for a
voyage with one of his old acquaintances. I turned
pale and trembled; my father told him, that he believed my constitution not fitted to the sea; and my
mother bursting into tears, cried out, that her heart
would break if she lost me. All this had no effect;
the sailor was wholly insusceptive of the softer passions, and, without regard to tears or arguments,
persisted in his resolution to make me a man.

'We were obliged to comply in appearance, and
preparations were accordingly made. I took leave of
my friends with great alacrity, proclaimed the bene-

ficence of my uncle with the highest strains of gratitude, and rejoiced at the opportunity now put into my hands of gratifying my thirst of knowledge. But a week before the day appointed for my departure I fell sick by my mother's direction, and refused all food but what she privately brought me; whenever my uncle visited me I was lethargic or delirious, but took care in my raving fits to talk incessantly of travel and merchandise. The room was kept dark; the table was filled with vials and gallipots; my mother was with difficulty persuaded not to endanger her life with nocturnal attendance; my father lamented the loss of the profits of the voyage; and such superfluity of artifice was employed, as perhaps might have discovered the cheat to a man of penetration. But the sailor, unacquainted with subtilties and stratagems, was easily deluded; and as the ship could not stay for my recovery, sold the cargo, and left me to re-establish my health at leisure.

' I was sent to regain my flesh in a purer air, lest it should appear never to have been wasted, and in two months returned to deplore my disappointment. My uncle pitied my dejection, and bid me prepare myself against next year, for no land-lubber should touch his money.

' A reprieve however was obtained, and perhaps some new stratagem might have succeeded another spring; but my uncle unhappily made amorous advances to my mother's maid, who to promote so advantageous a match, discovered the secret, with which only she had been intrusted. He stormed and raved, and declaring that he would have heirs of his own, and not give his substance to cheats and cowards, married the girl in two days, and has now four children.

' Cowardice is always scorned, and deceit universally detested. I found my friends, if not wholly alienated, at least cooled in their affection; the squire, though he did not wholly discard me, was less fond, and often inquired when I would go to sea. I was obliged to bear his insults, and endeavoured to rekindle his kindness by assiduity and respect; but all my care was vain; he died without a will, and the estate devolved to the legal heir.

'Thus has the folly of my parents condemned me to spend in flattery and attendance those years in which I might have been qualified to place myself above hope or fear. I am arrived at manhood without any useful art or generous sentiment; and, if the old woman should likewise at last deceive me, am in danger at once of beggary and ignorance.

I am, &c.   CAPTATOR.'

N° 199.　TUESDAY, FEBRUARY 11, 1752.

> Decolor, obscurus, vilis, non ille repexam
> Cesariem regum, nec candida virginis ornat
> Colla, nec insigni splendet per cingula morsu;
> Sed nova si nigri videas miracula saxi,
> Tunc superat pulchros cultus, et quicquid Eois
> Indus littoribus rubrâ scrutatur in algâ.—CLAUDIANUS.

> Obscure, unpriz'd, and dark, the magnet lies,
> Nor lures the search of avaricious eyes,
> Nor binds the neck, nor sparkles in the hair,
> Nor dignifies the great, nor decks the fair.
> But search the wonders of the dusky stone,
> And own all glories of the mine outdone,
> Each grace of form, each ornament of state,
> That decks the fair, or dignifies the great.

'TO THE RAMBLER.

'SIR,

'THOUGH you have seldom digressed from moral subjects, I suppose you are not so rigorous or cynical as to deny the value or usefulness of natural philosophy; or to have lived in this age of inquiry and experiment, without any attention to the wonders every day produced by the pokers of magnetism and the wheels of electricity. At least, I may be allowed to hope that, since nothing is more contrary to moral excellence than envy, you will not refuse to promote the happiness of others, merely because you cannot partake of their enjoyments.

'In confidence, therefore, that your ignorance has not made you an enemy to knowledge, I offer you the honour of introducing to the notice of the public, an adept, who having long laboured for the benefit of mankind, is not willing, like too many of his predecessors, to conceal his secrets in the grave.

'Many have signalized themselves by melting their estates in crucibles. I was born to no fortune, and therefore had only my mind and body to devote to knowledge, and the gratitude of posterity will attest, that neither mind nor body have been spared. I have sat whole weeks without sleep by the side of an athanor, to watch the moment of projection; I have made the first experiment in nineteen diving engines of new constructions; I have fallen eleven times speechless under the shock of electricity; I have twice dislocated my limbs, and once fractured my skull, in essaying to fly; and four times endangered my life by submitting to the transfusion of blood.

'In the first period of my studies, I exerted the powers of my body more than those of my mind, and was not without hopes that fame might be purchased by a few broken bones without the toil of thinking; but having been shattered by some violent experiments, and constrained to confine myself to my books, I passed six-and-thirty years in searching the treasures of ancient wisdom, but am at last amply recompensed for all my perseverance.

' The curiosity of the present race of philosophers, having been long exercised upon electricity, has been lately transferred to magnetism ; the qualities of the loadstone have been investigated, if not with much advantage, yet with great applause ; and as the highest praise of art is to imitate nature, I hope no man will think the makers of artificial magnets celebrated or reverenced above their deserts.

' I have for some time employed myself in the same practice, but with deeper knowledge and more extensive views. While my contemporaries were touching needles and raising weights, or busying themselves with inclination and variation, I have been examining those qualities of magnetism which may be applied to the accommodation and happiness of common life. I have left to inferior understandings the care of conducting the sailor through the hazards of the ocean, and reserved to myself the more difficult and illustrious province of preserving the connubial compact from violation, and setting mankind free for ever from the danger of supposititious children, and the torments of fruitless vigilance and anxious suspicion.

' To defraud any man of his due praise is unworthy of a philosopher ; I shall therefore openly confess, that I owe the first hint of this inestimable secret to the Rabbi Abraham Ben Hannase, who, in his treatise of precious stones, has left this account of the magnet : הקאלאמיטא, &c. " The calamita, or loadstone that attracts iron, produces many bad fantasies in man. Women fly from this stone. If therefore any husband be disturbed with jealousy, and fear lest his wife converses with other men, let him lay this stone upon her while she is asleep. If she be pure, she will, when she wakes, clasp her husband fondly in her arms ; but if she be guilty, she will fall out of bed, and run away."

'When first I read this wonderful passage, I could not easily conceive why it had remained hitherto unregarded in such a zealous competition for magnetical fame. It would surely be unjust to suspect that any of the candidates are strangers to the name or works of Rabbi Abraham, or to conclude, from a late edict of the Royal Society in favour of the English language, that philosophy and literature are no longer to act in concert. Yet, how should a quality so useful escape promulgation but by the obscurity of the language in which it was delivered? Why are footmen and chambermaids paid on every side for keeping secrets, which no caution nor expense could secure from the all-penetrating magnet? Or, why are so many witnesses summoned, and so many artifices practised, to discover what so easy an experiment would infallibly reveal?

'Full of this perplexity, I read the lines of Abraham to a friend, who advised me not to expose my life by a mad indulgence of the love of fame; he warned me by the fate of Orpheus, that knowledge or genius could give no protection to the invader of female prerogatives; assured me that neither the armour of Achilles, nor the antidote of Mithridates, would be able to preserve me; and counselled me, if I could not live without renown, to attempt the acquisition of universal empire, in which the honour would perhaps be equal and the danger certainly be less.

'I, a solitary student, pretend not to much knowledge of the world, but I am unwilling to think it so generally corrupt, as that a scheme for the detection of incontinence should bring any danger upon its inventor. My friend has indeed told me, that all the women will be my enemies, and that however I flatter myself with hopes of defence from the men, I shall certainly find myself deserted in the hour of danger. Of the young men, said he, some will be afraid of sharing the disgrace of their mothers, and some the danger of their mistresses; of those who are married, part are already convinced of the falsehood of their wives, and part shut their eyes to avoid conviction; few ever sought for virtue in marriage, and therefore few will try whether they have found it. Almost every man is careless or timorous, and to trust is easier and safer than to examine.

'These observations discouraged me, till I began to consider what reception I was likely to find among the ladies, whom I have reviewed under the three classes of maids, wives, and widows; and cannot but hope that I may obtain some countenance among them. The single ladies I suppose universally ready to patronise my method, by which connubial wickedness may be detected, since no woman marries with a previous design to be unfaithful to her husband. And to keep them steady in my cause, I promise never to sell one of my magnets to a man who steals a girl from school; marries a woman forty years younger than himself; or employs the authority of parents to obtain a wife without her own consent.

'Among the married ladies, notwithstanding the insinuations of slander, I yet resolve to believe, that the greater part are my friends, and am at least convinced, that they who demand the test, and appear on my side, will supply, by their spirit, the deficiency of their numbers, and that their enemies will shrink and quake at the sight of a magnet, as the slaves of Scythia fled from the scourge.

'The widows will be confederated in my favour by their curiosity, if not by their virtue; for it may be observed, that women who have outlived their husbands, always think themselves entitled to superintend the conduct of young wives; and as they are themselves in no danger from the magnetic trial, I shall expect them to be eminently and unanimously zealous in recommending it.

'With these hopes I shall, in a short time, offer to sale magnets armed with a particular metallic composition, which concentrates their virtue, and determines their agency. It is known that the efficacy of the magnet, in common operations, depends much upon its armature, and it cannot be imagined, that a stone, naked or cased only in the common manner, will discover the virtues ascribed to it by Rabbi Abraham. The secret of this metal I shall carefully conceal, and, therefore, am not afraid of imitators, nor shall trouble the offices with solicitation for a patent.

'I shall sell them of different sizes, and various degrees of strength. I have some of a bulk proper to be hung at the bed's head, as scare-crows, and some so small that they may be easily concealed. Some I have ground into oval forms to be hung at watches, and some, for the curious, I have set in wedding-rings, that ladies may never want an attestation of their innocence. Some I can produce so sluggish and inert, that they will not act before the third failure; and others so vigorous and animated, that they exert their influence against unlawful wishes, if they have been willingly and deliberately indulged. As it is my practice honestly to tell my customers the properties of my magnets, I can judge by their choice of the delicacy of their sentiments. Many have been contented to spare cost by purchasing only the lowest degree of efficacy, and all have started with terror from those which operate upon the thoughts. One young lady only fitted on a ring of the strongest energy, and declared that she scorned to separate her wishes from her acts, or allow herself to think what she was forbidden to practise.

I am, &c.   HERMETICUS.'

considered, how I should repress it without such bitterness of reproof as I was yet unwilling to use. But he interrupted my meditation, by asking leave to be dressed; and told me, that he had promised to attend some ladies in the Park, and, if I was going the same way, would take me in his chariot. I had no inclination to any other favours, and therefore left him without any intention of seeing him again, unless some misfortune should restore his understanding.   I am, &c.   ASPER.

Though I am not wholly insensible of the provocations which my correspondent has received, I cannot altogether commend the keenness of his resentment, nor encourage him to persist in his resolution of breaking off all commerce with his old acquaintance. One of the golden precepts of Pythagoras directs, that *a friend should not be hated for little faults ;* and surely he upon whom nothing worse can be charged, than that he mats his stairs, and covers his carpet, and sets out his finery to show before those whom he does not admit to use it, has yet committed nothing that should exclude him from common degrees of kindness. Such improprieties often proceed rather from stupidity than malice. Those who thus shine only to dazzle, are influenced merely by custom and example, and neither examine, nor are qualified to examine, the motives of their own practice, or to state the nice limits between elegance and ostentation. They are often innocent of the pain which their vanity produces, and insult others when they have no worse purpose than to please themselves.

He that too much refines his delicacy will always endanger his quiet. Of those with whom nature and virtue oblige us to converse, some are ignorant of the arts of pleasing, and offend when they design to caress; some are negligent, and gratify themselves without regard to the quiet of another; some perhaps, are malicious, and feel no greater satisfaction in prosperity than that of raising envy and trampling inferiority. But whatever be the motive of insult, it is always best to overlook it; for folly scarcely can deserve resentment, and malice is punished by neglect.

N° 201. TUESDAY, FEBRUARY 18, 1752.

——Sanctus haberi
Justitiæque tenax factis dictisque mereris?
Agnosco procerem.—Juv.

Convince the world that you're devout and true,
Be just in all you say and all you do;
Whatever be your birth, you're sure to be
A peer of the first magnitude to me.—STEPNEY.

BOYLE has observed, that the excellency of manufactures, and the facility of labour, would be much promoted, if the various expedients and contrivances which lie concealed in private hands, were by reciprocal communications made generally known; for there are few operations that are not performed by one or other with some peculiar advantages, which though singly of little importance, would, by conjunction and concurrence, open new inlets to knowledge, and give new powers to diligence.

There are, in like manner, several moral excellences distributed among the different classes of a community. It was said by Cujacius, that he never read more than one book, by which he was not instructed; and he that shall inquire after virtue with ardour and attention, will seldom find a man by whose example or sentiments he may not be improved.

Every profession has some essential and appropriate virtue, without which there can be no hope of honour or success, and which, as it is more or less cultivated, confers within its sphere of activity different degrees of merit and reputation. As the astrologers range the subdivisions of mankind under the planets which they suppose to influence their lives, the moralist may distribute them according to the virtues which they necessarily practise, and consider them as distinguished by prudence or fortitude, diligence or patience.

So much are the modes of excellence settled by time and place, that men may be heard boasting in one street of that which they would anxiously conceal in another. The grounds of scorn and esteem, the topics of praise and satire, are varied according to the several virtues or vices which the course of life has disposed men to admire or to abhor; but he who is solicitous for his own improvement, must not be limited by local reputation, but select from every tribe of mortals their characteristical virtues, and constellate in himself the scattered graces which shine single in other men.

The chief praise to which a trader aspires is that of punctuality, or an exact and rigorous observance of commercial engagements; nor is there any vice of which he so much dreads the imputation, as of negligence and instability. This is a quality which the interest of mankind requires to be diffused through all the ranks of life, but which many seem to consider as a vulgar and ignoble virtue, below the ambition of greatness or attention of wit, scarcely requisite among men of gaiety and spirit, and sold at its highest rate when it is sacrificed to a frolic or a jest.

Every man has daily occasion to remark what vexations arise from this privilege of deceiving one another. The active and vivacious have so long disdained the restraints of truth, that promises and appointments have lost their cogency, and both parties neglect their stipulations, because each concludes that they will be broken by the other.

Negligence is first admitted in small affairs, and strengthened by petty indulgences. He that is not yet hardened by custom, ventures not on the violation of important engagements, but thinks himself bound by his word in cases of property or danger, though he allows himself to forget at what time he is to meet ladies in the Park, or at what tavern his friends are expecting him.

This laxity of honour would be more tolerable, if it could be restrained to the playhouse, the ballroom, or the card-table; yet even there it is sufficiently troublesome, and darkens those moments with expectation, suspense, and resentment, which are set aside for pleasure, and from which we naturally hope for unmingled enjoyment and total relaxation. But he that suffers the slightest breach in his morality, can seldom tell what shall enter it, or how wide it shall be made; when a passage is open, the influx of corruption is every moment wearing down opposition, and by slow degrees deluges the heart.

Aliger entered the world a youth of lively imagination, extensive views, and untainted principles. His curiosity incited him to range from place to place, and try all the varieties of conversation; his elegance of address and fertility of ideas, gained him friends wherever he appeared; or at least he found the general kindness of reception always shewn to a young man whose birth and fortune gave him a claim to notice, and who has neither by vice nor folly destroyed his privileges. Aliger was pleased with this general smile of mankind, and was industrious to preserve it by compliance and officiousness, but did not suffer his desire of pleasing to vitiate his integrity. It was his established maxim, that a promise is never to be broken; nor was it without long reluctance that he once suffered himself to be drawn away from a festal engagement by the importunity of another company.

He spent the evening, as is usual in the rudiments of vice, in perturbation and imperfect enjoyment, and met his disappointed friends in the morning, with confusion and excuses. His companions, not accustomed to such scrupulous anxiety, laughed at his uneasiness, compounded the offence for a bottle, gave him courage to break his word again, and again levied the penalty. He ventured the same experiment upon another society, and found them equally ready to consider it as a venial fault, always incident to a man of quickness and gaiety; till, by degrees, he began to think himself at liberty to follow the last invitation, and was no longer shocked at the turpitude of falsehood. He made no difficulty to promise his presence at distant places, and if listlessness happened to creep upon him, would sit at home with great tranquillity, and has often sunk to sleep in a chair, while he held ten tables in continual expectations of his entrance.

It was so pleasant to live in perpetual vacancy, that he soon dismissed his attention as a useless encumbrance, and resigned himself to carelessness and dissipation, without any regard to the future or the past, or any other motive of action than the impulse of a sudden desire, or the attraction of immediate pleasure. The absent were immediately forgotten, and the hopes or fears felt by others, had no influence upon his conduct. He was in speculation com-

pletely just, but never kept his promise to a creditor;
he was benevolent, but always deceived those friends
whom he undertook to patronise or assist; he was
prudent, but suffered his affairs to be embarrassed
for want of regulating his accounts at stated times.
He courted a young lady, and when the settlements
were drawn, took a ramble into the country on the
day appointed to sign them. He resolved to travel,
and sent his chests on shipboard, but delayed to follow them till he lost his passage. He was summoned
as an evidence in a cause of great importance, and
loitered on the way till the trial was past. It is said,
that when he had, with great expense, formed an interest in a borough, his opponent contrived, by some
agents who knew his temper, to lure him away on
the day of election.

His benevolence draws him into the commission
of a thousand crimes, which others less kind or civil
would escape. His courtesy invites application; his
promises produce dependance; he has his pockets
filled with petitions, which he intends some time to
deliver and enforce, and his table covered with letters of request, with which he purposes to comply;
but time slips imperceptibly away, while he is either
idle or busy; his friends lose their opportunities, and
charge upon him their miscarriages and calamities.

This character, however contemptible, is not peculiar to Aliger. They whose activity of imagination
is often shifting the scenes of expectation, are frequently subject to such sallies of caprice as make
all their actions fortuitous, destroy the value of their
friendship, obstruct the efficacy of their virtues, and
set them below the meanest of those that persist in
their resolutions, execute what they design, and perform what they have promised.

N° 202. SATURDAY, FEBRUARY 22, 1752.

Πρὸς ἅπαντα δειλός ἐστιν ὁ πένης πράγματα,
Καὶ πάντας αὐτοῦ καταφρονεῖν ὑπολαμβάνει.
Ὁ δὲ μετρίως πράττων περισκελέστερον
Ἅπαντα τ' ἀνιαρὰ, Δαμπρία, φέρει.—CALLIMACHUS.

From no affliction is the poor exempt;
He thinks each eye surveys him with contempt.
Unmanly poverty subdues the heart,
Cankers each wound, and sharpens ev'ry dart.

                              F. LEWIS.

AMONG those who have endeavoured to promote learning and rectify judgment, it has been long customary to complain of the abuse of words, which are often admitted to signify things so different, that instead of assisting the understanding as vehicles of knowledge, they produce error, dissension, and perplexity, because what is affirmed in one sense, is received in another.

If this ambiguity sometimes embarrasses the most solemn controversies, and obscures the demonstrations of science, it may well be expected to infest the pompous periods of declaimers, whose purpose is often only to amuse with fallacies, and change the colours of truth and falsehood; or the musical compositions of poets, whose style is professedly figurative, and whose art is imagined to consist in distorting words from their original meaning.

There are few words of which the reader believes himself better to know the import than of *poverty*; yet whoever studies either the poets or philosophers, will find such an account of the condition expressed by that term as his experience or observation will not easily discover to be true. Instead of the meanness, distress, complaint, anxiety, and dependance, which have hitherto been combined in his ideas of poverty, he will read of content, innocence, and cheerfulness, of health and safety, tranquillity and freedom : of pleasures not known but to men unencumbered with possessions ; and of sleep that sheds his balsamic anodynes only on the cottage. Such are the blessings to be obtained by the resignation of riches, that kings might descend from their thrones, and generals retire from a triumph, only to slumber undisturbed in the elysium of poverty.

If these authors do not deceive us, nothing can be more absurd than that perpetual contest for wealth which keeps the world in commotion ; nor any complaints more justly censured than those which proceed from want of the gifts of fortune, which we are taught by the great masters of moral wisdom to consider as golden shackles, by which the wearer is at once disabled and adorned ; as luscious poisons which may for a time please the palate, but soon betray their malignity by languor and by pain.

It is the great privilege of poverty to be happy unenvied, to be healthful without physic, and secure without a guard ; to obtain from the bounty of nature, what the great and wealthy are compelled to procure by the help of artists and attendants, of flatterers and spies.

But it will be found, upon a nearer view, that they who extol the happiness of poverty, do not mean the same state with those who deplore its miseries. Poets have their imaginations filled with ideas of magnificence ; and being accustomed to contemplate the downfal of empires, or to contrive forms of lamentations for monarchs in distress, rank all the classes of mankind in a state of poverty, who make no approaches to the dignity of crowns. To be poor, in the epic language, is only not to command the wealth of nations, nor to have fleets and armies in pay.

Vanity has perhaps contributed to this impropriety of style. He that wishes to become a philosopher at a cheap rate, easily gratifies his ambition by submitting to poverty when he does not feel it, and by boasting his contempt of riches, when he has already more than he enjoys. He who would shew the extent of his views and grandeur of his conceptions, or discover his acquaintance with splendour and magnificence, may talk like Cowley of an humble station and quiet obscurity, of the paucity of nature's wants, and the inconveniences of superfluity, and at last, like him, limit his desires to five hundred pounds a year; a fortune indeed not exuberant when we compare it with the expenses of pride and luxury, but to which it little becomes a philosopher to affix the name of poverty, since no man can, with any propriety, be termed poor, who does not see the greater part of mankind richer than himself.

As little is the general condition of human life understood by the panegyrists and historians who amuse us with accounts of the poverty of heroes and sages. Riches are of no value in themselves, their use is discovered only in that which they procure. They are not coveted, unless by narrow understandings, which confound the means with the end, but for the sake of power, influence, and esteem; or, by some of less elevated and refined sentiments, as necessary to sensual enjoyment.

The pleasures of luxury, many have, without uncommon virtue, been able to despise, even when affluence and idleness have concurred to tempt them; and therefore he who feels nothing from indigence, but the want of gratifications which we could not in any other condition make consistent with innocence, has given no proof of eminent patience. Esteem and

influence every man desires, but they are equally
pleasing and equally valuable, by whatever means
they are obtained; and whoever has found the art
of securing them without the help of money, ought,
in reality, to be accounted rich, since he has all that
riches can purchase to a wise man. Cincinnatus,
though he lived upon a few acres, cultivated by his
own hand, was sufficiently removed from all the
evils generally comprehended under the name of
poverty, when his reputation was such, that the
voice of his country called him from his farm to
take absolute command into his hand; nor was
Diogenes much mortified by his residence in a tub,
where he was honoured with the visit of Alexander
the Great.

The same fallacy has conciliated veneration to the
religious orders. When we behold a man abdicating
the hope of terrestrial possessions, and precluding
himself, by an irrevocable vow, from the pursuit
and acquisition of all that his fellow-beings consider
as worthy of wishes and endeavours, we are immediately struck with the purity, abstraction, and firmness of his mind, and regard him as wholly employed
in securing the interests of futurity, and devoid of
any other care than to gain at whatever price the
surest passage to eternal rest.

Yet, what can the votary be justly said to have
lost of his present happiness? If he resides in a
convent, he converses only with men whose condition is the same with his own; he has from the munificence of the founder all the necessaries of life,
and is safe from that 'destitution, which' Hooker
declares to be 'such an impediment to virtue, as,
till it be removed, suffereth not the mind of man to
admit any other care.' All temptations to envy and
competition are shut out from his retreat; he is not
pained with the sight of unattainable dignity, nor

insulted with the bluster of insolence, or the smile of forced familiarity. If he wanders abroad, the sanctity of his character amply compensates all other distinctions; he is seldom seen but with reverence, nor heard but with submission.

It has been remarked, that death, though often defied in the field, seldom fails to terrify when it approaches the bed of sickness in its natural horror; so poverty may easily be endured, while associated with dignity and reputation, but will always be shunned and dreaded, when it is accompanied with ignominy and contempt.

N° 203.   TUESDAY, FEBRUARY 25, 1752.

Cùm volet illa dies, quæ nil nisi corporis hujus
Jus habet, incerti spatium mihi finiat ævi.—OVID.

Come soon or late death's undetermin'd day,
This mortal being only can decay.—WELSTED.

IT seems to be the fate of man to seek all his consolations in futurity. The time present is seldom able to fill desire or imagination with immediate enjoyment, and we are forced to supply its deficiencies by recollection or anticipation.

Every one has so often detected the fallaciousness of hope, and the inconvenience of teaching himself to expect what a thousand accidents may preclude, that, when time has abated the confidence with which youth rushes out to take possession of the world, we endeavour, or wish, to find entertainment in the review of life, and to repose upon real facts and certain experience. This is perhaps one reason among many, why age delights in narratives.

But so full is the world of calamity, that every source of pleasure is polluted, and every retirement of tranquillity disturbed. When time has supplied us with events sufficient to employ our thoughts, it has mingled them with so many disasters, that we shrink from their remembrance, dread their intrusion upon our minds, and fly from them as from enemies that pursue us with torture.

No man past the middle point of life can sit down to feast upon the pleasures of youth without finding the banquet imbittered by the cup of sorrow; he may revive lucky accidents and pleasing extravagances; many days of harmless frolic, or nights of honest festivity, will perhaps recur; or, if he has been engaged in scenes of action, and acquainted with affairs of difficulty and vicissitudes of fortune, he may enjoy the nobler pleasure of looking back upon distress firmly supported, dangers resolutely encountered, and opposition artfully defeated. Æneas properly comforts his companions, when after the horrors of a storm they have landed on an unknown and desolate country, with the hope that their miseries will be at some distant time recounted with delight. There are few higher gratifications than that of reflection on surmounted evils, when they were not incurred nor protracted by our fault, and neither reproach us with cowardice nor guilt.

But this felicity is almost always abated by the reflection, that they, with whom we should be most pleased to share it, are now in the grave. A few years make such havoc in human generations, that we soon see ourselves deprived of those with whom we entered the world, and whom the participation of pleasures or fatigues had endeared to our remembrance. The man of enterprise recounts his adventures and expedients, but is forced, at the close of the relation, to pay a sigh to the names of those

that contributed to his success; he that passes his
life among the gayer part of mankind has his remembrance stored with remarks and repartees of wits,
whose sprightliness and merriment are now lost in
perpetual silence; the trader, whose industry has
supplied the want of inheritance, repines in solitary
plenty at the absence of companions, with whom he
had planned out amusements for his latter years;
and the scholar, whose merit, after a long series of
efforts, raises him from obscurity, looks round in vain
from his exaltation for his old friends or enemies,
whose applause or mortification would heighten his
triumph.

Among Martial's requisites to happiness is, *Res
non parta labore, sed relicta,* ' an estate not gained by
industry, but left by inheritance.' It is necessary to
the completion of every good, that it be timely obtained; for whatever comes at the close of life, will
come too late to give much delight; yet all human
happiness has its defects. Of what we do not gain
for ourselves we have only a faint and imperfect fru-
ition, because we cannot compare the difference between want and possession, or at least can derive
from it no conviction of our own abilities, nor any increase of self-esteem; what we acquire by bravery
or science, by mental or corporeal diligence, comes
at last when we cannot communicate, and therefore
cannot enjoy it.

Thus every period of life is obliged to borrow its
happiness from the time to come. In youth we have
nothing past to entertain us, and in age we derive
little from retrospect but hopeless sorrow. Yet the
future likewise has its limits, which the imagination
dreads to approach, but which we see to be not far
distant. The loss of our friends and companions
impresses hourly upon us the necessity of our own
departure; we know that the schemes of man are

quickly at an end, that we must soon lie down in the grave with the forgotten multitudes of former ages, and yield our place to others, who, like us, shall be driven awhile by hope or fear, about the surface of the earth, and then like us be lost in the shades of death.

Beyond this termination of our material existence, we are therefore obliged to extend our hopes; and almost every man indulges his imagination with something, which is not to happen till he has changed his manner of being: some amuse themselves with entails and settlements, provide for the perpetuation of families and honours, or contrive to obviate the dissipation of the fortunes, which it has been their business to accumulate; others, more refined or exalted, congratulate their own hearts upon the future extent of their reputation, the reverence of distant nations, and the gratitude of unprejudiced posterity.

They whose souls are so chained down to coffers and tenements, that they cannot conceive a state in which they shall look upon them with less solicitude, are seldom attentive or flexible to arguments; but the votaries of fame are capable of reflection, and, therefore, may be called to reconsider the probability of their expectations.

Whether to be remembered in remote times be worthy of a wise man's wish has not yet been satisfactorily decided; and, indeed, to be long remembered, can happen to so small a number, that the bulk of mankind has very little interest in the question. There is never room in the world for more than a certain quantity or measure of renown. The necessary business of life, the immediate pleasures or pains of every condition, leave us not leisure beyond a fixed proportion for contemplations which do not forcibly influence our present welfare. When this vacuity is filled, no characters can be admitted into the circulation of fame, but by occupying the place of some that must be thrust into oblivion. The eye of the mind, like that of the body, can only extend its view to new objects, by losing sight of those which are now before it.

Reputation is therefore a meteor which blazes awhile and disappears for ever; and if we except a few transcendant and invincible names, which no revolution of opinion or length of time is able to suppress; all those that engage our thoughts, or diversify our conversation, are every moment hastening to obscurity, as new favourites are adopted by fashion.

It is not therefore from this world, that any ray of comfort can proceed, to cheer the gloom of the last hour. But futurity has still its prospects; there is yet happiness in reserve, which, if we transfer our attention to it, will support us in the pains of disease, and the languor of decay. This happiness we may expect with confidence, because it is out of the power of chance, and may be attained by all that sincerely desire and earnestly pursue it. On this therefore every mind ought finally to rest. Hope is the chief blessing of man, and that hope only is rational, of which we are certain that it cannot deceive us.

N° 204.   SATURDAY, FEBRUARY 29, 1752.

Nemo tam divos habuit faventes,
Crastinum ut possit sibi polliceri.—SENECA.

Of heav'n's protection who can be
So confident to utter this—?
To-morrow I will spend in bliss.—F. LEWIS.

SEGED, lord of Ethiopia, to the inhabitants of the world: To the sons of Presumption, humility and fear; and to the daughters of Sorrow, content and acquiescence.

Thus, in the twenty-seventh year of his reign, spoke Seged, the monarch of forty nations, the distributer of the waters of the Nile; ' At length, Seged, thy toils are at an end: thou hast reconciled disaffection, thou hast suppressed rebellion, thou hast pacified the jealousies of thy courtiers, thou hast chased war from thy confines, and erected fortresses in the lands of thy enemies. All who have offended thee, tremble in thy presence, and wherever thy voice is heard, it is obeyed. Thy throne is surrounded by armies, numerous as the locusts of the summer, and resistless as the blasts of pestilence. Thy magazines are stored with ammunition, thy treasuries overflow with the tribute of conquered kingdoms. Plenty waves upon thy fields, and opulence glitters in thy cities. Thy nod is as the earthquake that shakes the mountains, and thy smile as the dawn of the vernal day. In thy hand is the strength of thousands, and thy health is the health of millions. Thy palace is gladdened by the song of praise, and thy path perfumed by the breath of benediction. Thy subjects gaze upon thy greatness, and think of danger or misery no more. Why, Seged, wilt not thou partake the blessings thou bestowest? Why shouldst thou only forbear to rejoice in this general felicity? Why should thy face be clouded with anxiety, when the meanest of those who call thee sovereign, gives the day to festivity, and the night to peace? At length, Seged, reflect and be wise. What is the gift of conquest but safety, why are riches collected but to purchase happiness?'

Seged then ordered the house of pleasure, built in an island of the lake Dambia, to be prepared for his reception. ' I will retire,' says he, ' for ten days from tumult and care, from counsels and decrees.

Long quiet is not the lot of the governors of nations,
but a cessation of ten days cannot be denied me.
This short interval of happiness may surely be secured from the interruption of fear or perplexity,
sorrow or disappointment. I will exclude all trouble
from my abode, and remove from my thoughts whatever may confuse the harmony of the concert, or
abate the sweetness of the banquet. I will fill the
whole capacity of my soul with enjoyment, and try
what it is to live without a wish unsatisfied.'

In a few days the orders were performed, and
Seged hasted to the palace of Dambia, which stood
in an island cultivated only for pleasure, planted with
every flower that spreads its colours to the sun, and
every shrub that sheds fragrance in the air. In one
part of this extensive garden, were open walks for
excursions in the morning, in another, thick groves,
and silent arbours, and bubbling fountains for repose
at noon. All that could solace the sense, or flatter
the fancy, all that industry could extort from nature,
or wealth furnish to art, all that conquest could seize,
or beneficence attract, was collected together, and
every perception of delight was excited and gratified.

Into this delicious region Seged summoned all the
persons of his court, who seemed eminently qualified
to receive or communicate pleasure. His call was
readily obeyed; the young, the fair, the vivacious,
and the witty, were all in haste to be sated with felicity. They sailed jocund over the lake, which seemed
to smooth its surface before them : their passage was
cheered with music, and their hearts dilated with
expectation.

Seged landed here with his band of pleasure, determined from that hour to break off all acquaintance
with discontent, to give his heart for ten days to ease
and jollity, and then fall back to the common state

of man, and suffer his life to be diversified, as before,
with joy and sorrow.

He immediately entered his chamber, to consider
where he should begin his circle of happiness. He
had all the artists of delight before him, but knew
not whom to call, since he could not enjoy one, but
by delaying the performance of another. He chose
and rejected, he resolved and changed his resolution,
till his faculties were harassed, and his thoughts
confused: then returned to the apartment where his
presence was expected, with languid eyes and clouded
countenance, and spread the infection of uneasiness
over the whole assembly. He observed their depression, and was offended, for he found his vexation increased by those whom he expected to dissipate and relieve it. He retired again to his private
chamber, and sought for consolation in his own mind;
one thought flowed in upon another; a long succession of images seized his attention; the moments
crept imperceptibly away through the gloom of pen-
siveness, till having recovered his tranquillity, he
lifted up his head and saw the lake brightened by the
setting sun. 'Such,' said Seged sighing, 'is the
longest day of human existence: before we have
learned to use it, we find it at an end.'

The regret which he felt for the loss of so great a
part of his first day, took from him all disposition to
enjoy the evening; and after having endeavoured,
for the sake of his attendants, to force an air of
gaiety, and excite that mirth which he could not
share, he resolved to refer his hopes to the next
morning, and lay down to partake with the slaves of
labour and poverty the blessing of sleep.

He rose early the second morning, and resolved
now to be happy. He therefore fixed upon the gate
of the palace an edict, importing, that whoever, du-

ring nine days, should appear in the presence of the king with dejected countenance, or utter any expression of discontent or sorrow, should be driven for ever from the palace of Dambia.

This edict was immediately made known in every chamber of the court and bower of the gardens. Mirth was frighted away, and they who were before dancing on the lawns, or singing in the shades, were at once engaged in the care of regulating their looks, that Seged might find his will punctually obeyed, and see none among them liable to banishment.

Seged now met every face settled in a smile; but a smile that betrayed solicitude, timidity, and constraint. He accosted his favourites with familiarity and softness; but they durst not speak without premeditation, lest they should be convicted of discontent and sorrow. He proposed diversions, to which no objection was made, because objection would have implied uneasiness; but they were regarded with indifference by the courtiers, who had no other desire than to signalize themselves by clamorous exultation. He offered various topics of conversation, but obtained only forced jests and laborious laughter, and after many attempts to animate his train to confidence and alacrity, was obliged to confess to himself the impotence of command, and resign another day to grief and disappointment.

He at last relieved his companions from their terrors, and shut himself up in his chamber to ascertain, by different measures, the felicity of the succeeding days. At length he threw himself on the bed, and closed his eyes, but imagined, in his sleep, that his palace and gardens were overwhelmed by an inundation, and waked with all the terrors of a man struggling in the water. He composed himself again to rest, but was affrighted by an imaginary irruption into his kingdom, and striving, as is usual in dreams, without ability to move, fancied himself betrayed to his enemies, and again started up with horror and indignation.

It was now day, and fear was so strongly impressed on his mind, that he could sleep no more. He rose, but his thoughts were filled with the deluge and invasion, nor was he able to disengage his attention, or mingle with vacancy and ease in any amusement. At length his perturbation gave way to reason, and he resolved no longer to be harassed by visionary miseries; but before this resolution could be completed, half the day had elapsed: he felt a new conviction of the uncertainty of human schemes, and could not forbear to bewail the weakness of that being, whose quiet was to be interrupted by vapours of the fancy. Having been first disturbed by a dream, he afterward grieved that a dream could disturb him. He at last discovered, that his terrors and grief were equally vain, and, that to lose the present in lamenting the past was voluntarily to protract a melancholy vision. The third day was now declining, and Seged again resolved to be happy on the morrow.

N° 205. TUESDAY, MARCH 3, 1752.

> ———Volat ambiguis
> Mobilis alis hora, nec ulli
> Præstat velox fortuna fidem.—Seneca.
>
> On fickle wings the minutes haste,
> And fortune's favours never last.—F. Lewis.

On the fourth morning Seged rose early, refreshed with sleep, vigorous with health, and eager with expectation. He entered the garden, attended by the

princes and ladies of his court, and seeing nothing
about him but airy cheerfulness, began to say to his
heart, ' This day shall be a day of pleasure.' The
sun played upon the water, the birds warbled in the
groves, and the gales quivered among the branches.
He roved from walk to walk as chance directed him,
and sometimes listened to the songs, sometimes
mingled with the dancers, sometimes let loose his
imagination in flights of merriment; and sometimes
uttered grave reflections and sententious maxims,
and feasted on the admiration with which they were
received.

Thus the day rolled on, without any accident of
vexation, or intrusion of melancholy thoughts. All
that beheld him caught gladness from his looks, and
the sight of happiness conferred by himself filled his
heart with satisfaction: but having passed three hours
in this harmless luxury, he was alarmed on a sudden
by a universal scream among the women, and turning back, saw the whole assembly flying in confusion. A young crocodile had risen out of the lake,
and was ranging the garden in wantonness or hunger.
Seged beheld him with indignation, as a disturber of
his felicity, and chased him back into the lake, but
could not persuade his retinue to stay, or free their
hearts from the terror which had seized upon them.
The princesses enclosed themselves in the palace,
and could yet scarcely believe themselves in safety.
Every attention was fixed upon the late danger and
escape, and no mind was any longer at leisure for
gay sallies or careless prattle.

Seged had now no other employment than to contemplate the innumerable casualties which lie in am-
bush on every side to intercept the happiness of man,
and break in upon the hour of delight and tranquillity. He had, however, the consolation of thinking,
that he had not been now disappointed by his own

fault, and that the accident which had blasted the
hopes of the day, might easily be prevented by future
caution.

That he might provide for the pleasure of the next
morning, he resolved to repeal his penal edict, since
he had already found that discontent and melancholy
were not to be frighted away by the threats of authority, and that pleasure would only reside where she
was exempted from control. He therefore invited
all the companions of his retreat to unbounded pleasantry, by proposing prizes for those who should, on
the following day, distinguish themselves by any
festive performances; the tables of the antechamber
were covered with gold and pearls, and robes and
garlands decreed the rewards of those who could refine elegance or heighten pleasure.

At this display of riches every eye immediately
sparkled, and every tongue was busied in celebrating
the bounty and magnificence of the emperor. But
when Seged entered, in hopes of uncommon entertainment from universal emulation, he found that
any passion too strongly agitated, puts an end to
that tranquillity which is necessary to mirth, and that
the mind, that is to be moved by the gentle ventila-
tions of gaiety, must be first smoothed by a total
calm. Whatever we ardently wish to gain, we must
in the same degree be afraid to lose, and fear and
pleasure cannot dwell together.

All was now care and solicitude. Nothing was
done or spoken, but with so visible an endeavour at
perfection, as always failed to delight, though it
sometimes forced admiration: and Seged could not
but observe with sorrow, that his prizes had more influence than himself. As the evening approached,
the contest grew more earnest, and those who were
forced to allow themselves excelled, began to discover the malignity of defeat, first by angry glances,

and at last by contemptuous murmurs. Seged likewise shared the anxiety of the day, for considering
himself as obliged to distribute with exact justice the
prizes which had been so zealously sought, he durst
never remit his attention, but passed his time upon
the rack of doubt in balancing different kinds of
merit, and adjusting the claims of all the competitors.

At last, knowing that no exactness could satisfy
those whose hopes he should disappoint, and thinking that on a day set apart for happiness, it would
be cruel to oppress any heart with sorrow, he declared that all had pleased him alike, and dismissed
all with presents of equal value.

Seged soon saw that his caution had not been
able to avoid offence. They who had believed themselves secure of the highest prize, were not pleased
to be levelled with the crowd; and though by the
liberality of the king they received more than his
promise had entitled them to expect, they departed
unsatisfied, because they were honoured with no distinction, and wanted an opportunity to triumph in
the mortification of their opponents. ' Behold here,'
said Seged, ' the condition of him who places his
happiness in the happiness of others.' He then retired to meditate, and while the courtiers were repining at his distributions, saw the fifth sun go down
in discontent.

The next dawn renewed his resolution to be happy.
But having learned how little he could effect by settled schemes or preparatory measures, he thought
it best to give up one day entirely to chance, and
left every one to please and be pleased his own way.

This relaxation of regularity diffused a general
complacence through the whole court, and the emperor imagined, that he had at last found the secret
of obtaining an interval of felicity. But as he was

roving in this careless assembly with equal carelessness, he overheard one of his courtiers in a close
arbour murmuring alone: 'What merit has Seged
above us, that we should thus fear and obey him, a
man, whom, whatever he may have formerly performed, his luxury now shews to have the same
weakness with ourselves.' This charge affected him
the more, as it was uttered by one whom he had always observed among the most abject of his flatterers. At first his indignation prompted him to severity; but reflecting that what was spoken, without
intention to be heard, was to be considered as only
thought, and was perhaps but the sudden burst of
casual and temporary vexation, he invented some
decent pretence to send him away, that his retreat
might not be tainted with the breath of envy; and
after the struggle of deliberation was past, and all
desire of revenge utterly suppressed, passed the evening not only with tranquillity, but triumph, though
none but himself was conscious of the victory.

The remembrance of this clemency cheered the
beginning of the seventh day, and nothing happened
to disturb the pleasure of Seged, till looking on the
tree that shaded him, he recollected, that under a
tree of the same kind he had passed the night after
his defeat in the kingdom of Goiama. The reflection
on his loss, his dishonour, and the miseries which his
subjects suffered from the invader, filled him with
sadness. At last he shook off the weight of sorrow,
and began to solace himself with his usual pleasures,
when his tranquillity was again disturbed by jealousies which the late cont st for the prizes had produced, and which, having in vain tried to pacify
them by persuasion, he was forced to silence by
command.

On the eighth morning Seged was awakened early
by an unusual hurry in the apartments, and inquir-

ing the cause, was told that the Princess Balkis was
seized with sickness. He rose, and calling the phy-
sicians, found that they had little hope of her recovery. Here was an end of jollity: all his thoughts
were now upon his daughter, whose eyes he closed
on the tenth day.

Such were the days which Seged of Ethiopia had
appropriated to a short respiration from the fatigues
of war and the cares of government. This narrative
he has bequeathed to future generations, that no
man hereafter may presume to say, ' This day shall
be a day of happiness.'

N⁰ 206. SATURDAY, MARCH 7, 1752.

——Propositi nondum pudet, atque eadem est mens,
Ut bona summa putes, alienâ vivere quadrâ.—Juv.

But harden'd by affronts, and still the same,
Lost to all sense of honour and of fame,
Thou yet can'st love to haunt the great man's board,
And think no supper good but with a lord.—Bowles.

When Diogenes was once asked what kind of wine
he liked best? he answered, ' That which is drunk
at the cost of others.'

Though the character of Diogenes has never excited any general zeal of imitation, there are many
who resemble him in his taste of wine; many who
are frugal, though not abstemious; whose appetites, though too powerful for reason, are kept under
restraint by avarice; and to whom all delicacies
lose their flavour, when they cannot be obtained but
at their own expense.

Nothing produces more singularity of manners

and inconstancy of life, than the conflict of opposite vices in the same mind. He that uniformly pursues any purpose, whether good or bad, has a settled principle of action; and as he may always find associates who are travelling the same way, is countenanced by example, and sheltered in the multitude; but a man, actuated at once by different desires, must move in a direction peculiar to himself, and suffer that reproach which we are naturally inclined to bestow on those who deviate from the rest of the world, even without inquiring whether they are worse or better.

Yet this conflict of desires sometimes produces wonderful efforts. To riot in far-fetched dishes, or surfeit with unexhausted variety, and yet practise the most rigid economy, is surely an art which may justly draw the eyes of mankind upon them whose industry or judgment has enabled them to attain it. To him, indeed, who is content to break open the chests, or mortgage the manors, of his ancestors, that he may hire the ministers of excess at the highest price, gluttony is an easy science; yet we often hear the votaries of luxury boasting of the elegance which they owe to the taste of others, relating with rapture the succession of dishes with which their cooks and caterers supply them; and expecting their share of praise with the discoverers of arts and the civilizers of nations. But to shorten the way to convivial happiness, by eating without cost, is a secret hitherto in few hands, but which certainly deserves the curiosity of those whose principal enjoyment is their dinner, and who see the sun rise with no other hope than that they shall fill their bellies before it sets.

Of them that have within my knowledge attempted this scheme of happiness, the greater part have been immediately obliged to desist; and some, whom their first attempts flattered with success, were reduced by degrees to a few tables, from which they were at last chased to make way for others; and having long habituated themselves to superfluous plenty, growled away their latter years in discontented competence.

None enter the regions of luxury with higher expectations than men of wit, who imagine, that they shall never want a welcome to that company whose ideas they can enlarge, or whose imaginations they can elevate, and believe themselves able to pay for their wine with the mirth which it qualifies them to produce. Full of this opinion, they crowd with little invitation, wherever the smell of a feast allures them, but are seldom encouraged to repeat their visits, being dreaded by the pert as rivals, and hated by the dull as disturbers of the company.

No man has been so happy in gaining and keeping the privilege of living at luxurious houses as Gulosulus, who, after thirty years of continual revelry, has now established, by uncontroverted prescription, his claim to partake of every entertainment, and whose presence, they who aspire to the praise of a sumptuous table are careful to procure on a day of importance, by sending the invitation a fortnight before.

Gulosulus entered the world without any eminent degree of merit; but was careful to frequent houses where persons of rank resorted. By being often seen, he became in time known; and from sitting in the same room, was suffered to mix in idle conversation, or assisted to fill up a vacant hour, when better amusement was not readily to be had. From the coffee-house he was sometimes taken away to dinner; and as no man refuses the acquaintance of him whom he sees admitted to familiarity by others of equal dignity, when he had been met at a few tables, he with less difficulty found the way to more, till at last he was regularly expected to appear wherever preparations are made for a feast, within the circuit of his acquaintance.

When he was thus by accident initiated in luxury, he felt in himself no inclination to retire from a life of so much pleasure, and therefore very seriously considered how he might continue it. Great qualities, or uncommon accomplishments, he did not find necessary; for he had already seen that merit rather enforces respect than attracts fondness; and as he thought no folly greater than that of losing a dinner for any other gratification, he often congratulated himself, that he had none of that disgusting excellence which impresses awe upon greatness, and condemns its possessors to the society of those who are wise or brave, and indigent as themselves.

Gulosulus having never allotted much of his time to books or meditation, had no opinion in philosophy or politics, and was not in danger of injuring his interest by dogmatical positions or violent contradiction. If a dispute arose, he took care to listen with earnest attention; and when either speaker grew vehement and loud, turned towards him with eager quickness, and uttered a short phrase of admiration, as if surprised by such cogency of argument as he had never known before. By this silent concession, he generally preserved in either controvertist such a conviction of his own superiority, as inclined him rather to pity than irritate his adversary, and prevented those outrages which are sometimes produced by the rage of defeat, or petulance of triumph.

Gulosulus was never embarrassed, but when he was required to declare his sentiments before he had been able to discover to which side the master of the house inclined, for it was his invariable rule to adopt the notions of those that invited him.

It will sometimes happen that the insolence of wealth breaks into contemptuousness, or the turbulence of wine requires a vent; and Gulosulus seldom fails of being singled out on such emergencies, as one on whom any experiment of ribaldry may be safely tried. Sometimes his lordship finds himself inclined to exhibit a specimen of raillery for the diversion of his guest, and Gulosulus always supplies him with a subject of merriment. But he has learned to consider rudeness and indignities as familiarities that entitle him to greater freedom; he comforts himself, that those who treat and insult him pay for their laughter, and that he keeps his money while they enjoy their jest.

His chief policy consists in selecting some dish from every course, and recommending it to the company, with an air so decisive, that no one ventures to contradict him. By this practice he acquires at a feast a kind of dictatorial authority; his taste becomes the standard of pickles and seasoning, and he is venerated by the professors of epicurism, as the only man who understands the niceties of cookery.

Whenever a new sauce is imported, or any innovation made in the culinary system, he procures the earliest intelligence, and the most authentic receipt; and by communicating his knowledge under proper injunctions of secrecy, gains a right of tasting his own dish whenever it is prepared, that he may tell whether his directions have been fully understood.

By this method of life Gulosulus has so impressed on his imagination the dignity of feasting, that he has no other topic of talk or subject of meditation. His calendar is a bill of fare; he measures the year by successive dainties. The only common places of his memory are his meals; and if you ask him at what time an event happened, he considers whether he heard it after a dinner of turbot or venison. He knows, indeed, that those who value themselves upon sense, learning, or piety, speak of him with con-

tempt; but he considers them as wretches envious
or ignorant, who do not know his happiness, or wish
to supplant him; and declares to his friends, that he
is fully satisfied with his own conduct, since he has
fed every day on twenty dishes, and yet doubled his
estate.

N° 207. TUESDAY, MARCH 10, 1752.

Solve senescentem maturè sanus equum, ne
Peccet ad extremum ridendus.—Hor.

The voice of reason cries with winning force,
Loose from the rapid car your aged horse,
Lest, in the race derided, left behind,
He drags his jaded limbs and bursts his wind.—Francis.

Such is the emptiness of human enjoyment, that we
are always impatient of the present. Attainment is
followed by neglect, and possession by disgust; and
the malicious remark of the Greek epigrammatist on
marriage may be applied to every other course of
life, that its two days of happiness are the first and
the last.

Few moments are more pleasing than those in
which the mind is concerting measures for a new undertaking. From the first hint that wakens the fancy,
till the hour of actual execution, all is improvement
and progress, triumph and felicity. Every hour brings
additions to the original scheme, suggests some new
expedient to secure success, or discovers conse-
quential advantages not hitherto foreseen. While
preparations are made, and materials accumulated,
day glides after day through elysian prospects, and
the heart dances to the song of hope.

Such is the pleasure of projecting, that many con-

content themselves with a succession of visionary schemes, and wear out their allotted time in the calm amusement of contriving what they never attempt or hope to execute.

Others, not able to feast their imagination with pure ideas, advance somewhat nearer to the grossness of action, with great diligence collect whatever is requisite to their design, and, after a thousand researches and consultations, are snatched away by death, as they stand *in procinctu* waiting for a proper opportunity to begin.

If there were no other end of life, than to find some adequate solace for every day, I know not whether any condition could be preferred to that of the man who involves himself in his own thoughts, and never suffers experience to shew him the vanity of speculation; for no sooner are notions reduced to practice than tranquillity and confidence forsake the breast; every day brings its task, and often without bringing abilities to perform it : difficulties embarrass, uncertainty perplexes, opposition retards, censure exasperates, or neglect depresses. We proceed, because we have begun; we complete our design, that the labour already spent may not be vain; but as expectation gradually dies away, the gay smile of alacrity disappears, we are compelled to implore severer powers, and trust the event to patience and constancy.

When once our labour has begun, the comfort that enables us to endure it is the prospect of its end; for though in every long work there are some joyous intervals of self-applause, when the attention is recreated by unexpected facility, and imagination soothed by incidental excellences ; yet the toil with which performance struggles after idea, is so irksome and disgusting, and so frequent is the necessity of resting below the perfection which we imagined within our reach, that seldom any man obtains more from his endeavours than a painful conviction of his defects, and a continual resuscitation of desires which he feels himself unable to gratify.

So certainly is weariness the concomitant of our undertakings, that every man, in whatever he is engaged, consoles himself with the hope of change; if he has made his way by assiduity to public employment, he talks among his friends of the delight of retreat: if by the necessity of solitary application he is secluded from the world, he listens with a beating heart to distant noises, longs to mingle with living beings, and resolves to take hereafter his fill of diversions, or display his abilities on the universal theatre, and enjoy the pleasure of distinction and applause.

Every desire, however innocent, grows dangerous, as by long indulgence it becomes ascendant in the mind. When we have been much accustomed to consider any thing as capable of giving happiness, it is not easy to restrain our ardour, or to forbear some precipitation in our advances, and irregularity in our pursuits. He that has cultivated the tree, watched the swelling bud and opening blossom, and pleased himself with computing how much every sun and shower add to its growth, scarcely stays till the fruit has obtained its maturity, but defeats his own cares by eagerness to reward them. When we have diligently laboured for any purpose, we are willing to believe that we have attained it, and, because we have already done much, too suddenly conclude that no more is to be done.

All attraction is increased by the approach of the attracting body. We never find ourselves so desirous to finish, as in the latter part of our work, or so impatient of delay, as when we know that delay cannot be long. This unseasonable opportunity of discontent may be partly imputed to languor and weariness, which must always oppress those more whose toil has been longer continued; but the greater part usually proceeds from frequent contemplation of that ease which is now considered as within reach, and which, when it has once flattered our hopes, we cannot suffer to be withheld.

In some of the noblest compositions of wit, the conclusion falls below the vigour and spirit of the first books; and as a genius is not to be degraded by the imputation of human failings, the cause of this declension is commonly sought in the structure of the work, and plausible reasons are given why in the defective part less ornament was necessary, or less could be admitted. But, perhaps, the author would have confessed, that his fancy was tired, and his perseverance broken; that he knew his design to be unfinished, but that, when he saw the end so near, he could no longer refuse to be at rest.

Against the instillations of this frigid opiate, the heart should be secured by all the considerations which once concurred to kindle the ardour of enterprise. Whatever motive first incited action, has still greater force to stimulate perseverance; since he that might have lain still at first in blameless obscurity, cannot afterward desist but with infamy and reproach. He, whom a doubtful promise of distant good could encourage to set difficulties at defiance, ought not to remit his vigour, when he has almost obtained his recompense. To faint or loiter, when only the last efforts are required, is to steer the ship through tempests, and abandon it to the winds in sight of land; it is to break the ground and scatter the seed, and at last to neglect the harvest.

The masters of rhetoric direct, that the most forcible arguments be produced in the latter part of an oration, lest they should be effaced or perplexed by supervenient images. This precept may be justly extended to the series of life: nothing is ended with honour, which does not conclude better than it began. It is not sufficient to maintain the first vigour; for excellence loses its effect upon the mind by custom, as light after a time ceases to dazzle. Admiration must be continued by that novelty which first produced it, and how much soever is given, there must always be reason to imagine that more remains.

We not only are most sensible of the last impressions, but such is the unwillingness of mankind to admit transcendent merit, that, though it be difficult to obliterate the reproach of miscarriages by any subsequent achievement, however illustrious, yet the reputation raised by a long train of success, may be finally ruined by a single failure; for weakness or error will be always remembered by that malice and envy which it gratifies.

For the prevention of that disgrace, which lassitude and negligence may bring at last upon the greatest performances, it is necessary to proportion carefully our labour to our strength. If the design comprises many parts, equally essential, and therefore not to be separated, the only time for caution is before we engage; the powers of the mind must be then impartially estimated, and it must be remembered, that not to complete the plan, is not to have begun it; and that nothing is done, while any thing is omitted.

But if the task consists in the repetition of single acts, no one of which derives its efficacy from the rest, it may be attempted with less scruple, because there is always opportunity to retreat with honour.

The danger is only, lest we expect from the world the indulgence with which most are disposed to treat themselves; and in the hour of listlessness imagine, that the diligence of one day will atone for the idleness of another, and that applause begun by approbation will be continued by habit.

He that is himself weary will soon weary the public. Let him therefore lay down his employment, whatever it be, who can no longer exert his former activity or attention; let him not endeavour to struggle with censure, or obstinately infest the stage till a general hiss commands him to depart.

Nº 208. SATURDAY, MARCH 14, 1752.

'Ηράκλειτος ἐγὼ' τί με ὦν κάτω ἕλκετ', ἄμουσοι;
Οὐχ' ὑμῖν ἐπόνουν, τοῖς δὲ μ' ἐπισταμένοις·
Εἷς ἐμοὶ ἄνθρωπος, τρισμυρίοι· οἱ δ' ἀνάριθμοι,
Οὐδείς· ταῦτ' αὐδῶ καὶ παρὰ Περσεφόνῃ.——Diog. Laert.

Begone, ye blockheads, Heraclitus cries,
And leave my labours to the learn'd and wise;
By wit, by knowledge, studious to be read,
I scorn the multitude, alive and dead.

Time, which puts an end to all human pleasures and sorrows, has likewise concluded the labours of the Rambler. Having supported, for two years, the anxious employment of a periodical writer, and multiplied my essays to six volumes*, I have now determined to desist.

The reasons of this resolution it is of little importance to declare, since justification is unnecessary

* The number of volumes on the first republication of The Rambler.

when no objection is made. I am far from suppos-
ing, that the cessation of my performances will raise
any inquiry, for I have never been much a favourite
of the public, nor can boast that, in the progress of
my undertaking, I have been animated by the rewards of the liberal, the caresses of the great, or the
praises of the eminent.

But I have no design to gratify pride by submission, or malice by lamentation; nor think it reasonable to complain of neglect from those whose regard
I never solicited. If I have not been distinguished
by the distributers of literary honours, I have seldom
descended to the arts by which favour is obtained.
I have seen the meteors of fashion rise and fall, without any attempt to add a moment to their duration.
I have never complied with temporary curiosity, nor
enabled my readers to discuss the topic of the day;
I have rarely exemplified my assertions by living characters; in my papers, no man could look for censures of his enemies, or praises of himself; and they
only were expected to peruse them, whose passions
left them leisure for abstracted truth, and whom virtue could please by its naked dignity.

To some, however, I am indebted for encouragement, and to others for assistance. The number of
my friends was never great, but they have been such
as would not suffer me to think that I was writing in
vain, and I did not feel much dejection from the
want of popularity.

My obligations having not been frequent, my ac-
knowledgments may be soon dispatched. I can restore to all my correspondents their productions,
with little diminution of the bulk of my volumes,
though not without the loss of some pieces to which
particular honours have been paid.

The parts from which I claim no other praise than

that of having given them an opportunity of appearing, are the four billets in the tenth paper, the second letter in the fifteenth, the thirtieth, the forty-fourth, the ninety-seventh, and the hundredth papers, and the second letter in the hundred and seventh.

Having thus deprived myself of many excuses which candour might have admitted for the inequality of my compositions, being no longer able to allege the necessity of gratifying correspondents, the importunity with which publication was solicited, or obstinacy with which correction was rejected, I must remain accountable for all my faults, and submit, without subterfuge, to the censures of criticism, which, however, I shall not endeavour to soften by a formal deprecation, or to overbear by the influence of a patron. The supplications of an author never yet reprieved him a moment from oblivion; and though greatness has sometimes sheltered guilt, it can afford no protection to ignorance or dulne⸱⸱ Having hitherto attempted only the propagation⸱ truth, I will not at last violate it by the confession o terrors which I do not feel: having laboured to maintain the dignity of virtue, I will not now degrade it by the meanness of dedication.

The seeming vanity with which I have sometimes spoken of myself, would perhaps require an apology, were it not extenuated by the example of those who have published essays before me, and by the privilege which every nameless writer has been hitherto allowed. 'A mask,' says Castiglione, 'confers a right of acting and speaking with less restraint, even when the wearer happens to be known.' He that is discovered without his own consent, may claim some indulgence, and cannot be rigorously called to justify those sallies or frolics which his disguise must prove him desirous to conceal.

But I have been cautious lest this offence should be frequently or grossly committed; for, as one of the philosophers directs us to live with a friend, as with one that is some time to become an enemy, I have always thought it the duty of an anonymous author to write, as if he expected to be hereafter known.

I am willing to flatter myself with hopes, that by collecting these papers, I am not preparing, for my future life, either shame or repentance. That all are happily imagined, or accurately polished, that the same sentiments have not sometimes recurred, or the same expressions been too frequently repeated, I have not confidence in my abilities sufficient to warrant. He that condemns himself to compose on a stated day, will often bring to his task an attention dissipated, a memory embarrassed, an imagination overwhelmed, a mind distracted with anxieties, a body languishing with disease: he will labour on a barren ᵗᵒᵖⁱc, till it is too late to change it; or, in the ardour ᵒᶠ invention, diffuse his thoughts into wild exuberance, which the pressing hour of publication cannot suffer judgment to examine or reduce.

Whatever shall be the final sentence of mankind, I have at least endeavoured to deserve their kindness. I have laboured to refine our language to grammatical purity, and to clear it from colloquial barbarisms, licentious idioms, and irregular combinations. Something, perhaps, I have added to the elegance of its construction, and something to the harmony of its cadence. When common words were less pleasing to the ear, or less distinct in their signification, I have familiarized the terms of philosophy by applying them to popular ideas, but have rarely admitted any word not authorized by former writers; for I believe that whoever knows the English tongue in its present extent, will be able to express his thoughts without farther help from other nations.

As it has been my principal design to inculcate wisdom or piety, I have allotted few papers to the idle sports of imagination. Some, perhaps, may be found, of which the highest excellence is harmless merriment; but scarcely any man is so steadily serious as not to complain, that the severity of dictatorial instruction has been too seldom relieved, and that he is driven by the sternness of the Rambler's philosophy to more cheerful and airy companions.

Next to the excursions of fancy are the disquisitions of criticism, which, in my opinion, is only to be ranked among the subordinate and instrumental arts. Arbitrary decision and general exclamation I have carefully avoided, by asserting nothing without a reason, and establishing all my principles of judgment on unalterable and evident truth.

In the pictures of life I have never been so studious of novelty or surprise as to depart wholly from all resemblance; a fault which writers des... celebrated frequently commit, that they ma... the occasion requires, either mirth or abhorre... Some enlargement may be allowed to declamation, and some exaggeration to burlesque; but as they deviate farther from reality, they become less useful, because their lessons will fail of application. The mind of the reader is carried away from the contemplation of his own manners; he finds in himself no likeness to the phantom before him; and though he laughs or rages, is not reformed.

The essays professedly serious, if I have been able to execute my own intentions, will be found exactly conformable to the precepts of Christianity, without any accommodation to the licentiousness and levity of the present age. I therefore look back on this part of my work with pleasure, which no blame or praise of man shall diminish or augment. I shall never envy the honours which wit and learning obtain in any other cause, if I can be numbered among the writers who have given ardour to virtue, and confidence to truth.

Αὐτᾶν ἐκ μακάρον ἀντάξιος εἴη ἀμοιβή.

Celestial pow'rs! that piety regard,
From you my labours wait their last reward.

END OF VOL. XXII.

part of any work with pleasure, which no blame or
praise of man, shall diminish or augment. I shall
never envy the honours which wit and learning obtain
in any other cause, if I can be numbered among the
writers who have given ardour to virtue, and confidence to truth.

Αὐτὰρ ἐγὼ μακάρων ἐσσόμενος τὰ ἄκουα.

Celestial pow'r! that piety regard,
From you my labours wait their last reward.

END OF VOL. XXII.

Printed by J. F. Dove, St. John's Square.